SEX CRIMES OF THE FUTCHER

paperback editon published by the aquarium September 2005

ISBN 1 871894 82 4

First published as a hardback by the aquarium in 2004.
No ISBN, no barcode, no author.

The Aquarium
Woburn Walk, London, UK
www.aquariumgallery.co.uk

The short life

and

Strange and Exciting Adventures

of

William Loveday

Ex-student of C— town

Who, not being properly lookt after as a child, was sexualy abused by a 46 year old man, and his subsequent war with all education and authority.

Also including

An account of his sexual deviations and unjust expulsion from art school and his ultimate revenge.

Ritten by himself

Printed by The Aquarium, Woburn Walk

London MMIV

OUR STORY follows one persons struggle from a blited childhood into a damaged adulthood. It includes anal sex, hair burning, self mutilation and culminates in the senseless destruction of art. This will be quite familiar territory to many of us but as i point out – to friends and strangers alike – this does not make our novel a history or necessarily autobiographical. On the contrary, Sex Crimes of the Futcher is a product of the imagination and is completely fictitious. Characters and events are invented and even if time and place seem to point to a definite person, this is only coincidental, an invention, fancy, fiction, a story.

"And there can be no doubt that the Church would look upon the criminal and the crime of the future in many cases quite differently and would succeed in restoring the excluded, in restraining those who plan evil, and in regenerating the fallen."

The Brothers Karamazov.

Fyodor Dostoevsky

To The Public

It is my opinion that none of this could of happened if i had been lookt after as a child instead of being lead at an unnatural age into the dark world of adult sex. Also, if my psyche haddnt of been turned by the violent attempts of my parents and teachers to knock some of my sharp corners off, then maybe my anger would have been less. This being said, it is also my opinion that none of this could of happened if God himself haddnt intended it. Surly it was his wish that my sole and the sole of my accomplices should have been fated to meet and act out this dark but exciting episode. And maybe i am blessed, for who nos what extra unnown evil mite of come for me had i been lookt after and protected as a child? Instead, all i had to do was find my own painful way thru life without a good example or guiding hand of any kind. Some fanciful readers will no doubt see Gods mysterious lite in this.

I realise that its wrong to go feasting your mind on the murderous intentions of others, but also it is impossable to remain pure in a world which is not pure and was never designed to be so, or, as some would have it, is already perfect in its imperfections. And even the Great Book is littered with rape, incest and murder. In short – bathed in blud from cover to cover. And how many 9 year old children go stealing thru their fathers brief cases in search of that other hidden literature which is the staple diet of every doctor, cabernet minister and garage attendant of the land? I am of course speaking of pornography – the staple diet of every uprite citizen.

Reading thru my 'history' i see that ive again spoken out of turne, going into explicit details about a subject that 'thinkers' and 'liberals' dont even want mentioned, much less slit open and prodded. Certainly, riting it all down will only do me further harm. I no that im just storing up more misery for myself in the futcher. Riting and idears is the very stuff that ruined my young life in the first place. So without being at all facetious, i take this moment to ask that God, and you the reader, may forgive me. I rite this book in penance. With these words i pardon all those who have ronged me and smashed me, and i in turne seek pardon from those i have wronged and tried to smash. Is that too much to ask? Becouse as long as we human beings harbour grievances against each other we must remain trapped like snared animals. Thats only fair, isnt it? I have told tales and, as we all no, to tell tails is a sin that will get you nothing if not a smack in the face.

Anyway, once the lying, slagging matches and pain is over, the only person ive really hurt with my 'justified anger' will have been myself, wont it? By writing this little poem down it will be me who gets it in the neck again and i will see my tormentors go free, wont i? Yes, by trying to be honest and bearing my sole it is my hart that will be accused of being fouled and sullied. Ive found that out from hard experience: People will not kiss, love and bath the wounds of a broken and abused child but instead attack him as the monster. No, i should never have ritten a word, for it seems that to have 2 good ears, a pair of seeing eyes and a nose to smell shit with is just not allowed in this day and age.

But i carry on. Im a Claudius. I rite this not for the living but the dead and 'yet to be'. Thay can be my judges and i can be their hero. After all, how many other impressionable youths have fill'd their harts and heads with idiotic notions of 'truth' after reading the werks of mad Russians, insane Japanese and raving Norwegians? And how many of our great artists, after living poor and broken lives and being abused for their lack of modesty in life, have later been raised as geniuses in death? Yes, i hear myself, i am as guilty of vanity as the next man, probably doubly so, but that carnt stop me riting it down – its my bread and butter. So, without pretensions, without hiding of any kind and with the job of punching a few people on the jaw, here it is.

William Loveday. November 12 1998

1

Karima

YESTERDAY EVENING my father went into prison and i set my girlfriends hair on fire.

"Listen, Troll," i hissed, "do exactly as i say, or tomorrow you will die! "

I then took a single match, struck it and calmly plunged it into the vile nest of hair that sits on top of her stupid, grinning head. After putting the flames out, i maimed myself quite horribly.

"Look what you've done to me!" i shouted, jeering in her face. Then, puffing on my cigaret, stubbed it into the thin, papery flesh on the back of my poor hand. All the while she just sat there gloating at me maliciously, not uttering a single word of protest. Seriously, she made not one attempt to save me from harming myself.

I felt myself falling, reached out and dragged her to the ground with me.

I lie here with my face against the harsh carpet, scarcely breathing. It is true, if she comes at me in the nite again i will throttle the stupid cow! She tries to free herself so i tighten my grip, pushing my tear-stained face into her black, plastic smelling hair. Soon she stops wriggling and clings to me. I breath her singed hair and have to stop myself from pushing her roughly away or squeezing her in my arms untill she is dead. She dosnt hate me for my evilness but i do.

Actually, i want to hold her close to me, to kiss her and whisper that i love her and would never hurt her or leave her untill the end of time. I feel the downy softness of her ear lobe between my lips and gently draw it into my mouth, tasting it like a little live cockle, then suddenly bite down on it. Instead of whispering sorry and begging her for forgiveness, i somehow found myself hurting her yet again. I roll off onto my back nursing my poor hand. Over all i was pleased that i had re-confirmed my evil nature to myself.

I am above all else a sensitive person and have always required the sympathy of others, especially of women. The Troll loves and worships me, for which i despise her and it seems, will never be able to forgive her. Of course no matter what fairy tails she mite tell, i dont for one moment belive that she really, truly loves me and stare loathingly at her as she crawls towards me across the carpet and offers herself to me like some sort of disgusting dog. No, she only worships me becouse i treat her so viciously. I no that if i were to somehow start loving her in returne she would at once devour me and spit me out.

After my fathers arrest my mother went up to bed and the house was in silence. It was then that our terrible fight commenced. The reason that we carnt live peaceably is that

Karima has committed a sin against me: Things that i have said to her in strict confidence have been regurgitated, distorted and changed into something else, something quite different and grotesque from their original meaning. In short – she is a twister, turneing my honest and brave words of kindness into some kind of cowardly admittance of weakness.

I grab her by her dyed black hair.

"I told you that S— left me not so's you could ridicule me but to help you stop lying to yourself, you stupid bitch! I could see by your stupid face that you were lying. I knew instantly. I told you my story so's you'd no you diddnt have to lie to me. I made my confession for both of us!"

"But she did leave you, you said so." She whines in her strange, upper class, M— drawl.

"I no!" i shout, "I just fucking told you again!" I push her away from me. "I told you out of kindness, so's you could quit lying!"

The Troll bunches her red painted lips up under her nose and gurns at me."But im not lying, you did say it."

I lite another cigaret, take 2 deep puffs then, making sure that shes watching, rest the glowing tip into the wound on the back of my hand.

"Go home."

"Why are you doing that? – its stupid."

"You are making me do this." i tell her.

And its true, i have to punish myself for hurting her. Not only do i have to suffer her distortions about me in public but also i have to attack myself, wound for wound, as i defend myself against her onslaughts and false declarations of love.

The poor Troll just stares at me, her lips puckering.

"You really dont understand anything, do you," i speak "if you'd just realise how stupid you are, you'd be 1/2 as stupid imediately."

She smiles at me, thinking ive given her some kind of complement and comes across the floor on her hands and knees and tries to put her head in my lap.

"You give me your time, and time is more precious than anything else." she simpers.

I am about to attack her again when theres a sound from upstairs. I put my hand over her mouth and listen. My mother walks across the ceiling. She dithers about up there befor picking her way down stairs, crosses the hall and goes into the toilet. The toilet flushes, she re-crosses the hall, then the door handle turnes and her head pokes round the door frame.

"Are you still up?" she says in a hot whisper, "What's that smell?"

I release my hand from Karimas mouth.

"Nothing, i burnt something in the grate."

"Well shut up arguing and go to bed!"

"We're just talking."

"Well dont stay up all nite, and dont let my cat out!" She closes the door behind her and is gone.

So now Karima is making me catch her hair alite, maim myself, wake my own mother in the middle of the nite and lie to her in her own house. And all with my father barely

8

banged behind bars.

It seems that with every passing moment the Troll is turneing me from a gentle, God-fearing son into a vile, hiddious monster. I look down at the weeping wound in the back of my hand. How can i love myself, or even stand being alive in this world if i am such a spiteful being? One thing is for sure – Karima dosnt truly love me and i shall prove it. Soon i really will have to press her throat and kill her!

First off, if the Troll is in love with anything, it is with cigarets, money and some kind of grotesque caricature which she has forst me to become in order to save myself from drowning in her octerpus-like cunt. And i dont cear how often she offers herself up to me, becouse no man can tolerate such slutishness and dog-like devotion in another human being. In short – what has become of the sweet girl i met bearly 3 months ago, who, when she first visited my mothers house, offer'd to do the washing-up becouse 'washing-up was her favourite thing in the whole wide world?' No, not once since then has she so much as touched a cleaning cloth or ventured near the sink.

'You'll have trouble getting rid of that one,' my mother warned me, making a sign with her eyes.

Yes, since those olden days, Karima has evolved into something alltogether different and unrecognisable. Or, to be more specific, she has revealed herself as a blud sucker.

The true reason that i set the Trolls hair alite is becouse she has left me. When i say that she has left me, of course she hasn't really left me at all but she will leave me, becouse i will make sure that she leaves me, becouse if she dosnt leave me, i will cut her off her head and throw her rotting trunk into the river for the fishes to eat!

I reach out my damaged hand and gently take her into my arms. She shuffles between my knees.

"I love it when you put your big strong arms around me."

Again she is lying, for my arms are neither big nor strong.

I kiss her cheek but avoid her mouth. Kissing, afterall, is too intimate to do with someone you no and is something i will only do with strangers. When you look at Karimas face close up it really is quite abnormal. Her mouth is all the wrong shape and it seems that her upper lip glues strait onto her nose, and that nose is distinctly rat-like. Also, the hairs on her chin spread rite the way up to her side-burns. I am telling the absolute truth when i say that some people could say that she really is quite ugly. Whatever, if she dosnt stop scowling the way she does her face will become fixed like a monkeys for all eternity.

"Why dont you shave?" i ask her. And she glares at me.

If i can just make her despise me enough then maybe i will be able to drive her from me forever and my murderous instincts will subside and then maybe, just maybe, therell be a chance for me to re-find my good, gentle self and become almost human again. Only then will i search her out and try to win back her Trolls hart and make her love me all over again. Only this time it will be a true love, rather than her bogus, fake love; her love which is nearer to death than love; her love which is only designed to torture a man and drown him like a wasp in a jam jar.

She ducks out of my arms, slithers down onto the floor,

draws her knees up under her large breasts and sticks her wounderful arse in the air. Yet again she is enticing me to have anal sex with her, which i will refuse to do.

Yes, all of my evilness and unpleasant nature has sprung and become manifest becouse of you, Karima. It is true, if you wernt here, i wouldnt be able to treat you so rudely and i wouldnt hold such harsh judgements against myself either.

I walk to my fathers drinks cabinet, down a very hot glass of whisky then finger my stained flies. Quickly, i unbutton myself, lift my cock and balls out, then wanking myself, drop down on my knees, biting at the big split thru her knickers. I push my self against her, rolling on top of her, her dark hair spread out against the red spirals of my fathers stollen Persian carpet. Karima nos that if she can force me to enter her then i will not have the energy to escape and run away.

I pull her to her knees. She looks up at me with her hard eyes then takes my cock and balls into her long nailed hands, and i look down – i have to see myself in the Trolls hand to belive that i am alive. She holds me bctween her brown fingers, leans her head down and draws me into her mouth and a great well of love rises from withinside of me: that this dear girl could really love me and desire me, that i am not a lost human being after all, but one that is found, lov'd and adored.

I shuffle her backwards towards the settee. Now i must see myself framed in the vast, ornate, Victorian mirror that my father has hung above his drinks cabinet. I stand reflected amongst his whisky bottles like a brave soldier. I let Karima suckle on me then stand her to her feet, bend her over the arm of the settee and lick at her wounderful arsehole.

I put my tongue inside and she wriggles back onto it, pulling her cheeks apart and begs me to fuck it. I love to feel her muscular arse either side of my face as i lick at her big split. I run my tongue up and down from the black fuzz at the base of her spine round to where her cunt begins – its lips black and rubbery, hanging down in scary festoons. I stand and hold her tapering brown waist in my hands and ease the head of my cock into the dark split. I go extra gently, so's that i wont split my foreskin again (which is too tight), and all the while i have to look and see myself framed in my fathers mirror.

My mother is upstairs in her lonely bed and my father is in prison, reaping the rewards of his drunkenness and thievery. Yes, and everybody agrees that i am just like him, carved from the same rotting block, and that sooner or later, i will in fact become him. Thats my mothers prediction. 'Your just like your soddin' father!' And as i stair into my short life of alcoholism and sex, it is true – i have been cursed by them all; my father, my mother and all the generations of misfits and sodomites that pile up behind them. Each of them eager to see me trip and fall face down in the gutter and never come up.

So i look to the mirror and steady myself, not becouse i am a vain man – which i am – but out of fear. Yes, i look into the mirror to worry at my ugliness, not my buti; to hate myself, not love myself; to stare in disbelith at the hard knots of puss that push up beneath my shallow, white skin, and i want to cry and kill myself but be saved at the brink by angels. What has happened to the blond, friendly child i once was? It seems that he has been destroyed, scorched out from within. And at every turne i am confronted by my silly face and have to look at it and to study it, just so's i can mock myself for having the wrong hair, the wrong teeth, the wrong nose, the wrong lips and the wrong head. Yes, everybody agrees that i am a chip off of the same disgusting old block.

Karima pushes back onto me and her wounderful arse shudders and all of a sudden i no that i am wrong, that i have misjudged myself, that i am in fact handsome and brave and have been maligning myself needlessly.

I push into her and have to concentrate to stop myself squirting, then quickly pull my cock from between Karimas fat cheeks, pull her round by her hair and let her lick at me. My thighs tremble and i have to hold her small head in my hands as it jumps out of me, squirting over her hard, flickering tongue, across her face and eyes and into her dark hair. It dribbles from her chin and she smiles up at me, one eyelid glued together. And i look back to the mirror, to make sure that i really do exist, and instead of blushing and stammering like a hated and loathed youth, i take on the air of someone who is cock-sure and reckless. A man who has avenged the wrong doings of all women. A man who is wholly uninterested in the dull opinions of mirrors or others.

2

The Shell Grotto

THE TROLL originates from M—. A cold seaside town where her mother and grandmother live above a Kebab house. I have been there on the train and walk'd on its fake beach and lookt in thru the plate glass windows at its holliday makers putting food into their mouths, whilst their children push money into the machines in the vast amusement arcades. Later we too ate fish and chips and stepped thru those gray streets.

Rite after eating i have a headache. On the way up the hill to her mothers the Troll keeps on about some God forsaken 'Shell Grotto' she wants to take me to see.

"Its beautiful, its all lit up like fairies live in there – in the underground caves." I turn my face away in pain and try to concentrate on the sea gulls screaming at each other.

"We can go there now. Its on the way."

I stop walking, look at her and tell her flatly that we are not going to any shell grotto becouse there is no such place.

"Yes there is, ive been there hundreds of times. Me and Jango used to go there when we were kids."

Suddenly i have lost all patience. "Look", i shout "there is no Shell Grotto!" and turne and walk angrily ahead, even tho' i have no idear which direction her mothers house lies in.

I here her scampering behind me and smile to myself, hugely pleased with my cheep sneering. I let her catch up and even allow her to hold onto the sleeve of my coat. We are getting along quite famously when up ahead i see a sign that reads: Visit M—'s Famous Shell Grotto.

"There it is, look! Its in there." Karima points into a small park. "Theres the entrance."

I increase my pace untill she has to break into a run to keep up with me. No matter how many ostentatious signs these town folk display i still refuse to belive that such a shell grotto exists, let alone be tricked into visiting it.

"We've gone rite past it!"

"There isnt one," i tell her.

We reach the top of the hill and from rite down the end of the street i can tell which house is going to be Karimas mothers becouse of the big sign that hangs out over the road proclaiming 'Kebab and Chicken House'.

You have to go round the back to get up there, theres this endless red stairway that runs up 3 flites. Her mother and grandmother live in this masonet amongst the smell of old meat. Karima tells me that her grandmother – who is in her 80's – is 'unable to leave the building becouse if she goes down the stairs she mite never be able to climb back up them again'. Which is barbaric .

"Why dont thay move? i ask her.

"We've always liv'd here since we lost the hotel."

"Yeah, but now its time to move."

"She gets out sometimes. She went out last spring."

In the hallway i saw Karimas twin brother, Jango, and then had to kiss her mother and grandmother on their soft powdery cheeks. Her grandmothers skin smell'd of violets and i had to make my lips small. Then i escape to the toilet. The cubical is painted pink and there's a small, wicker basket of Highland heather tacked to the wall. I step up onto the toilet bowl and then, leaning with my hand on the sink, look out of the little top window. In the bottom corner i can see a small corner of gray sea, framed between the buildings opposite. There's an inordinate amount of screeching going on, on account of the seagulls. Already i was sick of this M— of theirs, with its stinking promenade, fake beach, none existent shell grotto and smell of old meat locked in above this stinking kebab shop. I pissed into the pan and plan'd to leave for home.

Another of Karimas stories is that her great grandfather was a slave of the Ottoman empire, was as black as the ace of spades and galloped about all over the island of Cypress on a black stallion.

"If he was a black slave from the Sudan, first thayd of castrated him and quaterised the wound with boiling tar, then buried him up to the neck in sand to see if he would survive."

"Yes, thats what thay did."

"Then he wouldnt of been able to have children," i explain to her calmly, liteing a cigaret and drinking from a cup of disgusting tasting tea. The Troll looks at me sulkily.

"Dont you like your tea?"

"Its too milky."

"Dont you like milk?"

"I dont like milky tea."

"I dont like anything red. I dont eat tomatoes, i only eat yellow food, like grapefruits, lemons, custard and bananas."

"You eat fish and chips," i point out.

"Yes, but the batters yellow."

I nod tho'tfully and flick the ash off my cigaret into my saucer.

"Biscuits are yellow. I like biscuits."

I look away trying not to hear her voice.

Theres a knock on the door and Karimas mother asks us who it can be, then gets up and goes and answers the door. I look to Karima. It is her uncle Reg. I see him taking his coat off in the hallway and then he enters the room. He kisses the grandmother, then starts molesting Karima.

"This is my uncle Reg."

Uncle Reg dosnt even look at me when he says hello. He smells of cigarets and has recently had a hart attack. I have to give up my seat. He sits himself down, surrounded by a plume of blue smoke, his eyes like bludy pin pricks. Karima fawns over him in a sickening way. I watch his hands linger on her shoulders.

"This is my new boyfriend. Hes a painter."

"Painter and decorator?"

"No, dont be silly, an artist."

Next, she flits off to get some photographs of a trip she made to Paris and leevs me standing here with this so call'd uncle Reg of hers.

"What do you paint?"

"Pictures."

"I guessed that. What of?"

"I dont no."

"Well if you dont no then God help us!" He looks around for someone to shear his cracking joke. The grandmother nods slitely.

"Have you sold anything?"

"No," i answer him. Uncle Reg shakes his head, turnes to look out of the window and lites up another cigaret.

Karima comes back in with her photos and all of them gather round the kitchen table clucking over them like a lot of mindless hens. Uncle Reg finishes his cigaret in 3 long draws, pushes it out in the ashtray and lites up another. As is the family tradition, he dosnt offer me one. Nor does any one offer to get me a chair, nor pass me one of the precious photographs to look at. It seems that now uncle Reg has turned up i am considered an outsider, and that Karima is somehow in love with this vile toad. His lips really start to drool as he examines her photographs. I too want to see the photographs, and lean over his square, padded shoulders to take a peek, but he manages to manoeuvre his fat fists so as to hide the picture from my view. I have to force myself not to laugh at them all, sat there drooling over some picture of Karima drinking a 'real French cup of coffee' and eating a 'real French croissant' in Paris.

The next picture is of Karima with a cigaret in her mouth sitting in the cafe bar of the P— Centre, a place especially built for bogus people who pretend to understand bogus art. I reach over and try to touch the corner of the photograph whilst it is still in uncle Regs hand but he pulls it away.

"Not so fast, sonny Jim!"

Uncle Reg is short, fat, surly and rude. I am deeply hurt by his unnessisary rebuke and carnt help but blame Karima for his arrogance. He will be top of my list when it comes to my acts of revenge. I stair into the back of his head, sat there with his preposterous backside filling the whole chair. I will him to drop dead of a hart attack, but he just keeps on mouthing off, another great plume of smoke billowing out of his fat gob and large gapping nostrels, and yet more bogus photographs clenched in his damp hands.

I take Karimas arm and drag her out into the hallway.

"We're going now." Karima nods obediently and goes to go back into the kitchen.

"Where the fuck are you going?"

"To say good bye."

"Your not allowed to say good bye!" i spit. I need Karima to prove to me that she loves me. To prove that she hates this vile uncle of hers who has had the effrontery to snatch photos from my fingers. Seeing as Karima is supposedly in love with him it seems reasonable to punish her.

"I will make him have another hart attack!" I shout at her in a violent whisper. Then the kitchen door opens and i drag her into the front room.

3

A Near Drowning

WE WAIT untill uncle Reg has picked his slow way down the flites of stairs, then me and Karima also leave the house. Karima wishes to go for a swim off the harbour wall. Along the way i force her to say bad things about her uncle. Also, she has to start hating M -, which she says she already does. Also, her brother Jango has been hanging around with a big blond, German queer named Tony.

"Your brother," i inform her, "is the person in films who gets stabbed. Not that i would watch any such film."

I watch her face thinking about what i have said. We pass back thru the town in silence. Then Karima comes up with the idear of asking me if i will help her with her drawings, which she says she carnt do on account of not wearing her glasses. She tells me that she will never be able to draw as well as i can. I listen to her cearfully but any attempts to ingratiate herself with me after virtually fucking her uncle in front of me are useless.

"If you want to draw, you dont talk about it, you just do it."

"But i could never paint like you. You use such thick paint. I could never paint like that. I've never used oil paint.

I carnt even draw. Its my eyes, i carnt see."

"Theres no need to be able to draw, particularly. Anyway. your drawings are good."

"Do you really think so?"

"Yes."

"Why?"

"Maybe becouse your blind."

She pouts.

"Im not joking. Anyway, if you carnt see, wear your glasses."

"I dont like wearing them. Thay dont werk properly. I'm sposed to get my eyes tested every year and the last time i had them tested was when i was eleven."

"I wouldnt bother, your pictures are fine."

Karima looks at me disbelievingly.

"Its true," i re-state it "honestly."

And Karima smiles and skips on ahead. The fact that she is so easy to please is the reason why i hate her. When i catch her up on the harbour wall shes already taken off her dress, folded it in a neat pile on top of her stiletto shoes, and is stood there in her performing bear costume. I look away from her body untill she turnes, then watch her arse fearfully as she dives from the harbour wall. I walk to the edge and wait for her to rise in the froth. She appears about 15 yards out.

"The ladys in Ankara told my father that he was blest with a daughter who can swim like a fish." I smile thinly, then she dives back beneath the filthy looking waves. I've always been afraid of water, especially sea water. My father and my big brother are also experts swimmers and have always enjoyed mocking me for my white body and fear of drowning.

"Come on!" She shouts up at me, "You arent scared, are you? Dive in, its brilliant!" She bobs in the heavy swell, and benith me, the waves lashing at the undercut of the sea wall: limpets and black, stinking sea weed. Under normally circumstances Karima would never shout at me. Like my father and brother befor her, she must have smell'd my fear and instinctively no that it is her job to imasculate me.

I watch as the sluttish waves lift her large breasts upwards towards me then lower them back down into the trough of the next wave. Thay lift towards me again and again untill i feel sick of them.

I unbutton myself and stand hesitatingly in the brite sun. The sea stinks of dirty salt and decaying fish and the great crescendo of gulls scream above my head. I hate the luminosity of my body compared to the dusky buti of her skin and i remember being ridiculed for my white legs and almost drowning in a swiming pool when i was aged 9.

Her head bobs up again bellow me. "Dive!" She screams over the screeching of the gulls and i jump. The water rushes up at me, slamming into my chest and body, filling my eyes and nose, and i go down into the cold gray depths. There is a strange silence in that darkness. It seems that an impossable amount of time has passed since i foolishly jumped into these waves, and still it seems that i am sinking to the bottom rather than floating back to the serfis. My hart pounding, i concentrate – counting the seconds in my head – holding my breath untill it feels like my chest will explode and my eyes pop out of my head. I strike out madly with my white legs. 'He has heavy bones.' My mother explained to my teachers. I am drowning.

And then suddenly i arrive back at the serfis. I reach out and grasp for the little patch of blue. A wave knocks me and fills my mouth with its bitterness and i choke and splutter. 'Please God, in your good sense, save me.'

From the crest of the next wave i catch a glimpse of some steps and some rusty railings that run down from the harbour wall. I kick out towards them with my doggy paddle. Now that i realise i have a few more moments befor i die, i allow myself to be cocky and put a certain arrogance into my stroke. All i have to do, it seems, is concentrate on saving myself.

Of course, i could of walk'd down those harbour steps and gently entered the water, but instead i had to wildly fling myself into the waves on the dare of some illergitamet mermade, who cannot even draw! Instead of risking the life of one of our soon to be honoured young artists - a boy of whom it was once said was 'touched with genius' – i could of calmly and gently lowered myself to the waves, or prehaps pretended that i diddnt feel like bathing at all. Or, simply pointed out that swiming is for idiots.

I push on, my thin, uninsulated body already chilled to the bone. At last i see the harbour wall rising high above me. My fingers – shriveled and lost all feeling – try to cling to its slippery serfis. I pull myself along by my finger tips, my thighs chaffing horribly against the barnical incrusted concreat.

In the first moments after i hit the water i beliv'd that if i could just make it to this harbour wall i would be saved. It would only be a matter of going hand over hand to the steps and i would be on dry land. But the waves harass me, bufferting me, pulling my legs from under me, smashing my chest against the dank smelling concreat. One large wave in particular lifts me and throws me against some rocks, scraping my boney chest quite badly. I try to cling on with my feet but the seaweed slips eerily between my white and tortured toes and i find myself back in the drink – in a very cold patch with no sun or lite, directly benith the sea wall; a large jellyfish blooming beside me. I am now bleeding into the water and am quite aware that i have made myself a target for any shark that happens to be swiming off M—'s beaches.

Suddenly, i feel its jaws on my legs and Karimas laughing face serfis's like a seal next to me. Her glee at my predicament is evident. I try to look at her but my eyes sting from the excessive salt and i sip and swallow another mouthful. She dives beneath me, her streaming hair brushing between my thighs. I grab for her but she slips from my grasp and serfis's behind me mockingly.

Once again i kick out in dessperation for the stone steps, finally getting a footing. I try to stand then slip down again into the tretcherious depths, swallowing another great mouthful of sea water and vomit, tears stinging my eyes.

'This is how i will die,' i tell myself, 'with this dark

mermade mocking my maleness'.

Where is the girl i met that nite in the fog, Karima? The girl who i beliv'd had come to save me? The girl who marveled at my 'wounderful paintings' and 'strong arms'? I was lonely and Broken, Karima, and i lov'd you despite the hiddious birds nest of your died black hair.

Ah, do you remember, i washed your hair for you, Karima? Combed out all the tangles and kissed you tenderly in your strange twisted mouth. I tasted the metal of your plate and then you clicked it out and grinned at me with no front teeth.

"Jango knocked them out. There wasnt enough room for us both in the womb. He was bigger than me so he used up all the calsium. Thats why all my bones and teeth are week. Thats why ive got a twisted spine. And when we were playing pillow fights on the bed, he bounsed across and head-butted me in the face and thay crumbled like chalk."

You could of talkt till the paint peeled off of the walls, Karima, i lov'd you for it, and tho't you so sweet and wounderful. But inside my hart was already hardened by the sharp blows of others of your tribe, Karima, and i vowed to never love or cry again. But even fearing you, i still sought you, Karima. And i spoke too you from my hart and i wanted you to speak to me from your hart too. To shear your truest fears and there by sign a pact with me in blud. To know each other and give up some vulnerable part of ourselfs; you to me and i to you, Karima; to tell you a secret of my fritened hart. For you to hold me and know me. And you said you lov'd my strong arms as i hugged you and kissed you and you wanted to live in my pocket. Why dont i hug you and kiss you any more, Karima? What evil spell have you put on me that makes me hate you? Is it becouse you think that you love men but in truth you hate men, Karima? And I, in my turne, hate you and all of the race of women? When we first met i told you my secret, Karima. And you threw that trembling, 1/2 formed foetus to the ground. This is why i am going to marry that girl whos name you despise, Karima. There is no sex between me and her, like your ugly mind imagines. I dont desire her like i desire you, but that is how i no, deep down in my impure hart, that i am still capable of simple love. Which beats you hands down, Karima, becouse a man needs to belive that he can love, other wise he is lost forever. Isn't that laughable? – So i will marry her.

Finally i manage to reach out and grasp the rusty railings and hall myself out of the briny sea. A wave lifts me and sends me sprawling higher up the steps. There is laughter coming from the sea behind me, from the air above me and from the ridiculous throngs of people who sprawl in the hot sun on that fake beach. The sun is laughing at me. The sea gulls are laughing at me and Karima is laughing at me, now imitating my crude doggy paddle thru the dull, stinking waves. Laughing so hard she sinks beneath the dirty froth. She is ridiculing me: William Loveday, the little boy who was sexually molested and almost drowned in a swiming pool aged 9. Me: William Loveday, who has nothing but encouragement for her in her uncertain, child-like doodling!

4

The Shell Grotto (Reprise)

THERE IS A STRANGENESS of being alive – and life smashing its reality into the faces of those who dare to cross its path – that makes it hard for a young riter to go on. Really, i stair at people as if i am a dreadful oga. It seems that i must have obedience at all times but none obey me and then i look quickly away. I am a coward.

We walk back towards Karimas mothers. Past the run-down greasy-spoons and hotels full of people who, it seems, life has cheated. But it is wrong to tell other people what thay feel or who thay are. It is me who feels cheated and deserted. I am those people.

"We used to live in that hotel over there when me and Jango were little. My dad owned all 3 of these hotels. Then he went bankrupt, his empire collapsed and he left M— and went back to L— to live in with his Turkish wife."

I look up at the white buildings, like big bits of old wedding cake rotting in the sea air.

"When we were little we had all the toys we ever wanted and all the sweets we could eat. I used to run up and down the corridors screaming, then we had nothing and had to go and live in the porters lodge with mum."

"My father left home when i was 6," i tell her, "but he still used to come home to make sure that us kids werent having any fun or dropping bits of litter on his fucking lawn."

She looks at me side ways, dragging on a cigaret, her chin small and jutting. She is hard and hateful, which is why i love her. I will make her my prostitute and become her pimp.

Then we meet one of Karimas old skool friends outside a closed down arrcade, and i look at her small breasts which are quite visible thru the arm hole of her T-shirt. I ask her about her display and she holds me with a very poisonous stare. I laugh in a hard unnatural way. Her name is Marina and apparently her breasts are not ment to be lookt at or mentioned, tho' it is quite obviously that she has arranged them for just such a purpose. Then we left her and headed up into C— Vill, back towards her mothers masonet. There were a lot of parked cars and lines and lines of lamp posts.

When she is well behind us Karima asks me if i like Marina, who she claims is her best friend from infants skool.

"Yes" i answer.

Karima flares her nostrels, which are like 2 torpedo tubes, and stairs ahead. There are other girls on the way back who i study. When i see a beautiful girl on the street it really is as if i am staring into a tin of disgusting, writhing worms. Which is quite true. But i not only stare at them but actually force myself to dip my trembling fingers into the tin, lift the worms to my mouth and kiss them.

Once again we walk round the side of the building and look up the steep, red, concreat steps. The thing that scares me the most is interacting; to be close to other human beings in their homes; to see their floral wall paper; to sit trapped in their kitchens or front rooms with their grandmothers miniature ornaments lined up on the mantelpiece with a photo of a dead sailor in a dark wooden frame and the central heating cranked up to full.

I drag my feet on those steps, the last of my energy draning from my tired legs. I put the back of my wrist to my mouth and tast the bitter salt sea and want to turne and escape to the train station.

I lean on Karima and make her help me up to the top of that impossable flite of steps, then stand breathless, the arroma of old meat coming up from bellow. Then we go in and once again thay crowed round me and once again i stoop my head forward at a sarcastic angle and kiss them in their doughy faces.

I am too tall and hate them for being meer midgets. Thay smile at me all over again and make tea and Karimas grandmother tells me that during the Great War, when she was a 12 year old skool girl, she saw a Zepplin raid over East L—.

"And thay must of shot it down or something becouse there was a terrible fire and all the little men fell down to earth in flames. And next morning, when thay lookt at their dead bodys, all their noses messured exactly 6 inches long! Becouse those Germans have long noses, dont thay? Or maybe it was the pressure? Anyway, my father wouldnt let me go out and look at them, becouse i was only a little girl, but the longest one mesured 6 inches! It was such a shock to my system that all my blud turned to water and thay put me strait to bed. I was under the doctor and wasn't allowed to get up or go outdoors for 6 months!"

I nod at her and dunk my biscit. It seems that she is as daft as her grandaughter. I look at their faces. Faces should somehow convay something of the person, or spirit, that lives inside. What does being alive mean? Who are these people on the inside? I for one can detect very little. I take a large gulp of tea and re-assure myself that i am quite cappable of out-witting this household of imberceals.

Next, thay talk about Karimas uncle John, who is dead. He was apprently kill'd in a car crash last summer. Then Karima goes to her room and the grandmother tells me that her husband was a 'huge man!'

"As tall as you but he waighed 22 stone! When he came home drunk i had to carry him up those stairs, all by myself. Single handed! " I look down at this tiny woman and smile and then Karima comes back in carring a small cardbored box containg dead uncle Johns personal effects.

"The police gave them to us after the inquest. This is everything from the cab of his truck. It was totally crushed, wasnt it mum?" Karimas mother nods.

"Oh yes, Kam," and she pushes her glasses back on her nose with her finger, "tottaly crushed."

Karima lifts out the objects one by one: a 50 pence pice, a single driving glove and a packet of Benson and Hedges ciggarets – which he was apparently clutching in his hand when he died. I pick it up and turne it over in my hand: a real packet of dead mans ciggarets, thats for sure. The packet is certanly very scrunched up.

"It could be any old box of ciggarets." I tell her, "maybe thay were sombody elses."

"Oh no, its uncle Johns, becouse he always smoked Benson and Hedges!"

"Yes, he allways smoked them, diddnt he Kam. Benson and Hedges were his favorite."

"Yes, but theres more than one packet of Benson and Hedges in the world," i reason.

Thay all look at me and the grandmother bows her head. Suddenly, i despise myself for my arogence and lack of humility. I hate myself becouse i am not capable of being soft and ordinary like them. I hate myself for not being capable of embracing this cigatret packet with a true Chistian spirit, for not being able to love uncle John, crushed in the cab of his truck, a last Benson and Hedges cigaret dangling from his broken scull. And i hate myself for not being able to love Karimas mother and grandmother, or to stand the smell of their food being cookt in stale lard – just as my mother cookt our food in stale lard. And i hate my mother and i hate myself for pretending that i am in anyway better than these people and their dead Uncle John, who i never even knew and is even now rotting in his grave.

I give back the crushed packet to Karima and she replaces it loveingly back into the box.

"I only smoke filterless cigarets," i say stupidly.

I follow Karima to the bathroom where she washes her

body at the sink. I whatch her towling her body dry, then i wash her hair for her. She wets it and it lies there like a black mess of seaweed. I wash it twice, cearfully comb out all the disgusting tangles and and she smiles timidly at me from the mirrior. Now she will always remember me washing her hair for her, as well as me holding her in my 'strong' arms.

Next, she sits on the tiolet and trims the hairs on her cunt. She stands to show me, the lips hanging down like the tentickels of an octipus.

"I askd my gran about them," she says, standing on tipi-toes and holding them in the mirror, "she said that thay were nothing to worry about. I call them the hanging gardens of babbilon."

I then unbutton myself and fuck her very expertly on the bathroom floor.

When we arive back in the living room Karimas mother takes Karima out into the hallway and tells her how she could here everything that we were doing, clean thru the kitchen ceiling. I look up at the ceiling thoughtfully. Karimas mother smiles at me falsly and asks me if i would like another cup of tea, which i would. I then lite another cigeret.

We sit there in silence for a few seconds. Naturally the sea gulls are still shouting their heads off outside the window.

"You should take your new friend to see the shell grotto," ventures Karimas mother.

"Yes," pipes Karima, "the shell grotto!"

I smile out of politness then, turneing to Karima, tell her in no uncertan terms that i am definetly not interested in visiting any of her fancyfull caves or imaginary grottos.

"But you must go and see them," interupts Karimas mother, "everyone who comes to M— visits the shell grotto!"

I stop drinking my tea and look at her molevently. "Not i," i tell her, "for 1, there are no such caves, And for 2, i am not the sort of person whos mind rests easy in a shell grotto." Karima stairs into her tea and takes a rodent-like sip.

"There is a shell grotto. I've been down there hundreds of times, havent i mum?"

"Oh yes, there is a shell grotto alrite. You should take him to see it, Kam. Its butiful isnt it?"

Karima slames down her tea cup. "Look mum, shut up! He dosnt want to go to the shell grotto, dose he!"

Karimas mother is genuinly startled. "But Kam, i was only saying how nice it is. You could take him and show him."

"Shut up! Shut up! You spoiling everything!" and she storms from the room.

Karimas mother looks to me. But i refuse to be drawn into the discussion. As far as i'm concerned there are no caves and there is no shell grotto.

On the train back to C— the Troll curls her head in my lap and i alow her to suck me off.

Of course, i havent always been a denier of the exitance of love and shell grotoes. And in my difence, i did once try to talk to Karima and for us to become intermert friends and speak of our truth and life but she refused me and humiliated me and now my hart is too knotted to forgive her her slite. In many ways i have lov'd and worshiped women far too much and for far too long, to the extent that i now resent being ask'd to visit fairy land.

It is my own mother who i blame for my anger and inapropreate behaviour. My mother 1st, followed by the whole catawulling gang of those who have humiliated me and smashed me for no good reason, it seems, than becouse i am sensitve. Yes, granted, i also am a lier and a thief but that dosnt mean that i will roll over on my back like some ingrashiating puppy dog and admit that this stinking Shell Grotto of theres really, truly exists, no matter how many signs in the park thay may erect proclaiming it.

5

A Man Who Kicks Sleeping Women From Their Beds

STRANGELY, tho' i persive all people as being less than myself, women i picture high above me, like a great, towering, indestructable bronse statue, sneering down at me with iron swords and clubs in its great fists. And if the truth be nown, the reason that i hate women is the very same reason why i love them and feel compeled to render Karima harmless.

Yes, it is Karima who has forst me to become evil. It

seems that i have become everything that is hard and broken in a young man and have now managed to cut myself from God himself. If Karima wasnt here then maybe i could be happy and become something like my old self again and would not in the futcher have to pay for crimes that i am unawear that i am even commiting in the present. Whatever, i am certanly not going to let down my guard, or alow myself a single nites rest from my endevour to become a man.

We sleep on an old matrice in my fathers empity studio. His expensive sable paint brushes – ruined by me not cleaning them properly after use – stand useless in an old copper pot. I have bandaged my hand with an old hanky and lie here in the dark lisening with hatred as the Troll drops into an easy sleep and then starts grunting at the moon. I stair at her dyed, matted hair.

If Karima haddnt of followed me home then it would not have been possable for me to abuse her and do errevicable harm to myself. But she really did trail behind me thru the nite streets, waited for me to enter the house, then threw small pebbles up at my window and demanded that i have sex with her, even tho' my father had been arrested and i was very tired.

She snorts like a pig, rolls onto her stomoch and pushes her arse against me. I reach down beside the bed, put my cock in her arse and slip a candle into her cunt. I hold onto her small waist but every time i push my cock in, the candle pops out again. On the whole i am very pleased with the strength of my erection and its thickness. It is quite something when a cock just entering her arse will not alow for the insertion of a candle.

Altho' in many ways Karima has become my enimy, i still love her for traveling thru the nite to awaking me by throwing stones up at my window; for being desperate to have sex with me and only me; for desiring my body to the exclussion of all others; for worshiping me and helping me belive that one as broken and as ugly as me could be at all lovable; for fooling me into believeing that i am God for the moments that her arse trembles on the end of my cock; for telling me that she has multipul orgasems just by me putting the fat head in there. And then i pull it out and feed it to her lapping tounge and i fall to the pillow kissing her lips in gratitude and tasting myself there, then to sleep a deathly sleep. Yes, even in the throws of my spite i no that deeper in my sole i am still that kind, gental, child i once was, even after beeing pawed by that 46 year old pervert.

I dream that i'm fighting my way up a strange river as broad as a sea, against tidle waves and thru terrible rappids. Many times my narrow dug-out canoo is almost capsized. I kneel in the stern up to my thighs in water, paddleing against the muddy torrents that smash down on me. Suddenly, there is a loud rendering of timber as the bottom of the canoo grinds over sharp, trecherious rocks. I battle on, dragging the canoo across the rappids by its paddle and every second the rocks threaten to slice thru the bottom of the hull and sink me to the bottom.

I awake in a heavy sweat with Karimas roasting body clinging to me in a hiddious death grip; her large breasts stuck to me with persperation; her troll-like nostrels snoring sourly in my face. I un-clasp her arms from round my neck and push her away from me across the damp sheets. She snuffles, rubs her nose with the backs of her paw-like hands, then carrys on sawing wood.

I lean over her and stare into her pug face lit up in the moonlite. She has drunk my seed and now she has the nurve to lie there with it smeered round her rediculouse mustash. Why should she sleep so soundly when it is me who has been drained and defiled? Me, who up untill this Troll latched onto me, never once sweated in the nite and allways maintained the perfect body temprichar? And now, here i am reduced to sweating, hateful sleeplessness by this over-heated dago! I poke her spitefully in her belly and she grunts, clings onto my arm and starts up a snoring noise to raise the dead.

I lay here and pray to God for her to shut up. Everytime there is a slite lull, i feel myself drifting off then suddenly she changes gear, theres an increase in pitch and a new level of grunting begins. I try to slap her face, gently at first. She hacks something up out the back of her throat, swallows it, smiles to herself, then starts off all over again. I feel that my body is an empited cylinder, the sound of her, reverberating thru my very core. I pinch her nose shut between my thumb and fore-finger. There is a moments silence, then she starts to gag, springs up in the air, flips over onto her front, ajusts her arse and just carrys on grunting.

Every time that i'm almost on the verge of sleep, she starts cleaning her drain. Suddenly, involentaraly, i spin on my back, hook my heels under her belly and push off, lifting her from the bed and sending her crashing out into the darkness. She goes flying across the room, knocks into the chair and comes to rest under the table, her head rebounding between the foot rails. I listen out into the nite. My mother calls from the other room, then silence. The Troll lies there groaning for a moment, sobbing to herself. She turnes onto her side and makes a pillow with her arms. Her breathing settles into a gentle rythem, then slowly builds and builds untill she is snoreing again at full throttle.

Yes, i am a man who kicks sleeping women from their beds in the middle of the nite then forses them to sleep under the table without so much as an old blanket to cover themselfs with.

6

A Familys Judgment

MY FATHER sleeps in his prison bunk and i sleep here with the Troll in his empity studio in his empity house. 'I dont want you bringing your whores home to A— Place!' He shouted at me several months back. That was just after i had been expelled from the Acadamy. I had walk'd 4 miles thru the ici snow looking for a bed with the Ice Queen, a woman both chased and pure and not in the least bit whore-like. But all that was long ago, in another age, another time, befor i lost her and the capasity to love. I could of stayed with the Ice Queen for allways becouse i wanted to be her slave and abase myself befor her ici butie. It was she who pulled herself away from me. When we parted i pretended that we were mearly going our separate ways and that it was a joint dessision to end our love. I was too ashamed to tell people i had lost her, so i lied. The truth is, she was sick of me and my base instinkts. So now, like my father befor me, i fall in love only with poisonus women who hate me. And i serviss them in his vast ornamental mirror, whilest he langashes in prison and pays the price for his crimes.

It is strange that my father should have call'd the Ice Queen a whore. Both my father and the Acadamy are obbsessed with apperences and both the Acadamy and my father have proved themselfs to be utterly bogus. In some ways it would seem that i have conqered over both of them. Yet even in victory there is still no food and no money. How is that whilest i starved, my father liv'd in the lap of luxsory? Whilest i struggled thru trecherious snow drifts, arm in arm with a delicate buti – who my father branded a whore – he was meanwhile being driven around in the luxsuory of a hire car, with a 1956 Rolles Royce sitting under its dust cover in the gararge?

I get up, step over the Troll and go down stairs. I take the torch from the kitchen draw, go out into the garden and lift the swing door of the grarage. The ghost of a car fills the darkness. I pull the dust cover up over the bonnet and try the doors but thay are all locked. I shine the torch in at the pale leather uphostery and across the walnut dashboard.

Even befor my father lost his licence for drunk driving he scearsly drove this precious car out onto the streets. Occasionally he would come home, cearfully unwrappe it, drive it out of its gararge then spend the whole afternoon massargeing its gray paint, then 'Haring' on the silver lady and all but licking at her tiny feet. After Sunday dinner, he'd reverse it back into its gararge, wrap it all up again and disapear up london to sleep with his mistress. My fathers moto in life is this: 'It is the presentation what counts!' His other great saying is 'It all adds to lifes rich tapistry'. Tho' ive only heard him use this maxim in regard to others peoples missfortunes, not his own.

Even when i was a kid i was never allowed in this car, on account of my muddy shoes and tendency to vomiting. Then my father left home and we diddn't see him anymore.

My hair is fair and people say that i am ugly. When i was still young i was brought up to belive i was somehow diformed and was trained to fret about my apperence. Back then i was forst to admit to myself that i was in fact ugly, but as i grew i came to question my famlys judgment and istead saw myself as ugly in an interesting way. This statement in itself will amuse my elder brother greatly, should he ever come to read this dark history.

It was when my father left home that my brother took it upon himself to reinstate my sureity of my own uglyness and genneral lack of worth. 'You will suffer violent achny!' – 'You are lucky you weren't born a phelidomide!' – 'You carnt read or rite, you are thick, thick-o!' – 'You eat with your disgusting mouth open!' And – 'You still piss the bed like a little baby!' At the same time he took every oppertunity to show off his inteligent and handsome head at every angle. Stood arrogently pouting in the Victorain gilt mirror that even then stood behind my fathers drinks cabbanit.

Probebly, my family are a bunch of liers and i am not really ugly at all. But that is not for me to no. All that can be said for certen is this – i have been given verious weeknesses. It is these weeknesses that my educators have chossen to exploit. Becouse as eveyone nos, librels are more vicous and scathing in their hatred than facist's can ever be.

Whatever else can be said about my young life, it is true that nobody ever lov'd me or protected me. Whether or not this has left me over sensitve and highly strung is debatable. But i do hunger for the good words and aprovel of others, tho' i will never bow down to acolayed or sucssess mesured out by another if it so much as smells slitely of condisention. My pride is what thay hate and my pride is what will ultimatly kill me.

What i despise about the world of adults – my father and Mister Bennit – is that thay are not adults at all, but meer children. Yet still thay hold power over me. Of course, Karima is in love with power and her puppy-like devotion to success is what will enable her to roll over and allow Mister Bennit to rub her tits.

Yes, i have learn'd to hate myself, my face and my hart.

Naturally, i keep my gob shut on this account and have learn'd to pose in photographs and not let people see my rancid sole. But whenever i am in some hiddious pub or other and am forst to look at my pale face, hovering ghost-like in the mirror, i am reminded by my profile and my hair, but more presisly by what lays hidden benieth and within, that i am ugly, that i am a fool, that i am a lier, and that i will forever remain un-lovable.

7

The Mad

SEEING'S THAT the world of the sain strives for fat, luxsorious cheeks, i will strive for the battered, hollow cheeks of a mad man. Where as the employed dream of pink, gleaming faces, i will dream of drawn, gray faces and my eyes will stare hauntingly, peering after strangers on wind-swept streets.

Where as the fashionable ware long, generiously cut slacks, my trouser leg will be too short and skool children will no doubt call out after me, shouting 'Frankenstine!'

Yes, i will rite fantastic stories about love which people will presume are about hatred and death. My fame will grow and i will be talkt about the length and bredth of the entire country and beyond. Compleat strangers will presume to no me and walk up to greet me on street corners. But no matter what liberties thay may take with me, thay will never no the tresure that lies hidden within my hart.

To escape them i will travel abroad and amaze everyone. Who nos, even Mister Bennit, my tutor from the Acadamy, may come to contemplate my name and stroke his chin nurviusly, woudering when i will come for him. Afterall, nothing is as mysterious as a madman.

8

Art Skool Devil

NOW THAT we've started i will do my best not to tcll you too many tall stories or downrite lies. Its the truth that i catch young ladys hair alite in my fathers front room then fall to the floor and maim myself as punishment. It really is as if my mind is fill'd with poison. I took a single match, struck it and… Well, you no the rest.

Let the historians amongst you note that i use matches and not a liter. I have no interest in gimickry. What intoxicates the sain man, with his carreer, his social standing and his nessisary laws and beliths, leaves me cold. I have no curiosity about where he sleeps, the colour of his lungs or what type of shoe his wife wears. In short – i refuse to bow down to any form of modern cleverness, fashion or pretence. What i mean is, is that im not exactly a beliver in the triumph of tecknolagy. No, i have instead desided to align myself with the mad. This means that i must nessisarally refuse all medels and praise least i become contaminated.

Karima, who started off wanting nothing but to be 'a small person living in my pocket' and to design cloaths for the rich and wealthy, has changed her tune. The Trolls ambition is no longer content with her being a meer fashion student and now wants her to become an artist instead. She has made her pictures and applied to the same Acadamy from which i was so shamefully expelled. On the whole this is exerlent news.

Despite her attempts to drown me i have helped her with her drawing, as ask'd. To make pictures after all is what counts, becouse life is in fact poetry. It is just up to us to desipher and show what is in our true harts without making any of it up, nor leaving out any of the meaness that we disscover within. But as far as the Mister Bennits of this world are concerned poetry can go to hell! And as far as Karimas wish to ingrashiating herself with the idiots at the Acadamy are concerned... Well, she may forn and capitulate, i for one will remain angry and pure, becouse somone has to stand up and refuse to be an interlectual chimpanzee.

There is a big joke in regard to Mister Bennit, this is

how it goes: Back during the Boar War – or whenever it was that he was mistakenly sited for a meteoric carrear in the arts – Mister Bennit was actually a painter. Then, struggling in the teeth of fashion to remain young and exciting, he gave up painting altogether and instead feverishly exhibited a lemon with 2 bits of wire hanging from it that, when connected, lit up a single lite bulb. This was not done, i mite add, to illustrate the tremendous elerctric current that circulates thru a lemon, but to show how imense Mister Bennits brain was.

So, to think that Karima now eagerly skips up those same hatefull steps that i once reluctently dragged my feet up. That she now stands there in the que for the canteen, chatting with the other brite students, awaiting there cookt meals in the very same canteen where i sulkerly stood to one side and refused to eat their stinking food and instead subsisted on an old banana, a packet of monky-nuts and a cup of hot water for my ginsing tea.

The floor tiles in there have a gray marble effect. I staired from them to the faces of my fellow students. I studdied their lips and the shapes of their eyes and sculls, but not one of them, to my eye, had the countence of a true artist. It seemed that i had given up my position in Her Majistys Dockyard (aprentice stone mason, £16.50 per week) for nothing.

By the end of that first day i had been summond into the office of Mister Bennit several times and denounced as the worst student who had ever soiled the threshhold of their pox-ridden Acadamy. Yet only 3 weeks earler i had been accepted – despite my lack of formel qualifications – into the bossom of their skool on the grounds of what thay described as my 'exceptional artistic ability'. What had happened to my genius in the meantime? Imediately i was banned from 3 dimensional studies and then thrown out of the print making rooms for back-chatting a man call'd Ralph with eyebrows the size of large hedges. I was then told that i was to be put on probation and would have to report to Mister Bennit every 2 weeks to have my progress monitored and see what steps mite need be taken in regard to my forthcoming expulsion and the curbing of my 'eccentric behavior'.

Returning home that first evening i was crest fallen. Where were all the brave artists and poets of the past? All the heroes of all the colourful books id seen in the library? Artists who diddnt become famous, i mite add, by bowing down to the fashions of the day and by fawning to the first man thay met who offer'd them a degree. Where were the men and women whos harts heaved and sobbed when thay happened across an old photograph of their mother as a beautiful young woman in the arms of a man not there father? The sensitives who could not pass a simple cherry tree in blossom without tears gushing from their eyes, who diddn't feel strange sensations of poisonous insects creeping all over their flesh when passing some chisel-faced prostitute on the High Street? Where were my brothers and sisters in arms who i had forsaken my life in the Dockyard for? Where were the ones who slept in bedsits with the stink of oil paint filling their nostrels and dreams? – Thay were pen pushers, my friends. Graphic designers, model makers and fashion designers. Corn flake packets, vile dresses and scale models of shopping arcades with miniature banks, small dogs and tiny people… Little trees made out of puffs of cotton wool… Bludless, sanitized and dead – There wounderful vision of the futcher. No, thay weren't painters of life nor God but career artists, baby tutors, burocrates and aspiring little Mister Bennets.

And so i must paint on my own, in the outside world forever. And then my little Troll came along. Someone to keep me company. But now she too belives in them and not in me. When she returned from her first day at the Academy, she was not in the least bit dispirited and instead of running into my arms crying and sobbing that she was never going back there, she sat, lit a cigaret and started singing their praises to high heaven.

She even spoke in a mysterious new language: in place of her usual M— drawl, she now talkt with a dull haughtiness about subjects quite at odds with the actual size of her brain. Watching me slyly from the corners of her dark eyes, she began denouncing my werk, suggesting that i used to0 much black, a trait which she had previously elevated. It also transpired that it was wrong to paint on white backgrounds and i should try some primrose yellow. It seemed that instead of denouncing the world of the sane, she was wholly in love with it.

I sat eating a dry crust as she moved about the dark flat searching out a missing packet of cigarets, then, still talking of art, went out into the kitchen (i had been teaching her how to cook). It really was as if Karima was dead and the wounderful Mister Bennit, or at least his fat ghost, had entered her sole and was now in the kitchen making leek and potato soup.

So, she had left the bogus world of fashion, only to bring fashion into painting. Black, it seems, was last years thing. It was then that i studied her face more closely and decided to name her The Troll. It was also then that i decided it was war and prehaps had the first notion of setting her hair alite.

To think, the Academy and Mister Bennit accepted her – the very same Mister Bennit who had expelled me, the young genius, William Loveday.

As i ate my soup i peered sulkily at the pulverised bits of potato floating about in the gray water. I had definitely liked her best back in the olden days, when she had lov'd my paintings and worshiped me of her own free will; when i had first broken her in, tho' of course i diddnt break her in, i failed.

It is a wounderful thing to have a woman lying at your feet, but also it is a terrible thing and really, all along, it was a lie. And really, she only gave herself to me so as to be able to smash me. And its all my own fault becouse it was me who encouraged her in all her idiotic notions and helped her with her feeble drawings and let her sleep with me in my small, coffin-sized bed. And then the other things i've already told you about happened and for that reason everything was already finished and i hated her.

After dinner she takes an old tobacco tin from her skool bag, opens it up with a 2-bob bit and commences to hand-roll a cigaret. I watch her in silence. What has happened to her belov'd Rothmans? Finally she gets the thing into some sort of cigaret shape and lites it up. As she puffs out the bitter smoke she wipes her dark fingers on the trouser leg of her rough werk overalls. And what has happened to her nice dresses? And instead of stiletto heels she now wears an old pair of scuffed army boots. Of course, this new uniform was quite familiar to me from my own days at the Academy, but it hurt me when she started to criticise my paintings in the idiotic voice of Mister Bennit.

Her brown fingers lift the cigaret to her twisted mouth and all tho' her nails are still quite long, thay were already beginning to look cracked and not cearfully manicured and filed as had previously been her obsession. Neither were thay painted their usual blud -red. I lookt to my own finger nails with their broken cuticles and felt a distinct unease rising in my chest.

I drag my chair noisily across the floor and stand to leave. I wait for her to speak but she says nothing. I even look pointedly towards the door so's she nos that i really am intent on leaving, but again shc ignores me. I cross the room stamping my feet, go out into the hallway, bang my way up the steps, open the front door and slam it behind me. I stop and listen. Rite on cue i hear her little cry of dismay when she realises that i really am leaving her for good. I here the quick scamper of her feet on the stairs and then her hand on the catch. I walk a little way up the entrance hall and pretend to be tying my boot laces. She comes thru the door way, drops to her knees and begs me to stay, her small fist clutching at the hem of my jacket. Then i stand and stride on, dragging her behind me. I am hard and arrogant, but on the inside i am happy and rejoicing. I can still smash this mere woman, for i am William Loveday, artist and poet, lover, sodermite and escape artist. I wait till she offers me her body and her purse. I look out into the inviting street then look at her in a most disdainful manner befor slowly turneing and reluctantly trudging back down the hallway into her flat, down the hatefull stairs, along the black damp corridor and into her bedroom.

Once there i sit on her bed morosely looking at her ferret- like face in the defused lite that trickles down from the grating above. Now i need to be drunk. There is nothing to drink in the house so i send her down the off- licence to buy me a bottle of rum with her grant check.

I lie here waiting for her to leave. First the door bangs, then her footsteps on the street and finally her shadow passes over the grating. I count to 10 in my mind then stand to the little chest of draws and start going thru her underwear. I fold one of her oversized bras into my pocket, the one for nursing infants, with the nipples missing. Next i take off my trousers and masturbate into the fire place.

When she returns she tries to kiss me but i take the bottle, shrug her off and walk back down the corridor to the front room. Only in the early hours of the morning do i pick my way back up the dark and scary corridor that leads to her Trolls cave. Very drunk i lean against the wall in the hallway to undress. I wank myself till i am hard then burst in on her and chaise her across the bed with my cock.

After sex i lay in the dark and smoke ciggerets. I have to

keep my eyes open or i will be violently sick. I sense the dark mass of her hair on the pillow beside me and can tell from her breathing that she is also awake. She lifts my arm and tries to snuggle up against me, but i hold my arms and body ridged and will not allow it. She asks me if i have drunk all of the rum.

"Yes," I say. There is a silence.

"That cost me 10 pounds."

"So?"

I listen out into the nite. After an impossable pause she starts up again. 1stly, about her lack of money, going into mindless detail about how much she spends on train fares a week. 2ndly, about how much tobacco she has to last her till the end of the week. And 3rdly, about how she has now wasted the last of her grant check on buying me a bottle of rum that i have drunk in a single evening without saving any for her. Not that she likes rum, its just that it was the last of her money for this term and now she is penniless.

"Im not complaining, i just want you to no that you've spent the last of my grant money, thats all. Now i dont no if ile have enough money for the buss, or the train. And i've got nothing left for ciggerets."

If i still had any strength left in my limbs i would kick her from the bed, but she has again robbed me of my precious bodily fluids and now of my will to live. And i must lie here, knackered, listing to her inane meanderings for all eternity. She keeps talking, and i stair blindly into the darkness. She has false front teeth and thay click as she speaks Finally, i roll out of bed, crawl blindly up the hallway and make myself throw up in the toilet. I kneel there shivering in the darkness with my head in the pan. I push my fingers down my throat and it jerks out of me in bitter spurts. Then the lite clicks on.

"What are You doing?"

"Throwing up."

"Its all that rum. I paid for that and now your just making yourself sick!" I lift my head from the pan and i shout at her to shut up. I also remind her that up untill now it is my money that she has been living off, for 6 whole fucking months! It has been my money that we've spent at the pub and my money that buys the food. Now get out!

There is a long silence. I lean back over the pan and throw up once more. I no that she is still there, i can feel her sulking in the gloom behind me and i realise that she has finnaly turned me into my father.

9

Of Terripins

I AM A TERRIPIN living in an old plastic washing-up bowl in the window of a pet shop. There are about 30 other baby terripins in here with me and every day, at about 3.30, many, many skool children come and bang on the window at us. I look at their giant faces and their pointing fingers. If one of those noses or fingers were to come within easy reach of our tank then as one we would swarm all over it and devour it. Out of all the skool children that come to view us, i recognise one. She pushes to the front and pinches the girl next to her with a horsey bite on her thigh. Of course, it is Karima i am talking of, and it is she who comes into the shop and buys me.

I look up at her out of our stinking water. Yes, it is definetly her. She is wearing platts and her front teeth are missing. Out of all of the others little terripins in the tank it is me she chooses becouse of my sexual nature. No doubt i am her favorite becouse of the boldness of the black and white stripes on my throat. Or prehaps becouse of the uneque way my teripin head bobs up and down and the special luster of my orange eyes and shell. Whatever her reason, it is clear that to her eyes i am a cut above all the other terripins that float aimlesly about in that bowl of teppid dish-water.

Karima points to me and the shop owner cearfully picks me up from behind so's i carn't give him a crafty nip, then drops me into a dark, carboad box. I am shaken about in there. I here the bell of the shop door and then it grows cold as we go out into the street. There's the screech of her skool friends and the close noise of trafic. From there i am jolted as Karima skips all the way home to her mothers masonet with me locked under her arm.

Once upstairs she sets my box down and i here her turne on the taps and the sound of running water. She then takes the lid off my box and emptys me into a clear tupper-ware bowl. The stupid girl hasn't even put a little stone in here for me so's that i can haul my tired body out of the water and have a little rest. No, i have to swim in little cirles, round and round forever. For several minits Karima stairs at me in child-like wonder as i splash helplessly about. It is up to me to try to keep moving thru the water or drown. She then lifts up my bowl, puts it up on top of the fridge, claps her hands and skips off. I dont even have a chance to bite her.

As soon as she is out of site i see about how to escape the walls of my glass prison. It is very hard to get anywhere on account of my body being encassed in its hard shell, but after 2 or 3 attempts, useing all of the strength in my small teripin body, i manage to get one flipper up over the lip of the glass and heave myself from the water. I sit here, see-sawing on the edge of the dish, the vastness of the kitchen swaying befor me. My idear is to drop down onto the top of the fridge and then plan my escape back to the giant sea. It is very hard to control my movements and as i tip myself over onto the fridge my wet shell skims off the plastic serfis and i feel myself spinning in space. There is a loud 'thack' as i hit the tiled floor and then darkness.

When i come to, i find that i am lying on my back. There is an enormous human foot stood rite there beside me. I twist my head round and look at the fat ankle, and above that, the towering legs of Karimas mother. I lie here motionless, my side is badly brused but it appears that my shell is not broken. Also my rite flipper is a little bent out of shape. Karimas mother passes back and forth from the sink, making tea. Twise she almost steps on me befor accidently kicking me under the fridge.

"Oh! What was that?" She asks herself and gets down on her hands and knees and peers in at me. It is dark under here and thick with fluff and black greece, but at least i am now the rite way up. I scrabble on the dirty tiles, trying to shuffel back up against the wall. Karimas mother disapears, then comes back with a fish-slice, and trys to scoop me out. I fight her off but it is hopless. Finnaly she weadles me out and tosses me into the rubish bin. Her face looms over me. I lie quite motionless, looking at her huge nose. Then she covers me with cold tea leaves and a great waight of potato peelings. Next a bag of old tin cans is dumped in on top of me and i am pinned here in the cold and dark. The stink of rotting garbidge fills my nostrels and i pass in and out of conciousness during the nite. In the morning i am taken outside and chucked in the dustbin. There is a faint lite of dawn filtering down to me, then some men come and haul me away in a dust cart where i am put thru the mincer.

Next, i am a terripin ghost watching Karima come into the kitchen, walk over to the top of the fridge to say hello to me but i am gone. All she finds is the empti, washed up tupper-wear bowl lying on the drainer. She call's to her mother.

"Mum, have you seen my terepin?"

"What, Kam?"

"What have you done with my fucking tererpin?!"

Karimas mother pokes her head round the door.

"Pardon, love?"

"My pet terripin, it was in here, where is it?" Karima holds up the empity bowl.

"That thing, Kam? It was a toy… Wasn't it? I kicked it under the fridge." Karima stairs at her.

"You kicked it?"

"I fished it out again, but then i threw it in the bin. I thought it was a toy. It was a toy wasn't it?"

"No, it fucking wasn't." and Karima rushes to the empti bin.

"Oh, sweethart, i kicked it under the fridge. I thought it was a toy."

"What have you done with it, you stupid cow?"

"Its no good swearing at me. I told you, i threw it away. It went out with the rubbish, i thought it was one of your jokes."

"It wasn't a joke, it was real. It was alive!" And she crosses her eyes in anger. Karimas mother rushes to the door.

"Ile go and look in the dustbin, maybe the dustman hasn't been yet."

But it is to late, i am already being carried away to the city dump. I lie on my dameged side, waving a torn flipper mournfuly in the air, my mouth caked with blud.

Karimas mother comes back up into the flat. "No, thay've already been. I really thought it was a toy… Are you sure it was alive?"

"Of course it was alive! It was my pet terripin and now you've kill'd it!"

"Im sorry Kam, How much was it? Ile buy you

another one."

"I dont want another one. I want my one!"

It is then that i wake up. She is on top of me, forsing her cunt into my mouth. I try to lift my head from the pillow but she has her knees on my shoulders. She rubs her cunt into my kisser, thrusting her hips at me. I reach up, grab her round the waist and topple her backwards. She paws at me but i push her off and sit on the edge of the bed, wiping the taste of her from my chin. I pick a hair from my teeth. She grabs me again from behind, wrapping her arms round my kneck and incircling my waist with her legs, her tounge worming at my ear. This time i stand and throw her off onto the bed.

"What time is it?"

Her face grows sad. "Why?"

"I've got to go."

"Carn't you stay? Please stay."

I sit back on the bed. "I carn't, im tired."

She snugles up to me. "I want to be a small person living in your pocket. Then you can take me with you and we'll be together for allways and allways."

I push her off and stand up. She tries to smile. Her dark lips, one moment a childs, the next like a sickening whores. Again she talks to me in her small, high pitched voice, like a glove puppit. Really, she holds up a small fluthy toy and makes it speak to me. I have to make a determind face not to smile. I turne away. No longer am i flattered by Karimas desire to be with me at all times, or her willingness to give her body to me. She lifts her face and reaches out her hands but i can not bring myself to kiss her or stay with her.

57

"You carn't go. You've got to stay with me." Her voice is saccharin.

I can now see that it was a mistake for me to get drunk and alow myself to be seduced and recaptured by her. I try to punch myself in the nose with full force but only hit myself a glancing blow in the eye. In futcher i must remember to get up and leave after sex, no matter what the houre. I go into the hall and bundel up my cloaths. Imediately she is on me.

"No," she wimpers, "you musn't leave!" I walk down the hallway, pulling on my trousers and stamp my feet into my old army shoes and all the time she is behind me, scampering on her fury Trolls feet, tugging at me and begging me to, 'please, please, please stay with her the whole nite'.

"You must stay here and fuck me!" I turne and look at her. Now that it is plain that i will not do her will, her voice has lost all of its cloying sweetness and instead screetches like chalk across slate. Once, it is true that i was inchanted by her troll-like charms, but now i must leave and presserve my honour, and i am not playing or pretending. I turne and leave and she springs from the floor and jumps onto my back. I walk on, ignoring her, dragging her waight out the door along the hall behind me. I feel a strange detachment, as if i am whatching the seen from above and it is not me who feels her arms tighten round my kneck as she leers into my face. It is not me who sees her dark mustash and her nostrels gapeing like torpido-tubes – her wet mouth with hardly any upper lip at all. It is not me who hates her intensly but somone else, somone who i can almost laugh at.

I get to the door and try to shrug her off but she clings

to me all the more tightly. I stagger up the unlit entrance hall that leads out onto the street. It is here that i run into a wheel barrow hidden in the darkness. I smash both my shines, then crying out in pain, roll her off my shoulder and storm out into the street to breathe the fog – which smells of piss, mud and the river. At the end of the road there is a street lite. I gingerly roll up my trouser leg and studdy my wound. Black looking blud trickles down my shin and into the top of my boot. Then Karima is upon me again. I hear her bare feet padding on the damp paveing stones and without turneing i run on. There arc 2 'Specials' stood by the castle gate. I slow down and keep my head down as i pass them, then hurry on down the little hill, Karima trailing behind me like a ghost.

"You musn't leave me!" Karima wails. The 2 'Specials' look nurvisly up the road and step further back into the shadows. I put on a spurt, cut up by the cathedral and into the V—'s. I get to the end of the avenue of trees then sit down on a bench, holding my shins which throb in the damp, nite air. Then there is another call in thc nite. I look up and Karima appeers at the far end of the park, her white nite dress, shimmering in the darkness. My mind is such that i love this game of hide and seek. Maybe i should of stayed with Betty, who it was easy to love. She was easy to love becouse she diddn't have hips and i diddn't desire her. Betty was my sister, but i left her to set some strange womens hair alite. For the thrill of having her chassing me, 1/2 naked thru this avenue of plane trees.

I now realise, Karima, that rather than being an

expression of your undying love, the charms you offer me are in fact an expression of your contempt. And all tho' you do say that you love me, in truth, Karima, your love has nothing to do with love at all, but rather with mindless goo. You dont no who i am or cear at all. Your love is like a small childs love for her pet hampster which she squeeses in her hands untill it is quite dead!

"You carn't leave me, you must stay. I will cook you something. Its too late to go home, you have to rest. I bawt food for brakfast tomorow!"

Sitting there on that cold bench i falter.

"Ile see you tomorow." I call back thru the fog, "I need my own bed!"

"Why, what's wrong with my bed?" And she comes closer.

"Are you all rite? Are you hurt?" There is hopefull concern in her voice. The truth is the Troll would rather i was a double amputy at her compleat mercey, unable to get up and walk away, strapped in a wheelchair in her damnable cave, having my stumps bathed by her brown turkish hands and forst to accept what ever love she dishes out, uncondishnally – smack in the kisser!

She is well into the avenue of trees now and no longer needs to shout. She steps closer and starts her insesent chattering again. Her nite dress is gaping open and i see her large brests dangling there, trying to eat each other. Her voice tells me about how one day, when she is rich, (and she will surly become rich), how one day she will metimorphasize from an insect into some stupendious, golden butterfly who will shower her frends with fragrant whisky and ciggarets.

"I will buy you bottles of scotch every week. I will buy all my friends their favorite drink and brand of cigarets. In hundreds!"

I stand and back away.

The reason i set fire to Karimas hair is becouse i have had to steal myself against her asaults upon my body and mind. She somehow belives that the more she offers me and debases herself in front of me the more i will love her and the more she can rob me of my hart. But even when i have taken her and conqued her, i dont feel like a hero, i feel like a fraud and a fake. She really belives that every time she lets me fuck her 'behind', as she redicliously calls it, that her perfetic whitchery will capture me for allways, redusing me to a gurgling cripple, tottaly at her mercy. And even after she has sucked me dry, she starts rite in tormenting me, trying to induce me to begin all over again. Yes, it is becouse of you, Karima, that i have become hard and un-loving. It is becouse of you that i have become a villan. It is becouse of you that i have hurt my shins so badly. I trip on the curbing and she almost grabs me. I move slightly behind a tree. She is hell bent on forcing me to live with her, to marry her and give her children, poisioning me to commit unnoable crimes against her and myself.

I scrabble to my knees as she reals off another great list of all the benifets that will flow into my life if i will agree to live in the same room as her for 24 hourse a day. Her face floats befor me. Certanly i need to have sex with her and have her worship and adore me. Also, i need to gaze on her wounderful Turkish arse, but since my father is now a gaol bird it is my duty to stay with my mother and suffer under her idotic juristictions, not Karimas. And so i push her away from me and start the long walk home.

Karima, if you diddn't degrade yourself befor me, then maybe i could love you, you Troll. But then you mite stop chassing me thru these streets in your nite dress as i stride away from you and never again would you throw stones up at my window in the middle of the nite. Never would you lift your arse in the air and ask me to fuck it, to hear you telling me that you want sex and you only want it with me, then drink every last drop of me.

Yes, it is exciting to no that you will allways chase after me.

10

A Game of Dockyard Chess

I PASS ON between the dark, somber trees and under this whitches sky. Quite soon i arrive at the bus stop. Hard, smudgy faces of werkers pass me by, some floating along on their bikes, others trudging by on foot. All of them disapear in under the vast, ornate doorway and into the shadows beyond. I recognise one old fellows face from the Rope Walk, nown as 'The Captin'. In those anciant days of old i played chess with him on my dinner houre. It seems strange now to concidor all those months that have passed since i liv'd in the world of werking men. Now i dont belong to them, but neither do i belong to the world of artists either.

It happened in the tearoom in the morning becouse i'm a show off. Some of the old boys used to play checkers and i bosted that i could play chess. Thay all lookt at me like i was lying. 'Chess?' Thay said, stroking their fat hooters. Next thay set up a match for me against 'the Captain'.

So come dinner time i knock off, borrow Bills bike and cycle all the way over to the Roapery with my flask and sandwiches. The Captain is short with fluthy hair sticking out round the sides of his cap and he has a one eyed cat call'd Nelson. Rite off he started complaining about the other apprentice, who mated him in eleven moves.

"Not becouse he could play chess, mind, but more becouse he couldn't!"

I nod. "He wasn't good then?"

"These kids, thay dont understand the true rules. Thay dont move the pieces in the propper order!" All the while the Captain plays with Nelsons torn ears. Nelson bites at the Captains thumb.

"I thought he was going to move his pawn but he'd go move his Queen instead! Next he'd move his Bishop when he should of moved his Castle! No, no, i couldn't play him, he was all topsy-turvy! Of course he won, but he diddn't no chess. I told him so as well, then i sent him packing. 'You can fuck off, yer little shit!' Never played him again. Next i heard he'd been laid off. And good bludy ridence, i say!"

I lookt at The Captains purple face, peeping out from benieth his cap, framed with white, candyfloss hair. I could tell that i was being given very explicit instructions not to win. It was very important that i made sure that i lost.

For a whole month i visted The Captain for our game of dinner time chess, and everyday i let him beat me. Not once did i dare win. After my defeat we sat and ate our sandwiches together and i fed Nelson some cheese. The Captain told me that i was a lucky sole, cos once your in the dockyard you have a job for life.

No, i diddn't belong with the simple, ritchious, werking men. Thay hated me becouse thay could smell that i was an artist; that i was special and cut from a different, more eligant cloth. Thay lookt at my long artistic fingers and hated me. Just as i was hated at skool and later by Mister Bennit at The Acadamy. Now i am free.

11

A Sensitive Sole

BACK WHEN i was still young and impressionable, back when i was new at the Acadamy, Mister Bennit used to get very angry becouse i refussed to visit any art gallarys – which as obedient students we were directed to do. Also, there was the case of the Paris trip.

"I can not possably go there, Sir, i have no money, Sir. Besides, it would make me ill and as everybody nos, the easyist place to catch a fever and die is in a French hospital, Sir."

"No ones asking you to go to hospital. It is quite sufficient that you go to the L— gallary."

"But art gallarys are like hospitels, only without the blud, Sir!"

"What pretentious rubbish you talk, Loveday! You will go to the L— gallary, along with everybody else. You are not a special case!"

"You can try and force me, Sir, thats your perogative, but i want it on record that if i do go, it is compleatly against my will."

Mister Bennit lookt at me with great violence and i realised that once again i had over stepped the mark. Actualy, i enjoyed his anger and whatched him cearfully.

"It is my oppinion that the so call'd art lovers who flock to the latest openings are not content to mearly marvel at the paintings, Sir, but have to find someway way of inverting everything into a means of congratulating themselfs for their own disgusting intelligence!"

Mister Bennit staired at me. "You can decide for yourself if you go or not, Loveday, but both visting gallarys and your ritten werk count towards your end of term mark. It is your choice!"

"Then i shan't go."

"You will go, Loveday, along with everybody else, and

thats an end to it!"

"No, Sir, i can not go into such a building!" And i swiftly ran from the studio giggling to myself madly. It was shortly after this that i ressived the first of a succession of mysterious notes aluding to my suspension.

The reason that i refused to go to any of Mister Bennits famouse gallarys or 'openings', is not becouse i was insensitive but completely the oppersite: i am overly sensertive. I refuse to enter the crowed becouse it is impossable for a sensitive sole, such as myself, to walk into an art gallary, gaupe at the horrible paintings that hang there, then to have to listen to the rubish that vomits from the open mouths of the likes of Mister Bennit. No, to my mind somone with a genuinely sensitive sole avoids such places. Unfortunattly, Mister Bennit does not understand such matters becouse he has not got a sensitive sole but the sole of a barberian! This is, i explain to Mister Bennit, not becouse i wished to attack him, but simply becouse Mister Bennit proclaims to be passionate about the truth. Anyway, if Mister Bennit did have a genuinely sensitive sole then he wouldn't be so quick to expel young students in his cear and cast them out onto the streets without a penny to their name without it niggling at his consionse. Nor, for that matter, would he be able to talk about art as if it were so much maggoty old meat lying about on a butchers block waiteing to be flogged off to the first idiot who carn't tell the diffrence between filet and carrion.

On the Monday after the excursion to Paris i was forst to go into the Academy to perchase some cheep paints from the college shop. This is where Bennit collered me and demanded to no why i had not gone on the skool trip with all the other fellows as directed. The reason was becouse i did not have a penny to my name, but i did not give Mister Bennit the satisfaction of this information becouse i prefer him to think badly of me.

12

We Catch Up With Some Further History

OTHERS IN THE STUDIO now wore berets that thay'd perchased in 'gay Parrie', worn in what thay smuggly imagined to be an ironical way. The fact that i am now an ex-student and the County Coucil is taking me to court to claw back the money thay advanced for my fees, mite be a sourse of worry to my mother but to me it is a sourse of great amusement.

This morning i lookt into the mirror and contemplated my triumphant fizog. All of my famileys grim prophersis about my doomed and dismal futcher are now bearing fruite and becoming manifest. Already i am becoming drawn and cear worn and, as predicted by my elder brother, my chin has been ravaged by acne. I stair at the pustuals in fear, loathing myself. Why am i ugly and despised? What has become of the vigerous young man who was accepted into the Academy on the grounds of his genius and who was marked to become some sort of Vincent van Gogh? Really, without a single qualifcation to my name i was awarded a place on account of my 'outstanding artist potential' And so entered into the Academy. And Mister Bennit himself was forst to mumble that i was 'the finest student ever to be accepted into their hallowed halls. And that if i could be accepted by a London skool (which i had), then i was certenly of a high enough ability to attend their provinacial Acadamy'.

In hatred i turne from the mirror and smash my head very purposly, 3 times, against the wall by the chiminy breast. I check very cearfully in the mirror but there is only a grased bruse – no blud.

I wounder if i was to go to Mister Bennit now – go down upon my bended knees, beseech him and humberely beg for his forgiveness – he mite just let me back into his wounderfull art skool? Even if only to sweep the studios, or prehaps bring him his nice cup of tea?

Of course, i am joking, It will be Karima who brings Mister Bennit his tea. Mister Bennit will no doubt lean over Karima as he advises her on her drawing. Certanly he will have one hand on her shoulder. At first, just the back of his hand will make casual and accidental contackt, litely caressing it, whilest his face will breath the fragrence from her hair. Meanwhile, his free hand will sturnely guid her brown fingers across the paper as she sketches with a pice of black chalk. His breath then will become thicker and within seconds the hand on her shoulder will slip down to her middrift and start inapropately brushing against the side of her heavy brest, as is the way with all male tutores.

How many times have i whatched a tutors jowls whilest he is lent over some female student – who, in fact i was in love with – and listened with dissbelith as he spoke of his sports car and 'real Tudor' house in the country. Intently, i also staired at his backside – crammed into its cream slacks, contained in what can only be described as a botty-bra – wishing him bad thoughts.

Not only are the sexuel ambitions of these 'gropers' in direct conflict with their duty as gaurdians, but thay are given postions of such power that thay become intoxcated with sex, and happily break any oppersition to their will by failing uncopperative femails and smashing any male student who thay persive as sexual or artisic compertition. In this way i was thrown on the scrap heap.

13

The Bridle Suit

IN MY SECOND week at the Acadamy a project was set by Mister Bennit entitled 'The Bridal Suit'. He stood there befor us, speaking in his inaudable Yorkshire whisper. Which, prehaps, was his witty way of letting us no that we had to be extra attentive. Anyway, i pricked up my ears and studdied his fat lips munching together. This is the gist of what he said, (viz). The bridal suit is a project in which the indervidual student can bring their own indervidual tallents to bear and interprite as they see fit. Werk can be either 2 dimenshanal in the form of graphics or a painting – or as a 3 dimenshanal model living in 'actual' space. All werk must be acompained by supporting drawings which must be compleated by the end of the 1/2 term break. All werk will then be exhibetted in the studios, being analised and marked on its own indervidual merrits by the great Mister Bennit.

As Mister Bennit whisped on i gazed out of the rain-flecked windows at the stretch of river below, which showed like a brown snake passin behind the hospital buldings on N— Road. There was some rusty barges out there being towed by a little black tug boat and something was following behind, moving benieth the serfis. I try to follow its progress, to see if a vast sea monster will show its self, raise its gigantic head and devour the barges and little tug boat in one gulp. When i next look up Mister Bennit has shut up and everyone has gone and sat down behind their desks to make their priliminary drawings. Mister Bennit looks questiononly at me and i realise that i too must now run along like a good skool boy and pretend to be inspired and motorvated by his maronic project.

Later, i am call'd to Bennits office. I knock and walk in. He is sat there massarging his large hands. He looks up and tells me to go back outside, knock and wait for him to give me permission to enter. He then stands from behind his desk, shoo's me out and closes the door behind me. I stand there for a moment then knock and wait. There is a short pause befor he calls out 'enter'. When i come back in he is stood by a small fish tank pretending to admire the fish. He dosnt acnolege me but sits himself down again, looks thru some papers in front of him, then looks up as if he is suprized to see me. He then carry's on reading a report and absently enquires how my project is progressing. The truth is, i havent been werking on his project at all but have been reading my book, 'Transcripts of the Trial of the M—'s Murderers'.

"No matter how special you mite think yourself to be, Loveday, The Bridle Suit Project is not some sort of joke that i have set for my own amusment. May i remind you that for better or worse, you are a student at this Acadamy and are there by bound to compleat all projects and course werk that is set by myself or any other of the tutors. You are not a special case!"

"I never said i was, Sir."

"Do not be inpertanent. The Bridal Suit Project must be compleated by all students, without exception! You understand that your mark will count towards you finnal degree?"

I shrug my shoulders.

"What exatly do you prepose to do when you leave art skool, Loveday?"

"Paint pictures, Sir."

"Paint pictures?" He shakes his head condisendingly.

"Couldn't i do some paintings of the M—'s murderers sir. That could go towards my degree instead, Sir."

"Dont be ridiclious, Loveday. You just wish to shock for the sake of being shocking."

"I could make some badges."

"Badges?"

"From their police photographs, Sir." I show him the cover of my book. "Miss H and Mister B, Sir. It would be like a club. Miss H's has been moved to C— Wood Prison. I'm going to rite to her and invite her to become the patron. Then, when shes released we could organise a coach tour to the Y— moors and she could be the guid and show people the whereabouts of the graves. You no the Y— Moors yourself, dont you, Sir?"

All along i had been looking at Mister Bennits shirt front, but now i focus on his eyes, which seem to have grown swollen and full of blud. His thick eyebrows, one of which is quite ruffled and already showing hints of gray, twitchs involentaraly. It is then that he stands and steps towards me. Already i have my hand on the door handle and in a flash am outside and in the corridoor.

"Get out!" He explodes "You cynical, nihalistic, child!" And comes after me.

I run a short way then wait for him. I walk backwards up the corridor.

Surly, it is Mister Bennit who is cynical, not I? If he would just stop and allow himself to concidor it, i'm sure he would agree with my view. It is true that my father is a nihlist and hates both God and myself, but nihilisim is for romantic youths and is merely a state of mind that proves nothing. I for one love God, though it is of course entirely possable that God hates me. Then i have to turne and run.

Just becouse i dont happen to hold the same beliths as Mister Bennit, it is no reason for him to have expeled me from his Academy. And so what if i have learn'd to hate the world of art? That dosnt make me a nihlist, as Mister Bennit has erroniussly claimed. He can pretend that i was cast out of the Acadamy becouse i am untalented, but the true reason for my expulssion – as both he and i no – is 1stly; becouse i refused to be obbedeant but most importantly; becouse of the riting of my 'true story', which i shall publish rite under his very nose!

It is interesting to note that in years to come Mister Bennit will be forst to enter into a bookshop against his will and then fearfully look between the pages of my book to see if it mentions his name in print. What is even more amusing is that it will be Karima who gets my 'poem' printed for me. The very same Karima who Mister Bennit dreams he could fondle. Mister Bennit may avoid bookshops for many years in his attempt to remain ignorent, but eventually, one day, he will have to give into his vanity, take my history from the shelf and read that i wanted to punch him on the bracket and knock him clean down 9 flites of stairs. Then, prehaps he will nurviously turne the page to see if it mentions him flicking my tie in my face and calling me a whipped dog with my tail tucked between my legs. And if he dare read on, he will see that i then tell the true story of his cowardness and betrail in brutel, sickining detail. Then he will nurviosly look over his shoulder – to see if he has been obseved reading my book –

73

turne up his coller and hurredly purchese it before scrurrying out onto the dark streets, woundering if history will ever forgive him.

Yes, this is the price Mister Bennit will have to pay for expelling the young genius, William Loveday from the Acadamys midst and daming him to a life of lonlyness and obscurity.

Why then, a historian mite ask, did i attend such an Acaddamy in the first place? The answeer is that it was my dream to be excepted: to be taken to the bossom of an artistic community and be cherrished, and above all else, slitely worshipped. Like Vincents dream of 'a studio of the south', i too dreamed of a community in the dreary suberbs of North K— . Instead of the Arles sun beating down upon our heads, we would live under the M— drizzel, bathing our cheeks in fog. Some readers may detect humour in my style, but i am sincer.

But once i'd left the Dockyards behind me and clawed my way into the Acadamy, i realised that my dreams were all impossable. I lookt instead to the girls. In the Dockyard there had been none and in my secondary skool the sexes were stricktly segrigated. The truth is, i'd never seen so many girls in such close proxsimity befor and it affected my mind.

I lookt at those women fearfully and hungryly but thay choose not to speak to me on account of my accent, my poor education and acned face. This is the reason i made myself vissable – to become truly hated rather than merly discarded. For this reason also, i allowed them to lable me a facist.

On my first day, after the incident in the canteen, i was

rude to a Jewish girl in the studios. She had never painted a picture before in her life, so instead of going to the effort of learning to draw, she hung stips of old cini film from the ceiling of her studio as a statement against the hollercorst. Later, in the corridoor, i overheard her and 2 friends organising a march against the Natinoalists. I waited for a suitable pause in their conversation, then told her that she should would do better to lern how to draw instead. In reply she shouted that her grandparents had been gased by the Natzis in Achewitz Concentration Camp. I lookt to group of nodding students that surrounded her.

"It's a pitty thay diddn't gas you too!" I repled. No one laughed at my joke and from that day on i was not spoken to.

Instead of striving to become clever, i have decided to remain ignorent. Becouse cleverness is applauded, i choose to become stupid. Becouse style is comended, i refuse to have style. I also refuse to be successful or interesting, and i refuse to rite what would be recognised as wounderful, pure and great, and instead hand the loaded revolver to my enimys. Also, i refuse to compleat Mister Bennits project, The Bridal Suit. In short, i forfill everything that is denied.

When once again i was repremanded for not producing my drawings for the project, i lookt at my nails and then at Mister Bennits tie.

"Do you not think that i no what you want me to say and what you want me to belive, Sir? Do you not think that i could say and do all of those things you ask of me, just like these other obediant monkys? No, Sir, i dont do these things, not out of disraspect, but out of respect for you. Becouse i dont wish to insult your inteligence, Mister Bennit, Sir. No, instead i trust that you will grasp that the reason that i do not say or do these things that you demand of me, is not becouse i carn't, but simply becouse i refuse. I simply won't. Not becouse i am stupid but becouse i am in fact magnifecently inteligent!"

On the morning that we are to hand in our Bridal Suit Project, i go to the gents toilets, masterbate into a durex and drop it into a plastic bag, which contains an indecent photograph torn from the pages of one of my fathers pornographic magazines. I then secure it with a pice of string and hang my 'sex mobile' from the cealing by the studio doorway.

Mister Bennit is a quarter of an houre late for his own tutorial. We all stand around waiteing for our master to appear. When Mister Bennit finnaly enters the room, my 'sex mobile' brushes indecently against his face. His fat hand comes up, stops it spinning, then looking at it, he turnes to me with flaming eyes befor ripping it from the cealing.

At mid-moring break i am again call'd to his office. I have to waite outside the dark wooden door. I read my book for over 1/2 an houre befor he finnaly ushers me in. Once the door is closed behind us he servays me very coldly. My sex mobile is lying there on the desk in front of him. The used durex now leeking slitely.

"My studio is not the place for your vulger jokes, Loveday! This... Thing... Is tottaly imatuer, pathetic and... Vulga!"

I watch his mouth as he speeks. "It is not a joke sir, it is my werk."

"Werk! You dont no the meaning of the word!" He really is angry with me and as allways – when i face orthority – i can feel my hart pounding fearfully, my lower lip starts to tremble and i have to concentrate not to start to cry.

He lifts my sex mobile and brandishes it at me. "This pieace of disgusting rubish could of only taken you 5 minits!"

No matter how hard he trys to intimidate me, i still refuse to appologise, or retract my prepossel for 'The Bridal Suit Project'.

"It is my honest responce to the project, Sir."

"Jouvernial rubish!" He spits.

Then Mister Bennit throws my 'sex mobile' into the bin and contemptiously wipes his hands on his handkerchife.

"Its sperm, Sir." I say very quietly. Evidently he dosnt here me.

"Your position is not as amusing as you may imagin, Loveaday. Since you've been here you've yet to compleat one piece of meaningfull werk."

"The true reason that i dont paint any pictures, Sir, is becouse i dont want to become contaminated." Then i look up at him and it seems that his face has again swollen to monsterious preportions. His eyes bulge out like those of an ornimental goldfish. I was at once remined of a story, where a Japanese brigand ambushes a man and his wife on the road, kills the man and steals his wife. He then takes her away to live with him in his moutain hide-away, where he resides with several other wifes whos hubands he has slaugtered. This new woman is very beautiful and very vain, and tho' she hates the brigand and refuses to love him, she can not bare that she is not the only wife in the brigands lair. So, out of jellousey, the new wife demands that the brigand kill all the other wives instantly by cutting off their heads. Thinking that if he follows her wishes, he mite there by win her monstrious love, the Brigand does her bidding and hacks away untill all of his cocubines are headless. But still the new wife is not impressed and refuses to let him have his way with her. Instead she amusees herself by playing childlike games with the severed heads; making them talk together and even encouraging the heads to have sex. But quite soon she grows bored and dispondent in the mountain hidaway only having the same old heads to play with, (which have anyway started to rot and fall apart), and the brigand, still intent on winning her love, is sent out on the road by her to procure some fresh heads. In evenings he cooks her meals, lavershes presents on her, but nothing he does pleases her. She tells him he can use his strength and bravery to surround her with every luxsory she may want. So he dose and he kills her some fat preist heads for her to play with. In the end, bored to distraction, she comands him to carry her on his back, away from the mountain lair, and all the way back to the riches of the capital city wear she comes from. Later, she turnes into a demon and he strangles her. Next up, her face turnes into a lot of cherryblossom petals and he feels a bit better. The point is, is that the heads in the story are all swollen and dead, much like Mister Bennits.

"Your ridiclious attitude is no way of going about getting

a degree, Loveday!" And Mister Bennit smiles smugly at me, hoping the words will cut me and wound me. I look to his blubbery jowles, which are all but blowing kisses at me. When ever i look into the face of a teacher, it really is as if a gang of devils has hold of me and are egging me on to steal the pencil from his top pocket, snap it in front of his face, then box his ears for him.

"Why would i want a degree? so's that i can teach students to get degrees, so that thay can teach students to get degrees, much like you do, Sir?"

I was already out the door when Mister Bennit lunged across the desk at me.

14

A Pscopath of Sex

MY MOTHER would agree that my biggest sin is arrogence. Next, she would list my sarcasim and how i like to rip everything apart. Also, she says that i havent got a good word to say about anything or anybody. 'You must lern not to antaganise people,' she admonishes me. Namely, she considers that doctors and teachers are to be obayed and respected regardless of their personal natures and that my holding my betters in contempt and smirking at their soft shoes and flabby behinds is what will get me smashed, and that is exactly what i deserve.

If i carn't be reminded that i am special and gifted, i would rather be beaten and abused, becouse i have somehow allowed myself to be tricked into hateing my own virtue. I may have turned my face from God, but one thing is for sure – i would rather be a true Devil than a fake Christian. Another reason for my sarcastic attitude is becouse i am shy of my talents and rather than show them off, i am happier to become some kind of sexuel genious, or 'phycopath of sex'. And so i walk the streets, empity and alone, the commaradery of my fellow students absent from my hart.

I was not the only uneducated wretch at the Acadamy, amongst those 'heros' of the gramer skool there was one other missfit from the 'outside'. When i say that he was uneducated, this could be missleading, for i dont no for certan that he was uneducated, let us just say that he was not educated in the manner of the English. This is becouse he was a real live Japanese from Japan.

Everyday Kajii arrived at the studio, took out his paints and painted another small section of yellow on his yellow coloured canvas and said nothing. He was small and wirey with a white faced and black, shinny eyes and he panted at the slightest exhurtion. It was said that he had terbeculosuse. Could he speak English? I certenly heared him say 'yes' and 'no' on several occasions. The fact that Kajji was silent and would never say boo to a goose, and painted meaningless rubbish is, as far as i can see, the only reason Mister Bennit did not have him removed from the painting department along with me.

One day, quite near the beginning of term, Kajii's sister came into the studio. Where as Kajii was twisted and sickly looking, his sister was quite tall, stood erect and breathed normally. She had 4 plats of hair on her head, like thick black ropes, which for some reason made me want to bite them. For this reason alone i went over and spoke to Kajii, on the pretexte of borrowing his pencil rubber. Whilest Kajii is rumaging about thru his desk i look intently at his sister, who keeps her eyes averted, only once glancing up at me thru her thick, black lashes. Her feet are smaller than my hands and i have to resist the urge to kneal and hold them. I ask her name and she says that her name in Japanese meen's Deep Snow. I reach out to touch her hand, which is 1/2 hidden up the sleeve of her Kamono. Her fingers are ici cold. Could this be where she gets her strange name from? I hold onto her icicel-like fingers and stare into the dark disics of her eyes for much longer than is decent. Then Kajii finds his pencil rubber and i have to turne from Deep Snow and accept it from his hot, feavcrish fingers and regretfully return to my allocated space.

For the rest of the week i make a special effort to turne up at the Academy every day in the hope of seeing Deep Snow standing in Kajii's space, her small feet and hands peeping from her kamono. When i came in, in the late mornings, i would walk over and say hello to Kajji, who diddnt reply to my greeting. All day i whatched his space most cearfully. He would twitch his head and nod very quickly but it was not possible to no if he understood my

81

questions. Even in the following weeks – when i had no intenton of attending the Acadamy at all – i would suddnly pop in on the off chance, just to see if Deep Snow was tying a green ribon round one of her extra heavy plats. But Deep Snow diddn't come in again and Kajii just carried on painting small yellow canvases that Mister Bennit declaired as 'having a certen lirical quality'.

No, rather than being ostraszied by Mister Bennit and the other students, this Kajii was actualy put up on a minor pedistal and admired. Then came the day that i recived my letter of expulsion.

15

A Certain Lyrical Quality

ON THE FRIDAY evening i leave my bedsit, walk up the hill and sneek in passed the doorman, old Merick. As usual hes sat in his cabin, the radio turned on and snoring his head off. I climb the high stairways up to the painting studios. All the lites are off cos the students have gone home early for the weekend as its the start of the 1/2 term break. I go to the bogs, take a piss then walk round the deserted studios. On the partition outside my old space is a passport-sized photo of the Jewish girl stapled to the wall. A fresh avalanch of old cini film hangs across the doorway. How has she, a girl who cannot draw, come to replace me? I go inside and finger her belongings: a chipped tea cup and an old radio that dosnt seem to werk. She is not even pritty. I step back out into the corridoor, then turne and rip the strips of film from the doorway and throw them to the floor. Near by is a jar of gray paint, i stick my fingers in and paint the sign of the swastica on her photograph.

Across the way is one of Kajii's idotic canvases sat freshly painted on an esil. I step from the shadows and peer into its serfis, trying to decern if it really dose hold some hidden meaning, but there is none. It is impossable, with my untutored eye, to desern any of Mister Bennits 'lirical quality' within its piss coloured paint. No, i can ditect nothing remarkable in its apperrence what-so-ever, the whole thing just lookt sarcasticly out at me thru the 1/2 gloom and made me aware that there is no point in living. I put my fingers to the wet paint, lift them to my mouth and taste them. No, this master piece dose not speak to me in the way that it does to Mister Bennit and the obedient, child-like minds of the students of the Acadamy. This painting is as silent as the tomb. Turneing, i walk away, then suddenly rush back and punch the canvas to the ground. It topples over face down. I look at it lying there, utterly vanquished.

"You are not equal to me, my friend, i am William Loveday!" Only then do i leave.

Whilest waiteing at the bus stop, a woman walks passed me and her small dog pulls on its string to sniff at my trouser leg. I move my leg away, but still it comes for me. I look up and its owner eyes me coldly. Could this tiny guard dog really detect that i am a destroyer of art and a painter of Natzi propogander? I check myself under a street lite, yes, i am covered in piss yellow paint. It was foolhardy of me to touch that lirical painting. It has marked me as its attacker for i have no doubt left my finger prints all across the jewish girls space and in Kajii's masterpice.

I turne and resinedly walk back up the hill, re-climb those hatefull steps and re-enter the Acadamy. I hide in an alcove under the stairs as old Merrick comes out of the toilets smoking a crafty cigaret. Once hes passed i hurry up the stairs, down the corridor and back to the painting studios. The painting is still lieing there, face down. Gingerly, i lift it from the floor and carry it at arms length to the basement where i fling it into the firy flames of the insinirator.

16

We Returne to the Subject of Madness

WHEN I LOOK BACK at my life at The Acadamy all those years ago, one face stands out from all the others in its intencity and harshness. Even tho' the female students were cruel and unkind to me, in so much as they ignored me, it is Mister Bennit who will be first to feel the waight of my wrath. (When i talk of years, of couse i mean months). You would think that being an artist, Mister Bennit would have simpathised and understood the troubles of a young man who was sexualy abused and trodden on in the course of his short life. But Mister Bennit did not see his job as protecting me and guiding me with a fatherly-like hand. No, rather he saw it as his job to smash me. In short – he was jellouse of my madness and was angry that my genuine insainty showed him up to be patheticly sain.

There's somthing disgusting and revolting about a bearded tutore pretending to be mad. In the real olden days it was the sole rite of genuine missfits and geniouses to bite at their own backs on the streets, not for burocrates. No, in the real olden days nobody dear'd to pretend to be mad. It wasn't untill the likes of Picaso came along that people like Mister Bennit started going out of their minds purly for the sake of vanity and artistic fashion.

Becouse in the olden days, and i mean the real olden days, Mister Bennit wouldn't of dear'd to pretend to be mad, becouse in the real olden days he would of been a bank clark, or a stock broker and wouldn't of been seen dead even looking at a painting that dipicted the living flesh of a woman. Becouse in the real olden days, to be a real artist, you had to be prepair'd to paint like an angel then take to the streets like a tramp, and Mister Bennit wouldn't of even had the guts to buy such a disgusting thing as a moldy old paint brush, or a tube of hidious paint, and go out doors like Van Gogh did and have everybody ridicule him for being useless, becouse Mister Bennit dosnt even no what courage is. No, if the real Jesus walk'd in to the Acadamy, Mister Bennit would be the first person to have him whipped, riddiculed, chucked out and burned at the stake. Yes, in the real olden days real madness was frowned upon. Only now that it is safe, do we see the faces of the mediocure stand bravely from behind the pulpit and declair themselves 'a little crazy'.

17

A Model Student

AS FAR as the dole office, the county council and my mother are concerned, i refuse to werk, i refuse to go to art skool and i refuse to repay my fees. When i was a child i refused to eat. Also, i refused to learn to read or rite. Also, even tho' my best friend at skool's father was a vica, i spat on the cruserfix just to see his freckley face trembling. Also, i refuse to apologise for my inflamitary ritings, weather or weather not, thay are responsible for my expelusion from the acadamy.

No one belives or understands that i am truely sensitive, that i love Vincent van Gogh for his humainty and courage, that i really did try to be a model student, rite up untill that gloryious day when Mister Bennit kicked me out onto the streets.

After that i contentdly signed back on the dole, and in my feverish state roamed the streets looking for Deep Snow, staring at the faces of unkonwn women, to see if thay were in love with me, or lov'd me not. But no matter how late i stayed out roaming, not one of them gave anything more than a fleeting glance at my hungry eyes. No, not one of them spoke to me or recognised my specialness. Becouse of my lack of a 'will to werk' my mother reffers to me as 'her son who dose nothing'. My father - when he was still at liberty – used to complain that i hung about with children from the criminal classes and that i'd wind up in prison. Which is amussing as it is him, not me, who is now languishing in gaol.

So, i wonder the horrible streets, surrounded by buildings that make my hart twist in on itself and recoil in pain. So, it is true: i belong no where on earth, not even amongst the artists. I have to hold my hand over my mouth and run down a back ally so as to be able to breath. Mister Bennit may have had me expelled from The Acadamy and welcomed Karima into its very hart, with open arms so to speak, but that wont stop me from printing my fantastic story.

All in all, i have become the master of refusel.

18

A Neon Hymn Book

NOW THAT i am at last free of Mister Bennit and his foul rageam, i have become more rakish than ever, spending my mega dole money with compleate abandon, like it was confeti in fact. This is an illussion to another tail which i will tell later, in its propper place.

Today i walk'd up to the top of the hill and staired out over this strange river that cuts thru these towns. At my feet was a greecy worm. I picked it up and let curle in the palm of my hand befor dropping it in some bushes where it would be safe. An icy wind was blowing in from Russia of all places, so i turned my back, hunched my shoulders and walk'd backwards along the bank. I clamp my arms to my sides but the wind still finds ways inside my jacket and blows between my ribs. Next, 3 crows fly up from behind some bushes, calling out in that gutteral tounge of theres. I try to imatate them but the wind carries my voise off (which is weak anyway on acount of my mastibating to often). Thay circle and fly off towards the art skool, flapping away in the wind like black rubbish bags. There upon i witnessed a strange and singular site: On the roof of the Acadamy is the siloet of an old lady, stood out against the racing sky. I recognise her at once as the serving lady from the canteen. The crows fly at her, as if she is a whitch, and appeare to settle at her feet and nestle at her ankles. My eyes were streaming in the ici wind but i was determind not to be fooled by what thay told me. She was, i presume, feeding them scraps from the kitchen bins. I could just make out her hook-like nose, and it appeared, from where i was standing, that she had a mop or a broom stick, tucked between her old legs. Upon her head she wore a black bonnet and her shawl billowed out behind her in the icy draft.

That old crone was certenly taking her life in her hands, balencing up there. Not only should a woman of that age not be allowed to go gallivanting about the rooftops, but to the best of my nolege the Academy is locked up for the hollidays with not a sole in the place. I wave but she dosnt notice me. Next, the old crone leans out over the parapit, peering down at something out of my site in the carpark bellow.

She was actually leaning her full waight into the wind, her bird-like shoulders bufeted and trembling in the icy gusts. Could this really be the same timid old lady who nervisly served me a rattling cup of hot water in a chipped sauser and a green banana all those months back? It was evident that if the wind subsided for just one 1/2 moment, the foolish old woman would be dashed to death in the carpark bellow.

I lookt nurviously around me but i was alone on that hill top, the field being utterly deserted. I walk closer, along a footpath by some trees. When i came out the other end the old crone raises a skinny old arm, and doubtlessly addressing the crows, points to some distant point on the herizon.

I turned, for just one second, the river, which was now the colour of gray iron, was partially obscured by a rain squall which appeared over U—. It seemed that there was nothing special to see and i was just going to turne away when a black and ancient squair rigger emerged from the squall. That it was a goast ship was obvious. There was a shreek from the crows and all of a sudden the old woman on the Academy roof, pitched forward and dissapeared from site. I saw her from the corner of my eye as she flew thru the air, rearly like a whitch. I listend out for the sound of her body being dashed to pices on the tarmac bellow, but the wind was blowing from the north east (from Russia), and must have carried the sound away.

The crows rose up then blew away across the fields. I watched them till thay were out of site. My eyes were still streaming from the wind and i had to dab at them with the course matterial of my cuff. Then, another old crone appeared on the rooftop in place of the first. She too wore a bonnet on her small head and she too had a shawl that billowed out behind her in the icy wind, and she too staired down curriously at something, possably the first dead old whitch, whos shattered corps was presumedly lieing in a heap bellow.

This time i wasn't going to be fooled and studied her most closely as she leaned out over the parapit, befor pitching forward, head first into the car park. Then i lookt at my wrist watch and had to leave.

I walk'd down the hillside to R— market, where somone had allegedly seen a neon bible floating in the sky above the Corn Exchange. One elderly gentlman had even heared it call out his name in Hebrew.

19

Under a Fathers Tyrany

I AM NOT RICH and have never had money. Even befor my father went into prison the only money i recived was that which my mother could aford to spair from his meeger handouts (£40 a month for house keeping – from which she had to clothe and feed us and pay all household bills). And when i was supposedly studdying under Mister Bennit at the Acadamy, i liv'd off of chocllet bars and slept on the floors of strangers, nursing my rotting teeth. Meanwhile, my father was eating in the finnest resteraunts, having his teeth capped by Mister Williams and beding short, stout whores. Now, he is in prison and i have instructed my mother to devorse him.

I am not the only member of the family to starve under my fathers tyrany. My big brother also goes hungry, but apart from wishing to inherrite the family silver he has no interest in the rites or wrongs of my father, and instead of hating him, he seeks his cold aprovel. But even tho' my brother is unlike me in every way – he is educated and obedeant – he never-the-less has to live like a scavanger, raiding the bins of supermarkets and dressing like a scear-crow. My big brother is also angry about everything about me: Since my expulssion from the Acadamy, his meeger grant check has been 1/2'ed. This is becouse the County Council say that, now there is only one member of our family studdying, our father is rich enough to foot the bill for his childrens educations (tho' he is in fact langishing in gaol). This must be the reason why my brother lookt at me darkly and told my mother that i must be stopped from writting my lies – i left the kitchen and went upstairs to the 'studio' – at least everyone is agreed on that.

My brother may be a poor, broke, art student but i on the other hand, ressive a handsome dole check every Wednesday morning, promt! Of course, i sleep in my fathers old, empity studio at nite. Also, our mother has suffered. Every evening she leaves the house, which she can no longer aford to heat, walks up onto the council estate and surves fish and chips to the drunken Irishmen who live there. 4 houres later – after the pubs chuck out – she returns to the house smelling of stale fat. All of the rooms are in darkness due to the fact that she carn't aford to replace the lite bulbs.

I lie up here in this empity space under the roof, drunk. Prehaps i have just let Karima in and we have just had anal sex in the front room and i have set her hair alite, fallen to

92

the ground and cryed in self pitty. Whatever, i am here against my mothers wishes. She dosnt like me staying the nite as she says that i wake her up if i get up, open the door, or take a piss. Also she dosnt like me drinking from the taps as that also causes a disturbence. She adds that i am as bad as my 'soddin father!' Karima has told her of my evilness and she, in turne, has advised Karima that like my father, i may be a homosexual and she should leave me.

Its true that on some nites i dont come back here and go and stay in the Troll's cave volenteraly, but that does not mean that i will marry her, or even consider moving in with her, no matter how many times she goes down on her kness befor me, takes my cock into her mouth and begs me.

My mother has a friend at the fish 'n' chip shop call'd Proffesser Kate. Her husbend werks at C— Wood prison, which is where Miss H— is incaserated.

"Does he no her?" i ask.

"Yes. He says that shes very nice."

"You no that the only reason shes still in prison is becouse shes a woman?"

"I thought it was becouse she was a murderer."

"No, that was I— B—. He did the killings. The only reason that Miss H— is in prison is becouse shes a woman. The papers dont like it that a woman was involved, so thay decided to get her." My mothers hand begins to temble.

"I dont no about that."

"That's why i'm telling you. The feminists should stand up for her. Okay, maybe she helped tie the children up and helped make the tape recordings, and maybe she held them down whilest I— B— attack't them. But its impossible to prove that she then helped suffocate them."

My mother fills the kettel then clangs it down on the stove. "Well, she would hardly be in prison if she haddn't of done anything wrong, would she!"

"But thats just it, if I— B— had done the murders on his own even he would'nt be in prison now. Its becouse shes a woman that the press want her dead. Thay wanted them hanged, or at least to throw them to the crowds and see them ripped apart."

"I dont want to argue about it."

"Im just trying to ask a question – why aren't the feminists up in arms trying to protect her? It's not rite that there is one law for men and another for women, is it? You would think that the feminists would be fighting for her release, for her rite to become mass murderer along with I— B—, without incuring extra punitive punishments, just becouse she's a woman."

I try to make my mother look at me, but she wont.

"At the court case the prosocution said to her 'If you never kill'd these children, then why are there photographes of you taken on the moors, standing over their graves, posing?' And she replyed 'I dont no, there could be bodies all over were i've stood!' So the police took her dog – which was posing in the photos with her – and x-rayed its teeth, to determing how old it was, to see if the photos dated from when the bodies were already in the ground." I look at my mothers hand, which is now rattling the teapot as she pours the tea, "thay couldn't really tell.

But the dog died under the anistetic and Miss H— acused the police of being muderers."

"Well, i supose thay were really."

"It was just a dog, mum and thay diddn't kill it on purpose."

"I wouldn't do anything so stupid! If i was going to comit a murder, id make sure no one found out."

"The reason thay wont let her out of prison is becouse women shouldn't be involved in killing other peoples children. Maybe if she'd just kill'd her own kids no one would of taken any notice!"

My mothers mouth twhitches, but otherwise there is no responce.

"You said that you thought about having me aborted when you first found out that you were pregnant?"

Finnaly she looks at me and holds me with her dark eyes. "Every mother considors abortion when thay first find out, its only natural."

I stair into the lite bulb above the kitchen table and a strange numbness travels up my arms and into my fingers.

My mother places a cup of tea befor me.

"B- is driving me to the prision to see your father on Thursday." Imeadiatly she mentions my father she reverts to her wisper, incase my father is listening, and i hate her for it.

Aparently, she has been smugling her miniscule ernings that she scrapes together at the chip shop, into my father's cell, so's that he can enjoy a nice bottle of whisky. I look at her with a new feeling. So, my fathers life of whisky, fat prostituets and yatchets in the south of France is not entirly over afterall, but my mothers pretence that their marrige is still somehow a marrage is a dirty, stinking, rotten lie.

When i was a child i had to watch my mother sat crying in her armchair evey nite – dabbing her dribling eyes and staring out through the vernition blinds – hoping and praying that that barstard would come back and make our lives even more missrable than they allready were... Fantersing that my father was going to go down on his knees, beg for her forgivness and that we could all then live happly ever after like in some retarded film... Even back then i was telling her to devorce him. Over the years she has agreed and agreed but not once has she had the courage to actualy tell my father to sling his hook. My mother is not nown to take advise and no matter what evidence presents its self to her, she is adiment that my father mite not be lying afterall, and in fact mite be on the verge of turneing over a new leaf and should therefor be given the benefit of the doubt. And so he was free to carry on abusing us.

"You cant give him your money to buy whisky with."

"Wheres my cat? Tig – Tig Tig Tig!" My mother stoops to look under the chair. "You didn't let her out, did you?"

"You cant give him your money to buy whisky with, you have to devorse him. Now, whilest you still can – befor eveything is gone!"

"I cant leave him now, can I? – not when he most needs me? He say's that he still loves me!"

I tell her that this is patent rubbish and that my father is a born lier. My mother turnes violently away from me and spits that it is not worth waisting her breath on me, which i find highly amusing. Meanwhile the whole stinking lot of them can go rot in hell.

20

The Only Type of Weding The Troll is Going to Get

WHEN I SAY that i am not rich and dont have any money other than my dole money, that isn't entirely true. Of course i have a small reserve, which i shall utterlise when the time is ripe. Namely, when i get my fantastic story printed in the very hart of the enimy camp, rite under the noses of the Acadamy.

When i say that i have a small reserve of money, this is not entirely true either, as i have already frittered most of it away on beer and cigarets. This was in the olden days – last summer to be precise – when Karima was broke and pennyless and i had to support her. Then she left me for the Acadamy, resived her grant check and started talking in the manner of a art skool phonie.

Altho' i have made Karima say that she will repay me the money she ows me, it is highly unlikely that she ever will. Yet her battle to try to make me marry her and live with her in her Trolls cave in marital bliss – which i shall never do – continues unabated.

1stly, i do not want her talking to me in her insessent baby talk. 2ndly, i will not tollerate her advising me how to paint, and 3rdly, she dosnt love me in the least. My book must be compleated befor i drive her from me compleatly and she is eaten out from the inside and becomes an 'artist'.

This afternoon, after having sex, we walk'd into C—. All along the way the Troll keeps up about how it would be in my best interests to move in with her and there by 1/2 the cost of living. Next she explains that she hasn't got any money left becouse i have spent the last of her grant on a bottle of rum that i vomited up.

The reason for our trip into town was this (viz). I have to go to the job centre for an interview.

My job is to prove that since being exppelled from the Acadamy, i have 'activly been seeking werk'. It is important, thay say, that i find a job 'sutable to my status'. As i do not have a qualification to my name 'suitable to my satus' means stacking shelfs in the supermarket or digging ditches in the road. All of my perents prophersuys of doom are coming true and bearing their fruits, but i can assure you that i will sleep in a carbored box on the street befor bowing down to the likes of my perents or the dole office!

Since going to the Acaddamy Karima has lernt another new word.

"You are a headonist." She tells me.

"I dont no what a headonist is," i tell her, "but i can

assure you that i certanly am not one."

I made several drawings of the Troll on the bus, then i let her reast her head against my kneck, then later in my lap. Afterwards i noticed that her mouth resembles more that of an old missers purse than that of a princess and i could no longer bring myself to kiss her.

We walk threw the crowds of the High Street, who jostel and push in from all sides, men and women alike, dressed in strange girl-like slippers, pastel coloured jackets and glittery earings.

"If these people are the sain," i tell her, "then i am doubly glad with my dession to align myself with the mad."

When we entred the Job Centre, Karima took off her coat and was very sexual in the manner in which she walk'd. A group of youths oggle her, then start to call out. (This was on account that she was wearing her performing bear outfit, which i had directed her to wear as oppossed to her art skool dungerees).

I join the que to see a lady in specticels who is not interested in my beliths in art, the fact that i am an impovershed young riter, or that i have no interest in werk. I refuse the seat offer'd to me and instead stand and look down at this old 'painted' dragon.

"You can put that you are an artist if you like but unless you are available for werk – and i mean any job that we choose to offer you – your claim shall be nullified!"

i sign away my sole just so's i can be free from standing in that depressing place. Anyway, i am quite certain that i will be quite cappable of failing any interview that thay send me to.

As we leeve the building, the gang of youths again leer at Karima. I notice their slack, girl-like mouths, turne, smile and make an indecent gesture at them as we exit thru the door. I see them jump to their feet and start rite after us. I hurry Karima along the pavement and instruct her to not look round, not to shout at them and to say nothing, as it will be me who get's my face smashed in, not her. I sqeeze her arm in my fist and force her to speed up, staggering along in her steletos.

Precently a large pebble strikes me between the shoulder blades followed by a tin can that whistles past my ear and rattles across the pavement in front of us. I try to steer Karima into the safty of a shop doorway, but a hard, red mitt drops on my shoulder and turnes me. I have to look into its face, which is not inteligent looking. There are 5 boy-men stood there and i realise that i have dissobayed the rules of the mob: It is perfictly fine for them to mock and humiliate me in public but it is not allowed that i should retaliate in anyway what so ever. It is then, with his face very close to mine, that i have to apologise for my missconduct. I tell them all that a i am extreamly sorry and diddn't mean to be discurtious in any way. I smile at them and appologise all over again, then make Karima offer each one of them a cigaret. I take cear to lite their cigarets and then have to promise to never do such a thing again.

It may surprise the reader that i am quite happy to provide this servus for them. This is becouse i am a coward and am quite happy to humiliate myself in any way the world sees fit, as this is the way in which i have been brought up from day one.

On the way home Karima tells me that i have given away the last of her ciggarets, which were to last her untill Wednesday. I nod. Also, she is still very insistant that i should marry her.

As we cross by the bus stop, i take my last 15 pounds from my pocket – 3 butiful blue ones – rip them up into tiny pices and sprincle them over her startled head like confettie. She gasps, falls to her knees and starts scrabling to pick up the pieces. I walk away.

This is the only type of weding the Troll is going to get.

21

A Pair of Boots

I ARRIVE at R— market in an agitated state. It seemed possible that the crew of the ghost ship may have already dissembarked and already be mingling amongst the crowds that gather there. I studdy the feet of the crowds, looking for seamens boots, but there are none.

My own shoes are worn, broken and in need of repair. I scan the stalls looking for a replacment. At first there are none, but gradualy i begin to see a pair thru the legs of the crowds. My first instinkt is to push in and snatch them up befor any one else can steel them away. With great restrant i waite till there's an ebb in the crowed then step in and kneel next to the boots – which were lying benith a trestle table. These are not sea boots but ancient army boots; the leather cracked and pre-historic looking, the hob-nails rusted and 2 thumping great horse shoes nailed to the heels. The only thing that isn't rotten about these boots is the laces, which are 2 pices of brand new string.

I lift one of the boots, smell at it and peer inside – there's a dead spider trembling in an sooty old web and something that looks like gravel in the bottom. I replace the boot to the ground and serch thru my pockets for my money. All the while the man whos stall it is, is whatching me very closely. He has undoubtedly noticed my excitement and has decided to take the oppertunity of my enfusiasim to overcharg me. Slyly, i pretended to be very unsure as to weather i really want the boots or not and ask the price very indifrently, thus beating him at his own game. He looks me in the eye and demands fiftey pence, the full 50 pence and refuses to come down a single penny. I point out that the boots are size 10s where as i am a size 8, or possably a 9, but he mearly sneers and turnes to serve another customer.

Reluctantly, i count out my coins, pay him the money and take my prize across to a quiet place by the railings, below the railway embankment. I bang the boots together to disloge the dead spyder, take off my shoes and socks and stuff them thru the railings into the stingers that grow there. The man from the stall peers at me between the passers by, so i turne my back. Looking at him over my shoullder i put my naked white feet fearfully into the greacy, black holes of the boots.

It is cold inside those boots and very rough. I tie them, stand up and take a few, hesitating steps. imediately the course leather cuts in to my white ankle bones. In short – i force myself to put on those ill fitting boots then painfully walk the several miles to my parents house.

I clank all the way there over the un-even pavements. Up M— Road, down R— Steet, along The D—, up onto C— Way and then P— Lane. I stick out my thumb but no one stops to offer me a lift or help me in any way. I am only shouted at twise in a rude manner from passing cars.

The boots waigh me down and blisters come so quickly that it takes me twise as long as usual to walk the 3 miles to the otherside of W— W— Hill.

By the time i get to my fathers house it is already dusk and the hob-nails spark in the gloom as i drag myself up the garden path. The house is in darkness. I go round the back and the dog starts barking its head off. I let myself in and have to stop the dog from wanking its self off in excitement. I step painfully into the kitchen and only then do i allow myself to site down and remove my new boots. I am pleased to see that i have large, bulbus blisters on the heal of each foot and my left ankle is bleeding slitely. I have waisted good money on useless, ill fitting boots from a war my grandfather fought in, and thrown a perfictly sound pair of comfutable walking shoes into some stingers bellow a railway embankment. This is something – for instance – that a sain man would never do.

22

The Fruit Factory

BEFOR THE ACADDAMY and Mister Bennit, my job was making fruit. I was 17 and had long left the dockyards and in my nieavaty beliv'd that my werking life had at last come to an end. For 3 months i relaxed myself and did nothing. It was at this point that i was forst by my mother – and the dole office – into accepting a job that, had i nown better, i would have refused to do.

It is hard now, from the point of view of my calousness, to explain what a soft creature i once was. It was whilst werking for the fruit packing agency that i discovered the true ghastliness of life.

Just now i said that i made fruit, which was facisious of me. Of course i diddn't 'make' fruit, i packed fruit. This was when i was still young and impressionable, otherwise i would never have allowed myself to have been tricked into taking such a job.

On that fatefull morning, my mother got me out of bed at 5.30. made me a flask of tea, cut me my cheese sandwiches and put 'a little something' in my lunch box for later, say a couple of digestive biscuits or a small chocolate bar. She was absolutely gleeful that i was to be made to werk for my miserable living again, and after packing my old army bag with her hateful cheese sandwiches she leads me to the front door to see me on my way. I peer into my bag befor stepping out into the cold morning. Yes, there are the cheese sandwiches, wrapped in tin foil, also the old flask from under the sink with the faded tartan pattern on it is there, and those are digestive biscuits, and this is some kind skool all over again from which i have only recently escaped.

She watches me go, giving me her worried expression, which i ignore becouse it is her jinx on me. Anyway, we both no that i am going to fail so why make a meal of it?

I walk reluctantly out into the pitch dark, her eyes burning into the back of my scull. I pick my way up the secluded garden, thru the garden gate and out onto the main road. Now i have to catch the bus into town and be picked up by the werks van at the top of S— Hill.

I wait by the H— Medow. There is frost on the grass. The moon is still up and there's a dog howling from behind the pub and a fireman goes past on his bicycle. I walk up to the library on the corner and peer up the road. There is a milk float up there but no bus. I walk very slowly back down to the corner dragging one foot in the gutter. I stamp my feet and blow on my hands. A man has appeared and is liteing up a cigaret. I nod to him but just blows out his smoke and looks disdainfully away. Quickly, i take my pipe from my pocket, stuff it with tobbaco and also lite up. I look at him again and cough, then the bus comes. I climb on board into the warmth. There are not many people in there but the conductor still makes me tap out my pipe on my heel befor he will allow me take a seat.

I find my fingerless gloves in my pocket and put them on. They have a fairisle patten on them, knitted by my mother and I sit there depressed: she has managed to make me soft and miss her and fear her death. Next, i get off at the station and walk over Jackson's field. That way, you have to pass the Acadamy and i peer jealously in thru the darkened windows. No body is there yet, it is only 1/2 past 6 in the morning and the students dont even bother arriving befor 10.

When i first left skool i aplyed to this Academy but was refused entry on the grounds that i have no qualifcations, they wouldn't even look at my wounderfull drawings. This was when i first started to feel that thay despised me and were planing to destroy me.

I cross the bottom 1/2 of the field and stand on the corner waiting for the werks van. It come up the hill from out of the mist. A man jumps out the cab and opens the back doors. There's a group of men sat in there, bunched up and staring at each others poorly shod feet. There's also 3 women who sit smoking by the door. Everyone ignores me, with the exception of the charge hand, who stares into my pale face and then at the gloves my mother has knitted me. Hes got a cap, much like mine, only mines pulled down over my eyes. He also wears an old teddy boys jacket, flecked with gold, which is fastened round his middle with a length of rope. He says his name is Dicky Bird. I, in turne, look cearfully at his stubbly face but there is no sign of amusement on his lips and no one else laughs, so i suppose that he is telling the truth. It is important to be cearful when you get a new job becouse people are allways on the look out to trip you up and trick you.

The others reluctantly make room for me and we drive on into the fog. Dicky Bird leans over the back of his seat and addresses me.

"So you are William Loveday?"

I nod and look out the back window at some car headlamps that are following us. Little do thay no that the mustash that i am wearing is a false and that i only paisted it on this morning.

"You'll be on grapefruits, only sorting them mind. Dot, Moreen and Babs will be bagging 'em up, thayre more experienced." He motions towards the 3 women who all have cigarets stuck in their painted gobs. The older looking one (Dot), squeezes him with her crinckly old eyes.

"Oh yes, we'er experenced, arn't we girls?" And she nudges the others who cackle as directed. Dot is wearing blue mascara and thick face powder. Dicky Bird smiles thinly and clears his throat.

"How do you do?" i say, to the lady with the blue eye makeup, "i am William Loveday."

She dosnt say her name but just looks at me. I smile rite into her face and can see that she has some unusual moles on the left hand side of her cheek. She takes a deep drag on a cigaret then grinds it out on the floor beneath her elegant foot.

"You a student?" she asks without looking up.

"No, no…I like drawing and painting tho'."

"Another poxy student!" Says her friend under her breath, and they all lite up another cigeret each. I can see that its pointless talking to them so i just pratice drawing in my note book.

Dicky Bird stands swaying in the ile.

"Not long now, we're almost there." he says comfortingly. "You stand by the conveyer belts and pull off any rotten or bruised grapefruits, lemons or pomegranates that go past. Dot and Miriam will bag 'em."

The fruit factory is just a giant hanger. There's no heat in there and there's a big black void up above, beyond the hanging strip lites.

The grapefruits run along a juddering conveyer belt driven by a large engine that lies hidden somwhere in the shadows at the far end of the nite. In other parts of the factory, oranges, apples and lemons trundle along on their own individual conveyer belts, to be sorted, boxed or bagged, by hawkish looking women with their hair tied up in nets. I stand and watch the little lines of fruit marching along but we'er not allowed to eat any of them.

My job is to make sure that none of the grapefruits which are undersized, brused or rotten, get bagged. Also, i must pick up any that fall from the convayer belt, as when thay are left to rot the fruits can become highly combustable. In this regard grapefruits are considered a minor hazard, whereas lemons are deemed the most lethal. Acording to Dicky Bird a lemon once brought the whole production line to a standstill when it lay unditected benith a 'bagger' for several days befor unexpectedly bursting into flames.

"Lemons are by far the most dangerous fruit, due to their highly acidic nature." he explains.

I look at him again, but he is deadly serrious. Then he has to go off into the dark area of the factory. I try to engage the lady with blue eye make up (Dot) into a conversation about the exploding lemons, but she pretends not to be able to hear me over the noise of the convayor belt.

All morning i stand there, occasionaly removing a moldy grapefruite, cearfully placing it into a cardboad box, then waiteing for the next ocurrence. At tea break i get another chance to ask Dicky Bird about the 'combustable lemon' but he tells me that he has already told me far more than he ought to of, and that if the 'govner' finds out about the production line being brought to a standstill due to neglegence, his job could be on the line. I ask him if he personaly has ever seen a lemon burst into flames but he shakes his head and refuses to be drawn on the subject.

"Only lemons are capable of it. Grapefruites, oranges and apples are quite harmless."

"What about pomigranits?" i ask him. And he looks me up and down, then just walks away.

You weren't allowed to eat so much as one piece of their stinking fruit at lunch break. I sat there the whole 1/2 hour chewing relentlessly thru my mothers cheese sandwiches.

One thing i dont like in a sandwich is butter, another thing is brown bread, or any kind of pickles. Also, i will only eat orange coloured cheese and no lettuce. Naturally the cheese should be finely grated and not cut in thick, inedible chunks which are then jammed into the bread with utter contempt. To be fair, my mother makes the most perfect cheese sandwiches imaginable. The bread is always white and soft to the touch and the cheese is never hard, the rind having allways been removed. It must be said that the cheese is sometimes a little on the strong side and burns the roof of my mouth, but, all in all thay are wounderful cheese sandwiches and i dont deserve a mother or the cear that she bestows on me and i carn't think why she should go to all the trouble of making me such fine delicacies when all i can do is find fault with them and toss them uneaten into the bin.

In the end i have to make do with the digestive biscuits. All tho' i would have prefered them to have been chocklet. Also, when i go to open my flask of tea, i find that it has been leeking. I shake the flask and it rattles. The plastic casing is full of broken glass. It has been smashed. I sit there alone and totally downcast. It is at this point that God smiles on me, (viz). Dicky Bird returns from the dark area, sits and pours me a cup of tea from his own flask so's that i can have something to go with my dry, inedible biscuits.

He lifts his cup and smiles at me. The tea is quite drinkable, tho' the milk is the disgusting UHT verierty, not that i mind in the least, as it is the gesture that counts and not the quality of the gift. I think that if you have to drink your tea second hand -from another fellow's flask for example – then you carn't really compare it to the taste of a nice fresh pot of tea that you would normally enjoy at home. Really, i force myself to drink it but tomorrow i will not come back to this hateful place.

In the afternoon i get taken off conveyer belt duty and am sent under the machines to clean out any clogged or rotting fruit that has fallen off the belts and accumulated there. Despite what Dicky Bird had told me, it looks like no one has been under these machines for decades. The fallen fruit – growing in black, living mounds – is piled up so high it almost touches the underside of the convayer belts. Long, green hairs pretrude all over these 'hillocks' and strange white worms poke their heads out at me and i knew that i had been sent under these machines as a hilarious joke by the 'regulars' and that rite now Dicky Birds harrium of shreeking ganits are holding their sides and laughing hysterickly at my missery and missfortune.

It was under those machines that i saw all the bodies hanging from the rafters; the corpses of all sorts of decaying delicacy's – others who'd been sent befor me to rumage amongst these smouldering fruits and never returned. It was then that i packed up, collected my bag and broken flask and vowed never to come back.

23

Stollen Cat

KARIMA HAS STARTED inserting more art words into her conversations. Words and sentences that mean nothing to me – becouse i refuse to understand their meaning or to speak in that manner. Already she smiles conceitedly after saying one of these meaningless catch phrases, which is ment to point to some vast expantion of her brain rather than to her gullability.

Also, she has brought back a cat to her Trolls cave. It is a small black thing and wears a red coller with a silver bell. It is a very nice kitty. I stroke its head. Karima says she found it on the towpath by the river.

"It was lost, so i brought it home."

"It has a coller on, so it belongs to somone," i point this out to her.

"No, its a little kitty-cat-kins and it was lost."

"How do you no?"

"It wasn't with anyone."

"Its a cat. Thats what cats do – walk by themselves – theyer not dogs"

"But it was lost!"

"How do you no?"

"I could tell."

"How can you tell?"

"Becouse it meowed at me."

"All cats meaow."

"But it came rite up to me and meowed. It said 'i'm lost' so i picked it up, put it in my coat and carried it home."

"You mean you stoll it?"

"No, i rescued it!"

"From what? It's got a coller, it belongs to someone. Thats someone else's little cat you've got. Its probly some childs pet. thay'll be missing it. The'll be thinking it been run over or drownd. You should put up a poster with a discription saying you found it."

Karima snatches up the cat and crushes it to her tits.

"Your not lost are you, Mooming? No! Youre my little cat-kins. You was lost, wasn't you, and now your mine!" She pouts at me and walks off into the kitchen still talking gibberish.

After dinner, Karima makes an outfit for the cat and dresses the terrified animal in a stripy hat with matching jacket and some wollen socks. Basicly, she tormentes the cat untill it jumps from her arms and runs smack into the door. From there it spins in circles trying to bite the jaket off, before dashing off again and banging into the lited gas stove and pissing itself. I finnaly corner the cat and untangle it. It mooches off crying to be let out into the back yard and to thereby return to its ritefull owner, which is something Karima will never allow.

"You have to make a poster saying that you have found a small black cat and pin it up by the towpath."

"But i love Moomin and she loves me. Dont you Moomins!"

"It probably belongs to a little girl. She probably loves it as well. Think of how she feels."

Karima picks up the cat and forces its paws back into the jacket's arm-holes.

"Ah, look at Moomin, she's got her little jacket on!"

Soon i will attack her.

24

A Rebuff

WHEN I FIRST attempted to gain entrance into the Academy i was refused on the grounds that i had no qualifications to my name whatsoever. I sent off my application in the spring, sure that my drawings would convince them of my worthyness. At the end of the summer i recived a brown envelope in the post. It was on the kitchen table when i came down for my tea – the Acadamys name embossed pretentiously across the top. Inside was a 3 lined, typed refusel. I sat down and put my toast back on my plate. Rite across the bottom of the letter, in his own handwriting, was

Mister Bennits signiture.

I read that rebuff, my hands shaking. Their refusel was not based on my artistic abilityies – thay had not seen my cearfully made paintings and drawings – but becouse i haddn't any exam results in quite un-related subjects to art. These people, who claim to love painting, wouldn't even give a fellow a chance, just becouse he can't read or rite.

Mister Bennits signiture, which was groteskly large, took up the whole bottom 1/2 of the page, leaving only the smallist arear near the top, for them to refuse me.

After this letter it was everyones unaminus oppinion (my father, mother and brother), that i forget any silly notions i once held of ever becoming an artist and instead enter into the dockyard, along with all the other no-hopers from the B stream of W— Secondary skool.

From then on my mother woke me at 6.30 every morning and i had to open my eyes, get dressed in the icey cold air and walk down to the bus stop at the H— Medow. Over my shoulder i wore my ex-army gas-cape bag, which contained my drawing pencils, a small sketch book, my cheese sandwiches, some digestive biscits and an occasional apple. My mother was doubly pleased that i was now being forst to werk in that same hatefull place as her father had once attended.

I stood by the roadside in the dark and rain with the other mournful figures untill the bus finnaly showed up. Then we all climbed on boared and paid our fares. If there was room i'd sit down at the back, above the engin, for warmth. I look round me at all the broken faces and the toothless gobs and no, deep down in my trembling hart, that no matter how hard i try, i will never be happy amongst the world of the sain and the living.

It was there – in the dockyard – that i learned to skive off, sitting in the tea hut drinking great mugfulls of that strong, sweet brew. My fellow werkers sit round me, stupifid by the heat and fumes of the calour-gas stove. I make drawing after drawing of them and dream of a life beyoned the dockyard gates with Vincent van Gogh and all of the other painters of hart.

It was shortly after this – enclosed in a thick morning fog -that i took up a 3 lb club hammer, purposly smashed my own hand and left werk for good. Next, i signed on at the dole office, did one day at the fruite factory, and that summer won a place at the Academy, but by default. This is how it goes, (viz). I applied to, and was accepted by, a far greater instituion than the Academy. I traveled to London, showed them my drawings that i'd made in those 'tea huts of hell' and was accepted on the spot. But as the greater instutuion was out of my catchment arear, the County Council decreed that i must instead attend the local Academy, regardless.

Shortly after this i recived a second letter from Mister Bennit, which was alltogether diffrent in tone to the first. In this letter i was not shunned, but invited to attend an interview at the Acadamy and to bring along all of my werk with me, which i refused to do. Instead, i went along empty handed and told Mister Bennit that i diddn't want to go to his pretencious Academy at all and would he please refuse

116

me again, so's i could attend the greater institution? He lookt at me from out of his fleshy face, placed the tipps of all his fat fingers together and told me that there was no question of me being refused entry, as 'if i had been offer'd a place at the greater instution, then i could certanly gain entrance to the Academy, and would have to attend the Acadamy weather i liked it or not!' He then sent me home to fetch my pictures. My face must have shown my dissmay, and this seemed to please him emencly.

I diddn't realise that i had upset him by not wanting to go to his shabby art skool, or that i would soon be made to pay the price for my honesty.

So that September i walk'd reluctantly up the front steps and in thru that marverlous doorway. Old Merick, the doorman, stopped me and demanded to see my pass, which i diddn't have. From then on it was war.

Despite my dissapointment at having to attend such a dump, i was happy that at last i was free from the mournful faces of the dockyard and was about to meet my brother and sister painters; people who ceared and lov'd painting as i did.

And so i came in off the streets and into the land of women. The canteen and studios were full of them. Most of them hand picked – for there looks rather than their ability – by Mister Bennit and the other male tutors. Those gray-beards were in direct compertion with us kids. Thay wanted to make sure that no student achive anything – in sex or art – that thay themselfs haddn't. As a student of 'outstanding artistic ability' i was not honoured, but seen as

117

a mear affectation, ripe to be smashed. I soon found out that all tho' the Academy is call'd a skool of art, it is infact a saussage machine.

As i wandered thru those morbid and desolate studios, all of my dreams of brotherhood and sisterhood were shown to be idiotic. Of course there were no great painters of the hart at the Academy, only obedeant students awaiteing their carrers in graphics, model making and fashion, prosided over by a handfull of frustrated tutors whos carreers had long fizzeled out into nothing, and all of them topped by the arrogant Mister Bennit.

I tried to speek with 2 boys in the canteen, but the rough accent i had picked up in the dockyard stood out harshly in that rearified atmasphear. Despite lacking real intelgence, any argument or obsevation i made would allways be torn down and shredded by their condicending looks, noing air, and surity of their rite to rule. No, i would never be able to speak with them or hold any comaradi.

When i was still a small child at home, i refused to eat food.

1stly, i diddn't like the feeling of things being squished up in

my mouth.

2ndly, washing up liqiud was on all the plates – i had seen the bubbles dying there and this was poison. Also, the toilet paper put bleach on your arse. Likewise, when i came to be in-tombed in the Acadamy, i refused to eat or to become contaminated by their poisonus dictates. In short – i refussed to take so much as one lesson from its trecherous officers or to paint one single painting within the confines of their sterile studios.

"I paint at home." I told Mister Bennit, but he refused to belive me. As i have already related, for my bravery and ethics, i was expelled.

25

Exploading Pomigranites

ALL THO' MY TIME at the Academy is officialy over and it is time for me to move on, it is now Karimas turne to walk into that world and pretend to be an artist. I still dream of destroying them. First, there will be my book. This will not only cook Mister Bennits goose for him but could also be seen as a general resistance to authority. Yes, i will make the cowards of the Academy regret their artistic snobbery, their foul gobs and their allegience to the status quo. Yes, thay will pay for their neglect. Mister Bennit, in particular, will pay for his unkindness to me.

I visit the flea market and look at the faces there. On the back of an envolope i draw a picture of an old woman selling pomigranits. Shes stood 1/2 hidden behind a huge pile of glowing lemons piled high into the harsh winter sun. I squint as the lite bounces off them and smashes into my pale face. Really i should eat something and not let my mind go spinning off in crazy directions. I am tired and hungry and just looking at the yellowness of those lemons makes me feel extreamly aggitated.

I put the envelope cearfully away in my pocket. I have a fairly good idear of the lay of the land; the comings and going of her cliental; the dirty bandages incasing her old legs; the way the old crone keeps her lose change strapped to her vast stomach. No, she will not escape me. I pass in front of her stall and she leans over her barrow and asks me, very pointedly, if she can help me. I look to her large breasts that nudge against the blud-red pomigranits that pile up in front of her.

"No!" i say – really too loudly – "i wish to buy nothing." The old crone looks at me curiously.

"Not yet" i stammer, "i'm still looking." I turn to walk on but then a piece of fruit – a pomigranit in fact – gets dislodged by her brest, rolls off the barrow and falls to the ground at my feet. I stair at it transfixed, but befor i can kneel to snatch it up, it is crushed benith a passing boot. I watch as its sexuel seeds and innards are pressed into the black tarmac. The old crone follows my gaze like a wretched hawk. Quickly, i step back into the crowed and melt from her penertrating gaze.

The air is ici cold and the sky is a clear, God-like blue. The vapour trails of 2 jets cross in the sky making an ominous X over the tower of the Corn Exchange. All i remember is that eveything grew very quiet and that the shape of all the bulidings stood out very sharply, the

120

yellownes of the lemons showing doubly strong, prehaps becouse of the blueness of the sky. The great X in the sky does not fade away and if anything, grows more robust and assertive, pehaps as a sign of Gods displeasure. Then a train goes by on the embankment and sounds its air horn, which brings the world back to normal.

Gathering my witts about me, i pull my hat down over my eyes and make another pass in front of the old crones barrow looking for an oppertunity to again stand close to the pile of lemons, but not once does she take her small, stone-like eyes off me.

I withdraw and stand by the railings of the railway embancment, her hord of lemons and pomegranets riseing up like a reef in front of her. Even when the crowed thins out and there's not a hells hope of her selling a single lemon, she still keeps survaying anybody who strays anywhere in the vasinity of her fruit barrow. The more i studdy her, the more i realise that even by the standereds of embitter'd old hags, this one is a champion: she is suspisious and tenatious by nature.

When i say that the old crone has bandaged feet, really it is her ankles and legs that are bound, not her feet. Her boots are made of black swade, with zips running up the front and little tuffts of fur sprout out at the tops and then there's the flesh coloured tights stretchethed over her swollen legs. I look at them fearfully as she hobbels about stuffing vegitables into peoples carrier bags and smiling at them with her cavernous mouth.

Twise now i have stepped forward out of the crowed and

brushed the frayed cuff of my jacket aganst the edge of her barrow, dearing myself to let the backs of my fingers stroke the cold, waxy skin of the lemons. Dareing myself to let my hand open and grasp one of them. But on both ocassions the old crone has gleared at me. When she serves the next customer she really does look me up and down in that manner peculia to old women who have grown to hate all young men becouse of our grace, inginuity and cleverness. She has a fearfull groth sprouting on her left eyelid, which actually seems to be the root of an old potato. Up in the sky the great X of God seems to have disintergrated and been blown away on the winds.

My fingers are cold and freezing on account that i wont let myself wear gloves or allow myself to even warm them in my pockets. My grandfather – who was in the Royal Navi during The Great War – was the only man on the Baltic run who refused to grow a beard against the cold. Every morning the crew had to go out on deck and smash the ice from the rigging with their bare hands. I am just trying to imagin the deck done out like a christmas tree when a lady wearing a faded, lite blue coat pushes in front of me and orders some potatoes. The old crone slings some newspaper on the scales, emptys the sack of spuds on top, wrapps them 'n' dumps 'em in the old womans hold-all. Wipeing her nose on her cuff, she counts out a few pathetic coppers worth of change from her stomach bag and looks at me again, trying to make me feel like some kind of shaby thife.

To show that i am not in the least bit interested in her lemons, i walk purposly over to the oppersite ile, where a man with a purple nose is selling domestic cleaning products. I have a feeling that it must be him who is the owner of this so-call'd 'neon hymn book'. And it is true that he has a certen religious conternance about him. He wears a brown wearhouse coat and his hair is hard, black and shiny almost like a hat.

Just in front of his stall there's a little row of plastic bins full of stuff. In one of them i find a pack of yellow dusters. I pick it up from the display and make a great show of examining the packaging. I take one of the dusters out of its celophaine packet, and shake it out into the lite. I smell at it susspisiously, then test its strength and durability between my cold fingers. All the while i am not really interested in the dusters at all but am secreatly looking under the crook of my arm, keeping whatch on the old crone and her pomigranets. Just then the man with the purple nose looms over me and tells me that if i want to buy the dusters thay are 20 pence each.

"Where are thay manifactured?" i ask him absently. "Manifactured? i dont no. What's it say on the packet? … China?"

"Are you sure there not Russian?"

"I dont no, there bludy dusters arnt thay!"

I lower my head sarcasticly and explain to the lady stood next to me that i am not going to spend hard currency on dusters of dubbious orrigin, probebly mass produced in a goolag by starving convicts fed on a diet of cabbage soupe and cockroaches.

"It would only be condoning state crulty." i explain.

The lady, it turnes out, is the very same woman who just now was served by the old crone. As well as wearing the blue faded coat, she also wears purple lipstick to match and has a satin headscarf with a blue buttifly motif on it. I try to peer down into her carrier bag to see exatly what fruite she has purchesed. What ever it is that she has in there is obscured by a cabbage which she has craftly placed on top.

"Did you buy any fruite?" i ask her roughly. She nods at me and moves her mouth silently. She is sceared of my emaciated mad-mans face, and really and truthfully, i am bullying her, stearing unashamedly into her hold-all like that. I look up into her old eyes which are almost trasparent and feel genuine and hart felt guilt for my actions. I show her the duster.

"I for one wouldn't buy any," i advise her, "thayre liable to molt!" I hold up the offending duster to the lite. "Look, you can see daylite clear thru it!" I say it loudly enough so's that the man with the purple nose, plastic hair and 'neon hymn book', can hear.

He stops in mid conversation with an old dad wearing a cloth cap and tells me that nobody is forcing me to buy anything.

"And i should hope not," i retort cleverly, "or we would all be complisite." At this the lady with the blue lipstick smiles at me. Taking this as encouragment, i carry on. "And i very much doubt weather this 'talking bible' of yours even speaks English!" Again the old lady nods, as if she really does no what a neon hymn book is.

"Have you seen it?" i ask her, "have you heard it sing?"

"Oh, I've seen it all, ducky." she says in a very thine, torn voice. She has papery white skin and her breath smells of gin.

"No," i retort iratably, "the hymn book, have you seen this mans neon hymn book?" She looks blankly at me thru her transparent eyes.

I fold the duster cearfully and replace it back in its celophain wrapper, all the while staring at the stall keeper. I will not let this sharlaten treat me as if i am of no consiquense, just on account of my frayed cuffs. I call out to him defieantly.

"I've heard much talk about this singing bible of yours, sir! About this piece of gimicary! But i dont think that our saviour would approve of it, and frankly, i doubt if it even actually speaks as such at all!"

The man with the purple nose ignores me and the lady with the blue lipstick turns to leave. Quickly, i pluck up the dusters once again.

"Of course, its possable that i was mistaken!" i shout, and examin the duster most minutly, untill i can again feel their curiosity drawing them back in. "Yes, yes, yes, look! These dusters arn't Russian, thayre of Polish origion! Well, this puts a compleatly different lite on the subject." I try to peek round the corners of my eyes, and can tell that all tho' the man with the purple nose is turned slitely from me, he is now listning to my every word.

"Reverand," and i snap my fingers – the purple nosed gentleman turnes on me with obvious displeasure – "i wish to buy these dusters of yours. Do you do house calls? ... I

125

mean do you deliver door to door? … Please have them deliver'd to my premisses forthwith, here is my card." … And i hold out the old enverlope i have in my pocket, but he refuses to take it, so i let it drop to the ground at his feet.

"Of course i will pay on delivery." My face has coloured up and i turne, walk a few paces then smack my forhead with my palm.

"Oh, i ment to ask you, are you giving any demonstrations of your talking hyme book, or neon bible, or whatever it is you call it? I'd be most interested in seeing it in action. To see if its predictions are false or true."

The man with the purple nose holds me with his gaze befor turneing his shoulder most rudly and starting to serve somone else who, in fact, was behind me in the que.

"I realise that now mite not be the best time to disscuss these matters, sir. I can see that youre obviously very bissy at the moment," i raise my voice, "but maybe we could organise a privat demonstration, one evening next week prehaps, at my bedsit? Or if not, then possably at the Quakers Meating House over the way?" I gesture across the road. "Not that the Quakers are nown for their love of gimickry. But who no's, maybe you've made the whole thing up from start to finish, just to drag lost sheep back into the fold." I turne to the crowed. "But i am quite prepair'd to give this gentlman the oppertunity of proving me wrong, i am not a disbeliver!" With that i reach down and pick up my envelope from the floor and hold it out to him.

"If you would just like to scribble your name and address on the back of this envelope, i can drop in on your home this evening and we can discuss Christ and weather he ever wanted a church that waged war on his behalf and indulged in pagen rituels of blud letting and canabelisim!" I hold out the crumpled envelope to him but he refusses to accept it.

"What are your views on the eucharist? Do you really think you are scoffing the literal, living body of the dead Christ? Or isn't that really just some barbaric reminent of Jewish fear of the mothers blud?"

i put these perfictly reasonable points to him, not as oppions but as subjects for discussion. I really try to engage him in a serious theological debate but some rough people jostle me from behind and i somehow get pushed to the back of the que.

"Do you think that it was moral of the church to force Christianity down the throats of the Godless heevens of the dark continant?" i shout over their heads. "What about the rites of the ignorent to remain ignorent?" I feel a sharp, intence pain as somone elbows me in the ribs, bend over double and have to concentrate just to be able to breath.

I can see that i have made a mistake coming to this flea market on such a cold morning. My nurves were shot thru and i have been opening my mouth just for the thrill of hearing what i mite say next. The best thing would be to leave now, returne to my room and eat something warm and nurishing; a glass of boiled milk for instance. Besides, it is obvious that i am waisting my time trying to hold an inteligent debate about theology with a man who perports to own something so vulga as a neon hymn book, or bible, or what ever it is he calls it.

"A man who dies his hair with ink and fools himself that Christ would be in anyway flattered by such a gaudy invention as a neon bible is deluded!" I gasp, still doubled over looking at the tarmac.

Slowly i recover, stand and turne to leave. It is then that i notice Kajii, the Japanese boy from the art skool.

He is stood slitely to the side of the old crones fruit barrow, and for all I no, has been there all the time, watching me and mocking me. He is holding a blue note book in his small hand and is obviously writing something down. I look at him envyiously and wish that i too had thought of bringing an important looking note book and inwardly curse myself. Quickly, i take the stub of a pencil from my pocket, lick at it, narrow my eyes thoughtfully – just like my Japanese friend – and pretend to rite something on my crumpled brown evelope. I hover on the outskirts of the jostling crowed, hateing him for his black, healthy looking hair and popularity.

Like me, he is an artist, only he is accepted and celibrated by the Acadamy, where as i have been rejected and abandoned. Just like me he is pale and unwell looking, tho' my hair is fine and brownish blond. Just like me he is looking hungrely at the magical lemons that pile upwards towards the winter sky.

Tucking my white hands out of site, i move round to the left of the fruit barrow and hang my head. I dont want that old crone looking me in the eye again. Still keeping my hand in my pocket i imperceptabley reach out towards the lemons. Just as i am within a fraction of an inch of touching its yellow skin a little girl starts shouting with glee and pointing at a train that comes trundleing along the embankment. It sounds its air horn and the childs mother – whos hair is dyed a filthy yellow – looks down at the little girl and tells her to 'shut her fucking gob!' She then yanks on the childs arm, making the little girl drop her ice cream to the dirty tarmack.

"Look what you've done now, Tracy!" She screams. The little girl looks from her ice cream and up into the contorted face of her tortuter, then bursts into tears.

"Thats fucking it, your going strait home to bed and youre not having any more fucking sweets!" The child starts howling. The mother then squats down in front of the little girl, grabs her by the shoulders and shakes her very vigerously, all the while shouting into her face at full volume.

"How dare you show me up in public, you little slut! Do you want me to have to pull your nickers down and smack your arse in front of all of these people!?" The little girls face contorts into the most hiddious mask and she shakes her head from side to side, green coloured snot sucking in and out of her nose as she bellows in missery.

Instead of holding and consoleing the child, the mother pushes her away. The little girl staggers into a mans legs then sits down in a puddle. She looks around her at the faces of the grown ups that stair on saying nothing. Her dress really is quite mudded.

"Get up, you little slut! For cring out loud, stand up and stop that God-awfull noise or ile give you somthing to cry about!"

But the little girl remains sitting in the puddle. Then her pink tounge comes out and trys to lap at the green strings of snot that hang from her nose. Involenterally, my own tounge comes out and i too gingerly tast my own upper lip, to see if it is me who is really crying and not the little girl, which is all a lot of sillyness.

My body jeks and twitches and i go to rush forward and protect the child from its babaric parent but my legs wont werk. I imagin punching the vile woman to the floor, snatching up her screaming infant and running thru the crowds to the safty of some back street, where i will nurture the child and become its father and protector.

"I said stand up!" The mother strides forward, pulls the little girl to her feet, slaping at her red, lunchon-meat coloured legs. She then drags her away still screaming, into the surging crowed.

No body is in the least bit bothered by this violent attack on this inosent child. Indeed, many of the elderly women nod their curly old heads in aprovel. An old man with quite a frendly expression on his face trys to get me to smile with him in a sick, noing manner, which i refuse to acnolege.

Yes, so everybody, it seems, is a coward. They are all in agreement that it is not the behaviour of the mother who is at fault but that of the inocent child.

I watch the mother and child disapear out onto the road and, finding my strength, push into one old lady on purpose – one who seems to be the ringleader of the facistic old whitches. I lower my head and kick out at the tarten pattened shopping trollie she drags behind her and knock it

130

slitely to one side. I appologise most profussly, looking agressivly into the baggy old eyes of this hag who condones such disgusting behaviour as child abuse. No wonder that she hates inocent children, for she has a nose like a man and has never been held or lov'd in her entire life and juging by her hatefull breath she dosnt deserve to be either! But far from being intimidated by my attack, the old whore merely sneers at me, snatches at the handle of her trollie and drags its wheels purpossly over the toe of my left foot.

I push her violently to one side and move towards the fruite and veg barrow. Thru the seething crowed i see the old crone stop to fill yet another trollie with contraband vegitables. This truck belonging to the same old man who grinned at me. Judging by his smiley mug, he thinks that the whole world is some sort of hellerious joke ritten just for him and that crying children being slapped into puddles have been placed here purly for his amusement.

Again, he trys to smile noingly at me, and again i refuse to let him. I put my hands on my hips and sneer at him openly. He lowers his head like a great cow and holds protectively onto the handle of his trollie, all the while still smerking to himself. The crone finishes filling his trollie with her great heavy, muddy potatoes, looks around nerviously, then taking 2 pomegranits and a lemon from the top of the pile, stuffs them down amongst the potatoes befor straping down the canvis lid.

She obviously thinks that no one has noticed her slite of hand, but in truth it is i who have outwitted her, for now i have my chance to strike.

I waite untill that disgusting old smiler is handing over his 50 pence peice, the old crone looks down just for an instant and i seaze my chance, pushing thru the crowed. I reach out my white hand, grasping at the pile of glowing pomegranits. I have won my prize and am just about to escape, but the fruit is much greecyer than i had imagined. The pomigranit jumps from my fingers. I here a small cry of angwish escape my lips as i madly flail for another fruit but it too manages to slither from my grasp. Apparently i am not the only bystander who has noticed the old crones momentraly laps of vigerlence. Kajii – who has untill now been scribbling in his pretencious note book and chewing on his feavered lips – suddenly steps forward and steals the falling pomigranit from out of the air, rite in front of me.

I stare into his Japanese eyes, thay have dark lashes and in a way are quite butiful. There is also a smile hidden in them, and prehaps a hint of triumph, which is accented by his strange oriental shyness. As he is poor and undernorrished, i too am poor and undernourished. As i am cold and my ribs poke falornly thru my shirt, he is wracket with tebuculosious and his ribs poke felornly thru his shirt. It really is as if we recognise ourselfs in each other and i let go of the pressious fruite and allow him to steal it from my grasp. I imagine that his Japanese eyes acnolege my gift, then he turnes and starts to run. I reach out to stop him but it is too late, he has got away.

Instantly a shout goes up and the old crone lunges at me across the lemons. It really is as if she belives that it is all my fault and that i am the villan of the day rather than the one who tried to save her rancid old lemons. The stall sags and teeters, the piles of yellow and red fruit swaying drunkenly in the brite sun lite, then – as one – casscade onto the cold tarmac, druming the ground like tiny, severed heads.

The man with the smiling face lets go his shopping trollie and blindly reaches out his old claw for my shirt front. I look down in horror as his hand inches towards me like a dark spyder. It so happens that i have to lean over and bite his blue-vained fist to make him let go, the cuff of his jacket tasts of cough sweets. He slaps at my face with his free hand, then we both go down, made unstable by the avalanch of pomegranits.

The man with the neon bible takes off after Kajii but i am sure that the Japanese boy is so hungry that he will never be able to catch him.

I pick myself from the floor, brush myself down and cassualy walk away. I let go my teeth on the old mans hand, spit and leave. Really, i hardly bit him at all and was really only playing, but he still looks at me darkly. I appologise and explain how i fell down and his hand somehow came into my mouth, and all tho' it seems that i did indeed bite his hand, this certenly is not the case, it just seems that way and i can only deni it.

I hurry off in the direction of the urinals by the Adult Education Centre, hoping to find Kajii hidding in there. I check all of the cubicals but he is nowhere to be seen. Somehow, i have been tricked. In my nievaty i beliv'd the Japanese boy was winking at me, making a silent signal that we were acomplaces; that if i caused a diversion and let him steal the fruit, then we would meet up later and share the spoils between us.

I walk up and down the High Street several times but there is no small, feaverish painter with black hair moving thru the crowds of shoppers. He has deserted me.

26

In The Trolls Cave

To MAKE SURE i'm not being followed i walk the long way back to C— Hill. On one occasion, i feel a hot pair of eyes stareing fiersly into the back of my scull, but when i turne there is no one there.

I cross The V–'s and some bushes move suspiciously. Out on the road there is a loud screaming of locked breaks. When i come to the junction, a black, German car pulls up and a man in dark glasses and a ginger mustash studdys me befor driving off, stinking smoke billowing from his screetching wheels. He go's down past the cathedral, then takes a left up the hill. Kajii is nowhere to be seen.

When i arrive back at the Trolls cave the black, German car is parked out front, its front wheels up on the pavement, the indicators flashing and a little blud-red Turkish flag drooped from an arial on the bonnet. The smell of burning breaks fills the air. The man in dark glasses has dissapeared.

Holding my shirt closed, i climb over the railings in front of the house, then bracing myself against the wall, lower myself down into the darkness. I feel out for the window sill with my toe. Behind me are the black mouths of 2 great coal holes, which in the olden days fed the fires when this was a grand, city house. Now thay are just 2 empity sockets which i refuse to look in to becouse of their sinister darkness. I find the window sill, quickly lift the Trolls window and scrurry inside.

Karima is not in. I cross the room turne the lamp on. Several lemons – that somehow found their way into my shirt – lie coldly against my ribs. I am just about to unload them onto her bed when there comes a loud banging on the front door. I walk out into the hallway, there is a bare lite-bulb hanging at the far end – at the bottom of the stairs – at the top of the stairs is the front door. I stop and listen. There are 3 more loud thumps then a mans voice shouts out 'hallo' in a thick accent. I deside not to open the door and am just going back into the Trolls room when i hear a key in the lock and the front door Bursts open. I stand hidden in the shadows. Shortly, a pair of stumpy legs come down the stairway. It is then that i am accosted, in a most brutel manner, by a man in a faded blue, 3-piece suit, and dark glasses.

"Good day to you my friend, i am Al Mersin!"

He has shiny hair, greaced back over his ears and a ginger mustash, which he puckers at me.

He thrusts out his hand and hobbles menicingly

towards me. In his hand he carrys a handfull of kitchen knifes and under his other arm a set of stainless steal sauspans.

"I am the new freind in the house! Allow me to introduce myself, i am Al Mersin!" He puts down his knifes and the stack of sauspans and again offers me his brown, pudgy hand. I have to try and shake it without dropping my stollen pomigranits.

"This is a very butiful house!" and he looks about the dingy hallway, nodding his head with satisfaction, but dosnt let go of my hand. He stares up at the cracked and cobwebed cealing.

"Yes, you are a very lucky young man!" he smiles at me in an overly familiear way and i try to pull my hand back and clutch my pomigranitss to my poor belly. Al Mersins finger nails are unussualy long and sinister. It is only with great reluctens that he lets go of my hand at all.

"Yes, my friend… i love your England… I love the English people with their fantastical sence of hummour! I love it very, very much indeed. But now, to be quite honest with you, i am sick to the back of my teeth with the place!… Of its petty rules and lack of butiful women!"

Somewhere behind his thick, black glasses, are his eyes.

"But you, my friend… i can see are… different. You understand taste and penashe… dont you?"

I look at him in silence. I can feel his eyes survaying my face. He licks his thick lips and nods. Aparently, i have given the correct answer.

"I wish for only one thing befor i die, my friend." I nod

my head looking at the purple tie that cuts into his neck. "To make my fortune… Returne home to my belov'd homeland and for my butiful princess to marry a Turkish husband. Then i can die in peace." Al Mersin coughs and looks at me slyly from behind his impenertrable glasses. I presume that he means his daughter.

"You, my young… English friend, still have your whole life befor you." Al Mersin bends in the middle and picks up a handfull of kitchen knives. He fondles the blade of the largest carving knife with his short fingers.

"These knifes are from my home-land… thay are all of them made from the finest Cypriet steel."

"I have no money for knives," i tell him quietly.

"Buy them for your… mother, then?"

"My father is in prison," i whisper.

Al Mersin looks at me doubtfully. "Of course thay are in the French manner, but dont let that fool you, thay are not Cypret knifes. No, not at all! thay are one hundred percent German knives… Made by German craftsmen!"

He stares down at the blade in his hand in utter amazement, as if he himself, Al mersin, has never seen such a set of sharp and sinister looking daggers.

"You see the price on these sauspans?" He kicks them with his gray, scuffed, slip-on shoe. "How much do you think such fine sauspans sell for in the shops nower days? That is if you can find such quality in this day and age!"

I shrugg my shoulders.

"3 hundred and 60 of your worthless English pounds!" I nod, as if i am perfictly aquainted with the cost of

137

sauspans. "We'll forget your 3 hundred and 60 pounds! I am not even asking 2 hundred and 60 pounds. Not even am i asking for 1 hundred and 60 pounds-No! All i'm asking for from you, my English friend – for these fine German, stainless steal sauspans – is 30 of your worthless English pounds! And why can i let you have these delux, gormat copper bottomed, stainless steel sauspans at such a cut throat price?" Al Mersin raises his eyebrows untill thay show clearly above his dark glasses. "Becouse i like your face, my English friend. Becouse this is the last batch i must sell befor i leave this stinking country of yours!" And he kicks the stack of sauspans and holds me with a very stern expression.

"Truthfully, my English friend, i must raise this last small sum of money so's that i can buy from the Turkish government... Land... For my wounderful Princess!"

I look at this Al Mersin cearfully. "Are you from Mersin?" i ask him, hestatingly. Al Mersin looks at me as if it is the most rediculous question he has ever heard.

"My friend, i am not here to be made a mockery of!" and he bends down as if to tiedy away the sauspans and leave, but then looks up at me sharply again.

"It is not my intention to sell you rubbish... I am only interested in selling you the best... These are the finest sauspans that money can buy, it is up to you to deside... Do you want gormat cook wear... Or do you want to eat out of an alimnum trough like an English pig!" Al Mersin makes a large gesture, denoting all the pigs that surround us.

"These pans arn't for eating your disgusting chip and

fish out of. No… These pans are for cooking a banquit in. Not that the English cear a damn about what thay stuff into their disgusting stomachs, or no anything of true Turkish quasine!"

Al Mersin holds me with the stern lines on his Turkish forhead, then relents slitely.

"Look, my English friend… If you buy these wounderful sauspans for just 25 of your worthless English pounds, i will give you these kitchen knifes for absolutly free!"

He brandishes them at me once again, but i refuse to take them and instead stroke my stollen pomigranets benith my shirt.

As he stands mesmerised by the blades, i slowly step back down the hall towards the bedroom. I go to close the door behind me but at the last second Al Mersin looks up and offers me a mint flavoured cigaret. I refuse but he insists. He lites up and trys to look behind me into the room.

"I have to go now, i carn't aford sauspans," and i try to shut the door on him. "I have no money, Al Mersin," i back him out the doorway, put the latch down and stand there listening.

"Money isn't everything, my English friend," Al Mersin calls out. "In this world there is also love and companionship… Are you truly in love with my daughter, my little English friend?"

"Go away, Al Mersin. You are not supposed to be here, this is a privat flat!"

"When will my little princess be home?"

"Shes in skool. She wont be home untill later."

"Well, i shall waite for her here."

"She's going to be very, very late."

"I can wait… I will relax myself in the sitting room." I hear his Turkish feet padding away up the hall, then thay stop and come back and there is a soft knocking. I stand very still and hold my breath.

"My friend, are you still in there? … You will regret your tone with me, i am an honest man… It will do you no good ignoring me, my English friend… I am the bissness partner of the Sultan of Mersin and personal friends with the Prime Minister of Turky! … I am not some English pig-dog, i am the son of a Muller!"

27

A Moment of Disapointment

I WAIT untill Al Mersin walks up the stairs and i hear the front door closeing behind him. His shadow passess over the grating above and i am alone. He gets in his car, starts it up and crawls away, the breaks still locked and screeching.

I undo my shirt front and cearfully count the lemons out onto the Trolls pillow. There are not as many as i had first hoped; just 3 lemons and 1 pomigranit in total. But one of the lemons is exceptionally large. As it comes out from its hidding place it leaps into the room like a lited bulb. It really is as if it is far too yellow to be real. I examin it, testing it with my mouth and smelling its magical aroma. I here a sound from the street and look fearfully up to the dark grating above, expecting to see the triumphant face of Al Mersin looming there, or prehaps the feverish face of Kajii, the lemon thief. No, no one is there and unless someone lies on the ground and peers in thru the narrow angle, or lowers themselves down in front of the filthy coal holes, thay will never be able to see anything.

I weigh the single pomigranit in my hand then pretend to lob it as if it was a handgrenade. I can honestly say that i have never in my entire life seen such magnificent fruits. I admit that it seems farcical and silly to imagin such a thing as an exploding lemon, but that dosnt make such a notion entirely implausable. For instance, there was once an incident in Japan – where a poor and starving student was forst by illness, poverty, and the indiffrence of the authorities – to let a lemon off in an art bookshop. Aparently, the entire premisses – and the intiraty of its heenious stock – were reduced to a heap of disgusting, smouldering rags.

I take my penknife and cearfully slice the top off the lemon and peer inside, lift it to my lips and suck. Rather than being plump and jucy this lemon is in fact quite dry and barron. Neither is it as large and dangerious looking as i first thought. I throw it down, scoop up the pomigranet and in turne studdy that; it too is rather small and on the shrivelled side. What at first had lookt so scarlet and threatening, now looks positivly dull and harmless.

I sit back on the bed. It is quite obvious that in my haste i have picked up 4 compleat duds. By the sorry state of these lemons – their dull, lifeless skins and their very aura's – even a novise can see that thay are not capable of blowing the top off a rice pudding, let alone destroying a bogus art skool. I fall back onto the pillow, beaten and exhorsted by the events of the day.

So, Kajii, my Japanese friend, you snatched the only truely explosive fruit on the whole market stall, from rite under my very nose, so to speak.

Just then there's a creek from the floor above. The hallway that leads to the front door runs directly above Karimas room and somone is standing up there, within 12 feet of me. Quickly, i wrap the incrimnating lemons in some old newspapers and stuff them at the back of Karimas wardrobe. I puff out the bottom of her dresses then quickly lie back on the bed and pretend to be sleeping.

28

Authenticity over Orginality

SOME PEOPLE have said that i havent got an original thought in my head, which is true, as their are no such things as orginal thoughts, or at least orginality is worthless if it is a meer gimick used to impress the gulable. No, truth is of value, not gimickry.

In the olden days it was recognised that it is impossable to make or do anything that was wholey original as it was understood that everything had already been something else befor hand and was meerly in the prosess of being something else in the present and becoming something else in the futcher. So nothing could be original, yet at the same time it was impossable to copy something to the extent that it became the thing it was copying. Something else cannot become the other thing but may meerly be assimilated or refrenced, which an honest artist dosnt lie about. Becouse an honest artist dosnt go striking stylish poses on the brink of hell just for effect, but speaks the truth.

Truth and authentisity are above fashion, lying and trying to apear interesting. Some things may apper to be the same as other things, yet thay aren't; and other things may appear to be seperate, but thay also arn't. This is becouse all things are joined by invisable threads and all things live in a state of flux, changing from moment to moment. Thay are not really solid or existing at all, but mearly appear to be so. But despite all this, you carn't walk on water or disapear thru brick walls. This is becouse reality is very stubon and insistant. Thats the whole truth, everything else is just a lot of sacasam, brought about by people reading too many books.

29

An old Spinner

THE TRUE REASON that i caught Karimas hair alite is not nown to me. Is it becouse she betraid me? Or, that she has gone to studdy under Mister Bennit at the Acadamy? No, it is becouse i am a spitful man. Becouse she has made me hate God and myself. Becouse i have given her gonareah.

It is impossably hard for a young man to no himself and even harder still for a young man who is not a man at all but a boy-man. The reason it is hard for a boy-man is becouse he is a man who is still a boy with no father above him and mistakenly belives himself to already be fully grown. So, becouse he thinks that he already nos himself, the imature youth smashes into life full of hatred and brevado and the imature youth never grows into a man at all but remains forver a boy, to the most pathetic degree. I am of course aluding to Mister Bennit, who belives himself imbuedly qualified to teach others, while he himself is still a child who nos nothing.

This is the reason that, in all matters of life, we are surrounded by ideocy. This is also why people belive in the supremisy of werk, the worship of the clock, the glorys of mindless consuption and the hatred of art! Yes, i walk'd into that building, a lost and trembling youth, looking for the guiding hand of a kindly father, but there was none. There was only middle aged boy-men, rubbing there dry hands together and licking their disguting old lips over the female students and hating me for my youth. No, there was not a grown man amongst them. We were children bullied by children. I could not flurish there under their jellouse gaze.

Yes, it is best that i have left the Academy, so that i mite walk a little in the fresh air and try to become a grown man, a whole person. So i walk'd out of that building and wondered the streets like a drunkard, marching along with one foot in the gutter. There i find a smashed wooden toy, pick up the pices and place them in my pocket. Catching site of myself in a shop window, i walk over and examin the open scars on my cheeks. I place my fingers where i cut the knotts of puss out of my skin. Also, my hair is cut like a madmans. It seems that i am the only person left in the entire M— Towns – other than in the asylum – who still has the sence to visit the barbers every 2 weeks and have a real haircut.

In the window are some very high class antiques. Notably, an old spinning wheel – that someone has ingeniously adapted into a standard lamp. The wood is old and sinew'y looking, where as the lamp shade itself apears to be made from dryed rabit skin. The whole thing stands there, sagging, on 3 wrickity old legs. I study it most meticliously for several minits. Shortly, an elderly gentleman joines me in admiring the magnifecent antique.

I drag my eyes from the spinning wheel and look at him sideways. The whites of his eyes are yellow and lumpy like old egg whites. The elderly gentleman notices me whatching him and i have to look away. Just incase i have offended him in some way i rub my breath mark from the window with my frayed cuff.

Next, the elderly gentlman raises his hands and touches his fingertips to the glass, as if in reverence of the magical spinning wheel. Judging by his old and knotted fingers – and by the pair of wooden clogs on his feet – he is an old weaver re-living his past triumphs. Shortly, he stops sighing, leaves his place by the window and clatters off into the shop. I watch him dissapearing into the gloom. At first i lose site of him, then a truly ancient scearcrow emerges from behind a barracade of old mattricess and radiograms and – looking for all the world as if he has just stepped out from out an explossion, the sparse gray hairs on his head all stood on end and his face smudged with soot and he wares a watch chain like my father and is evidently the proprioter – accosts him.

I try to read their silent lips threw the plate glass window. The proprioter then leads the old weaver into the window and lets him examin the spinning wheel.

I bite my lips as the old weaver fondles its gracefull lines, caressing the wheel in a way that is almost indesent. His greedy, eggy eyes gobbling up every contoure of that remarkable spining wheel. All i can do is stair in dessperation, willing the wretched thing to drop from his hands and smash to the floor in smitherines.

Finnaly, the old weaver lets go the damnable ornoment and alowes the owner to place it cearfully back into the window. Where upon, the old weever speeds off to the other end of the shop to molest some other piece of nonsence: a trashy looking drappery, dippicting a wild stag being brought down by a pack of baying hounds.

Again i am left to stand alone stareing at the spining wheel, dreaming of the day i will be rich enough to own such a rare and unusual ornament.

A little bell tinkles and the old weaver comes back out the door. He glances at me then looks away, hiding his knotted hands in his pockets. Meanwhile, the proprieter places a red painted sign on some object that lies their hidden in the shadows. Not the spining wheel but something entirly different, something entirly extaraoudenary and utterly unique. The sign reads: RESERVED and has been placed upon a book, but this is no ordinary book, this book has electric glass lettering. I stair in disbelith: it is an authentic Neon Bible.

I have been tricked by a con man! Messmerized by a slight of hand. Forced to oggle a vulga spining wheel, when all along there was a Neon Bible sat rite there in front of me – stareing me rite in the nose. I look up the street, the old weever is stopped at the curb, waiteing for a break in the traffic to cross the bissy road.

"Excuse me!" i shout, but he dosnt here me, or at least he pretends not to – this shape-changer – this 'weever', who sneeks around the streets at nite mascerading as an old spinner!

Excuse me!" i shout again, "you leave that Neon bible alone, you leave it exactly where you found it! It is against God!" He turnes and survays me with a quisical look about his brows.

"You think you can trick me by pretending you were going to buy that spining wheel?" I look at him imploringly, but he just shakes his head, spits in the gutter and clatters off.

Theres a lound thump as the proprioter bangs on the glass at me and 'shoo's' me away. I reluctantly cross the street and studdy his shop from a safe distance. The sign says 'House Clearensess, Quick Sales, Furnishings and Antiques'. It also says that the proprioters name is Wally Hangman. I amuse myself by making up storys about how this Wally Hangman erned his name, generaly dragging his buisness thru the dirt and proving, beyond doubt, that Wally Hangman is a murderer, a thief and an idiot!

Mister Hangman seems to attach quite some importance to the antique aspect of his trade, as this word alone is picked out in large, onstentashious, gold coloured lettering. Well, Mister Hangman, if you specialise in antiques then why is your shop full of such deplorable, festering old rags? When i am a rich and famouse artist, Mister Hangman, i will returne and buy anything that i so choose from your missarable shop and you will not be allowed to bang on your window at me then, my friend. Oh no, not by any mesure you wont!

After this experence i feel so melencolic and down at hart that i can scearsly drag myself along the street to the

Trolls cave. The traffic has died down and a lite drizzel has set in. It is then that i relise that i havent eaten anything since yesterday tea time. On the banks i find a sweet shop, but it is closed. Outside is a vending machine which steals 3 10 pences off me in a row. I pull at the little tray and bang the machine on its side with my elbow, but it is jammed. I peer into the little glass in the front, where you can normally see the stack of small choclet bars. It is empty. This is a choclet machine that hasnt vended any choclet since the Boer War. I stand back, look up and down the street and give it a tremendous kick. Imediately a window above the shop opens and a bald headed man shouts at me to clear off or he'll call the police.

"Your machine stoll my money!"

"Then you shouldn't be putting money in it, should you?!"

"I want my money back."

"It says out of order on it."

"No it dosnt."

"Well it should do." And he slams the window shut. I look at the machine. He is rite, there is a sign that says out of order. I look back up at the window and he is still standing there – just behind the curten – watching me.

"It dosn't werk!" i shout up at him. He opens the window again, this time in a real rage.

"Clear off! Rite, thats it!" He turnes and shouts for his wife to call the police, then looks back down at me.

"Rite, now the police are on their way. You just wait there!"

I ask the shop keeper for a cup of water.

"Bludy students!" He shouts down at me, "i'm not

made of money!"

"I havent any bus fair. You stoll all my coins!"

"I have to pay my water rates!" He says most haughterly and slams his window shut again.

"Im not a student," i shout back up at him, "and where is your Christain spirit!"

I turne and start walking off down the road. I am at the bottom of the Banks when i here the window being lifted up once more.

"There's no fucking Christains in here son, now piss off!" He slams the window again. It is true, he did look like he mite be of Indian origin.

I sit down on the curb and put my fingers into my mouth. Luckerly, i find a puddle, get down on my knees and lap at it like a cat.

There is a clack of heals and a prostitue apears. She slows as she walks past then dissappears into the nite. I stare after her. The old whore proberbly belives that i am drunk, purely based on my atire and the fact that i am kneeling to drink from a puddle.

"I am not drunk and not a student! I've been reading the letters of Vincent van Gogh and realise that i must improve my relationship with God! This is the reason that i drink out of puddles, madam!"

I call out to her in the nite but she is gone. I look down at my socklees feet, the bones of my ankles jutting out horribly against the course leather of my hob-nailed boots. I stand, painfully, and hobble off up to the other end of the High Street.

30

Stollen Brushes

AFTER MY EXCITING adventure with the puddle i go and try to get some sleep in the park. It is there that i lie awake all nite freezing and waiteing for it to be morning.

At 6.30 a.m. i am stood outside the art shop next to the Cathedral, waiteing for it to open its doors. My whole body is damp with due and shaking with cold. At 10 past 9 the lady owner comes along and opens up shop. She recognises me from my glory days at the Academy, the glory days, when i entered into this very establishment in my brand new blazer and bawt 2 new scetch books and a large pack of willow charchole.

She holds the door open as i enter and actualy smiles at me. I pass quickly on to the back of the shop where thay keep the cabinet of 1st quality, sable brushes. I keep my legs close together hoping that no one will notice my jutting ankle bones that crack loudly as i walk.

I lift the lid of the brush cabbernit, pick out a number 5 and put it to my mouth. I suck on the fine hairs and then paint my nose and lips with it. The hairs are ultra soft and caress my lips in a most sensuous manner. I stick out my tounge and paint all over it. I continue to suck on the magical brush as i walk round the ancient establishment examining their collection of over priced oil paints.

(When i was a little boy there was a small joke shop on G— High Street, run by an old soldier. I had to go to G–. every 6 months to have my teeth pulled, and my mother used to take me in the joke shop as a treet – to see the scary masks and other bits 'n' bobs he sold. It was the smallist shop you could ever hope to fit into – to the extent that even i, a missrable, toothless child – could feel my tiny shoulders brushing agaist the walls. I wasn't allowed to buy any of the masks or tricks as id allready spent all of my pocket money on a model Spitfire with retractable under carrage and a spining proppeller, but the the old soldier showed me a jagged scar on the back of his neck and a matching one bellow his addams apple. Apparently, he had been shot thru the throat at Dunkirk by a Stüka dive bomber.)

I check to see if the lady owner isnt whatching and tuck the wounderfull brush down the waistband of my trousers. I check again and it is true that no one is looking. My hart beats excitedly as i dip my hand into the cabinet and lift a whole handfull of the ginger looking brushes and stuff them down inside my knickers. 2 of them fall to the ground and i kick them out of site under the cabenet. Really, i would have liked to break them and fling them in sombodys face.

I walk cearfully passed the counter and smile in a fake way at the lady owner – who is stood behind the till – and leave the shop, cearfully closing the glass doors behind me.

I am free and out on the street again, breathing the ice cold air and ready to be recognised for my talent and geniouse.

I am a theif like my father is a theif. I imagine myself as a poor impoverished young artist (which i am), but now that i have stollen these special artists brushes i will be able to paint picture after picture that will force the girls of the Acadamy befor me on their knees, and Mister Bennit will have to look on jellously as thay kiss my loins and take me, not him, into their mouths. A real artist, after all – an artist who doesn't feel the need to be sanctioned by the Acadamy and isn't a mear teacher – has special rites and privaleges in this world, over and above the law and women. And besides, i am not really a thief, and even if i am, i am sure that i will be forgiven, and if not, then what is the point of having a Christ? This is how my feverish mind was werking.

I walk rite the way up to the bridge, where i stand and stair into the black flowing currents that tumble benith the arches. It is here that i realise that i have turned into the worst possable type of hypocrite imaginable and turne back down the High Street. I stryde in thru the glass doors and, looking at thc lady owner in a hard way, take one of the brushes from my jacket and place it on the counter in front of her.

"I havent paid for this," i tell her, then turne and leave.

Shortly, it starts to drizzel and then rain. I go into another shop, hoping to warm myself up a bit. On one of the shelfs i discover a book of photos. To be compleatly honest, it is not a book but really a cheep magazine full of indecent photographs. There are many young women in there but i have named my favourite Bernadet. She is, i would presume, of German origin, tho' there is something very dark about her eyes, espesherly in the way that she peers rite into my sole, as if she nos my deep rotting hart and is daring me to do some very indesent things.

Instead of placing the magazine back up on the shelf, pursing my lips and leaving that establishment for ever, as i should, i make a very bold mistake. Whereas i would normally never dream of stealing litrichar from a shop, Bernadet has taunted me into to taking her.

A surge of people suddenly enter the shop to escape the rain, and tho' very bissy, the lady on the till seems to be watching my every move. Even whilest she is serving some skool boy a packet of Gaurds cigarets, she still peers at me from between the newspaper racks. I walk up and down the row of magazines, my hart thumping away in my chest. In my efforts to remain anominus i pretend to be examining a magazine about 'The Lost Art of Balkan Cake Decoration'. I look at a recipe for Balkan souflay then place it back on the shelf and kneel to the floor where, in another magazine entitled 'Real Life Murder', i read a most interesting article about the exploits of a Victorain headless corpse and the fun it had scearing its killer. The account says that when the murderer tryed to burn the severed head in an open fire, its hair stood on end and it opened its dead eyes and laughed at him. I keep the magazine with Bernadet hidden benieth the murder book, then, with my back to the till lady, i quickly stuff Bernadet up under my jacket and clamp her there with my arm.

I lower my nose and whisper. "You are my SS princess Bernadet. Soon we will be alone together and i will possess you."

Still kneeling, i look back over my shoulder and have to smile thinly at the till lady, who is still studdying my every move.

Even if she has suspision that i am a thief – which she evidently belives me to be – i see no reason for her to look at me so pointedly. Surly, even an expelled student is inocent untill proven guilty. I stand, turne and march rite up to her counter, put my rite hand inside my jacket and nervissly feel the crisp, butiful pages of my stollen magazine. Suddenly, i realise that the till lady has come from behind her counter and is walking towards me. In a moment she will be upon me. I look around desperatly for an escape but she has contrived herself to stand between me and the doorway.

"Good morning." she says in an overly friendy manner, trying to trick me into giving up my dareing mission. I squeeze my arm to my side, feeling the pages of my SS princess heavy against my ribs, lift my free hand and stroke my chin in a nownchalant manner.

"Hello," i say stupidly.

"Can i help you?"

"No," i stammer, "Im fine, thank you."

"Oh, i thought i mite be able to be of assistance to you?" and she smerks at me hatefully.

"No thank you, i am perfictly cappable." And i, in turne, smile trumphantly at her.

So, Madam, you thought that you could terrorise

William Loveday – you and all the teachers who reduced him as a little boy to a crying reck becouse he couldn't spell – well, you were sorly mistaken!

I whatch as she nurvissly ajusts a magazine on the shelf between us.

"I have to go now," i speak, somehow beliving that i have to ask her permission to leave. I turne and she touches my arm.

"I just thought that prehaps you were dropping your magazine?"

My hart stops and i stare at her uncomprehendingly. Suddenly all of the saliva seems to have dryed up in my mouth.

"What magazine?" i stammer.

"The magazine under your arm, sir. I suppose that you are wanting to buy it?"

"You are mistaken, i have no magazine." And i walk quickly towards the doorway, looking back at her to see if she is following me. It is there that i collid with a tall black man. I go full tilt into his manly chest and my magazine flops from inside my jacket to the floor at his feet. I look down and see Bernadet smiling up at us. I try not to stare at her – lying there on the cold, tiled floor – looking over her shoulder with her magnificent German arse in the air.

The black man has a gray mustash. I try to step round him and abandon Bernadet, as if she is nothing to do with me what-so-ever but he holds me still with one of his massive hands, picks up my magazine and pushes it to my chest.

"Excuse me, sir, i think you dropped your book?"

I look at him in dessperation. His skin is purple-black and the whites of his eyes are rageing with a burst of red vains.

"I keep telling you all, this is not my book!" I sob, "i've never seen it befor! " And again i see Bernadet, smiling at me from his giant hand.

"I told him he was dropping his magazine," the till lady chimes in.

"What magazine?" I manage to speak.

"This magazine, sir, the one you just dropped."

She takes the magazine from out of his hand and places it in mine. I look at her dumbfounded as my hand closes around Bernadets nude middle. I realise that she really does belive that the magazine is mine, belongs to me and that i have not stollen it. I nod, turne on my heal and walk out into the street which is now teaming full of cars, busses and people.

31

Willhelm Leibertag

HORSES REAR UP at me out of a vile, spurting fountain and thrash their giant fish-like tails at me and i run on breathless thru the German nite. My hart races untill it feels like a windmill in my chest. I will do anything to destroy this black void of my sole.

Please be kind to me you God, send me your hartless whores, for i am a stranger in your town. And i run from dark street corner to dark street corner in serch of love, or sex or blackness.

My name, by the way, is Willhelm Liebertag. Already i have sinned against your race with one of your hot, German Whores. Do you think that i can ever forgive myself? Let me assure you that she was as complicet as me, and i am, if i am not mistaken, a man of Kent, so come out of your silly looking gingerbread houses, pull your knickers to one side and let me lick at your arse holes!

Oh Karima, i have sinned aganst you. Karima, sweet Turkish girl, i have sinned aganst the entire race of women. Forgive me my sweetharts, obsolve me, drink my seed, brest feed me, let me be you, let me become a woman!

And i dash off again thru the black nite, my eyes hungry for the friendly site of a neon sign glinting in the rain, where i can wank to the site of a black girl having her buttocks parted and her arsehole licked by a butiful SS princess and i will die of orgasem and shame, my hart fluttering in my throat.

"So your hart is in your neck now, is it, you imberseal!" i yell at myself and cower from this new asault, then run off down another blind ally.

If, for instance, i had been a common foot soldier in the Vermarcht, sent by the Furhurer to strike a blow at the hart of the Russian bear, we would now be sleeping in the open, in our summer kit, whilest its 15 below. Never have i nown such cold. My teeth ache in my scull. After brakfast, we aproach a farmhouse in line abrest, crunching thru that ici wilderness. Just as we are drawing close to that black building something flys thru the air towards me – a small bird? But Hans shouts 'granade!' and there's a flash and the 'crump' of an explosion. I feel the snow thrown in my face. I open my mouth, bite a mouthfull and let it dissolve, the world has gone very silent. Shortly, i manage to sit up. I look round but my comrades are no where to be seen. Then i notice a boot lying on the snow some meters away, and then that it is my boot and that my left foot is missing. I hold the tattered end of my trousers as my raggedy stump twhitches and pumps scarlet across the white, virginal snow. Next, i must have fallen unconcious, becouse when i open my eyes i see my enimy grinning down at me from behind his great shaggy beard – an Ivan! He must have come to finish me off. Qiuck as a flash i pull him to the ground and cut off his leg with my black-forest hunting knife. Later that week – at the red cross station – i beat the same bearded Russian at a game of chess. Then, after drinking tea, we lay like brothers, side by side on the same bed, our twin stumps seeping into an old horse hair mattrice.

I rush on thru the nite – my string laces have snapped in 2. I have contrived to tie them decently but the tounge of my left boot lolls out insulently.

"No wounder that no decent, uprite women will ever love you!" i scream.

Both of my legs are made of tin. I kick them out in front

of me, clanging along the vast, empity streets. I wimper feebly in protest.

"You hair burner!"

Under a crumbling bridge i stumble over a sleeping corps. It is hard to belive that this bundle of rags is really a human being at all, or that thay ever had a mother and father, or were ever a child in the cear of adults who would never let them starve or sleep in the rain. That thay too sung hyms to God and once were virgins. A whole town of the disspossesed.

One day i will lose an arm or a leg, of that much i am certen. I lite up a cigaret and my breath and the tobbaco smoke are as one. I studdy the blisters between my poor white fingers. (When i'm drunk i forget that i'm smoking. Actually, i burn myself on purpose, dropping the ciggaret onto my hand in slow motion, then grinding it out).

If you really look at the world and see it for what it is, the streets are like black oily rivers and the rivers like concreat motorways and all of them are taking us away from who we truly are towards a mechanical hell. I peer over the edge into the black water. I have to stay awake to make sure i dont fall asleep, drop off and freeze to death. One old fellow motions for me to come in out of the rain and and sit next to him on his mouldering mattrice. His wife is with him, drinking beans from a tin. This is the place for Wilhem Libertag: i am not a king but a begger! No, i am an artist and artist's are not special, thay belong here – close to the ground.

As we sit thru this nite, strange signs loom at me from

out of the darkness: A panther the size of a juggernaught slinks across the motorway, and a knite in full armour rears up on his white stallion, brandishing a broad sword, and 10 severed heads laugh at me, stuck on posts on the road side. One head speaks to me in a dry, hot whisper, 'I can order you to kill yourself if i so wish'.

All the while the ici wind blows in at me. I loosen my coller and stick my neck out into that gale. I stay there, my eye streaming, the chill-blains in my ears burning like coals. In the distance i see a dark ridge running across the horizon and beyond that, the lites from one of the great citys of the British Empire. R—, i should imagin. The whole sky stained orange.

I find my little bottle in my pocket, still 1/2 full. My hands are frozzen and can hardly twist off the useless, tin lid. I stand here, clinging onto the bottle as it dances in my hands, jets of wisky squirting down my neck and trouser leg. I lift the bottle to my lips, it tips and glugs, foul, bitter stuff. I sive it thru my back teeth, my stomach revolting, hot sick pushing up into my nose. I have to swallow it and wash it back down with another bitter mouthfull.

The wind peircess every part of me. I have to protect my poor white cock. Walking on thread-bare feet, the soles of my boots flapping aganst the tarmac, i stagger in the road

It is only after walking for several houres that i notice someone has joined me. I look to his face but it is allways in darkness. He wears a black cap and the coller of his cloak is pulled up. I can see the backs of his fingers, yellowed. Sometimes his pale eyes glint in the glear of the headlamps of a passing truck. It would be true to say that he is somehow bathed in shadows. I look at him and tho' he says nothing, i no that he hates me, in that respect he is my true brother.

32

A True Story

AS A CHILD my father impressed upon me, most violently, that i must allways tell the truth – this great lier and bender of the truth. I looked at his baggy, blue eyes and hated him, yet this is the one comandment that i have followed: truth. I have followed it to the extent that i show every sickening part of myself, so's that i can be scortched clean in Gods firery furniss. So i tell tails against myself, telling the 'truth' but moor so: inventing lies so that people can hate me with impunity and blame me personally for all the sins of the world.

This is the true story of how i gave Karima gonareah. Of how i betraid her. Of how i betraid my own hart. Of how i hurt myself. Of how – becouse in my childhood something in my sole was snapped, broken and lost – i have not been able to become whole. Of how i have grown into a desperate man intent on destroying myself and anyone who mite dare love me. This is the true reason i set Karimas hair alite. Not becouse i am angry but becouse i am a romantic, becouse i wish to be rescued from myself at the brink of hell – caught by my sleeve as i teeter over the pit. The truth is, i dont love evil at all but actualy love God and goodness, tho' i loath goodness becouse goodness and kind sentiment cut me to the quick. Becouse it seems that this world, tho' made by God, is not after all perfict, possably becouse it was never ment to be perfict. Which is all very well for God but is wholely unacceptable to me, becouse for me nothing but pefection will do. In short – i have tried to become my Father and have failed missarably and now i roll crying in the filth, becouse failer is glorious and is next to the real Jesus, whereas success is in leage with the Devil.

33

Bernadet

YES, I HAVE FAILED YOU, Karima. Please, dear God, protect me. I swear never to set lite to a girls hair or wank myself off over the pages of deceptfull pornography ever again – on my honour!

I fall to my knees licking at the beautiful blond hairs

around Bernadets arse, her cunt peeping out from beneath, playing hide and seek, if you like. Such a lovely blond arse, a Nazi arse, an arse of the Third Reich. Not like my sweet Karimas arse, not in the least. Her arse is of the Otterman Empire. Rite now its back in England, doing the hoovering, or making some toast i should think. An arse that will damn us all to hell!

When it comes to anal sex, i am what my mother would call 'a sodding bugger.' Serriously, when i was 10 years old she frew the chip pan at my head and shouted those exact words: 'You sodding bugger!' and i ducked just in time. It took a lump of wood out of the door frame the size of my thumb. If she'd of hit me then, it would have been all over.

I dribble in the split, biting at the quivering cheeks. I stick my tounge in there as well, thats the sort of fellow i am – i sin against love. Karimas arse is a soft, dusky brown, not at all Nazi-ish. A heavenly arse with a spray of black, downy hairs just at the base of her spine. How i love to kiss those soft, rude hairs and then spray my seed on them – God, save me from the Ottoman Empire!

The reason i have to kiss the arse of this German whore is to make myself less, to dissapate my energy. To run from Karima and my foul abuses of her. I look around me, studying the cealing. Since i was a child i have beliv'd that people were filming me on the toilet; to see if i have a split when i stand to wipe my arse. This is becouse me and my family are the only people in the world who have splits, everybody else has no arse, just a solid lump of flesh.

I have to stop myself from coming over Bernadets

buttocks. Really, my cocks so hard it could spit any second, without me even touching it!

Just now i said that Karima is probably back home in England doing the hoovering, which is a down rite lie as she dosnt even own a Hoover. Oh, Karima, i love you! If you did own a hoover i would stand behind you as you hoovered and press my body against yours, push you down onto your knees and then… You see, Karima, i do love you.

I lift my whisky bottle to my lips and lap at it like as if it is one of Bernadetts wounderfull, girl-like teets. I take a hot swig and look down at myself. Thats something i love to see – my cock swaying about like a dagger, ready to stab your butiful arse. This time i must be cearful that i dont split my foreskin again.

Back home in England, in her trolls cave, Karima fits it in for me. Thats another site i love to see, but in fact she carn't manage on account that its too blunt and i have to help her ease it in. Just fitting the knob in takes some manoeuvring but then its held there like in a vice and she pumps up and down on it, her big arse cheeks shuddering as she goes into multiple orgasms.

"Just as soon as it goes in i start coming," she says in my ear and hearing her talk that way makes my cock grow another inch.

"You can get it bigger than that," she says, pulling on it, "thats it, make it nice and thick!"

The Trolls bed is so narrow that i can stand with one foot either side, put my hands on my hips, and lower myself in there, my thighs and calves juddering. I spit on her arse and slap at it and Karima looks over her shoulder, pulling at her arse cheeks.

"Its too big" she says, "i want more of it in there but it just wont fit." And i just keep staring at myself in disbelith, the veins popping.

"Its gonna come, where do you want it?"

"In my mouth!"

"Say please."

"Please!"

Quickly, i pull the head out, step forward and, squirting, feed it into her mouth. I'm on my tipy toes, her little tongue flickering at the spunk hole like a kitten. It feels like the top of my scull is going to rise and come off and i nearly fall as it leaps out of me. I stagger and collapse onto her. She rolls over, gurgling on the juce, smiling up at me like the cat thats got the cream and i kiss her rite in the mouth.

Karimas 1/2 Turkish with tits like a pair of crashing Zeppelins, where as Burnadet has the breasts of a skool girl.

When i first saw you across the room Bernadet, the scent of danger and sex fill'd my nostrels. I pretended not to be afraid of you, yet all along i knew that you could crush me at will, for you are butiful and i am nothing but a poisonous insect.

Please, you must want me and desire me, Bernadet, i live thru you, you hold my life in your masterful hands, will you give me sex, or will you reject me? Do i live or die? – Bernadet, you must decide.

I smile weakly at my SS princess, hoping for just a hint of a smile in her cold, flint-like eyes.

I sit here in the toilet shivering, whispering to this sad girl, untill really i have to laugh at myself for pretending that i am a man at all. I whisper to her flesh.

Its true that i wish to conquer you, Bernadet. To pull you from your pedestal and drag you to the ground. I wish to be your King and for you to hold me and desire me. But have no fear, i will be a merciful ruler, if you in turne will only surrender yourself whole to me.

Actually, Bernadet, i am a poet, which is a crummy trade. Really, i am a painter, which is even worse. And i read you 2 of my poems, here in this toilet, 2 beautiful poems from my damaged hart. And you lookt out at me from beneath your insolent fringe and said that you had read stuff like mine befor. And when i showed you my drawings you raised your painted eyebrows dismissivly. So, you are also at war with man, Bernadet, and hate me. And i lift your face with my hand and try to brush the hair from your eyes but you pull away and snap – 'Dont do that!'

You are German, or Polish, or possibly both, Bernadet. You, like me, like Karima, are damaged and can therefore be forgiven. Now turne to me, Bernadet and i will bite your lips and spread your cherry-red lipstick rite across your fucking mouth! Did anyone ever tell you that you look like a murderess Bernadet? Such a cold, hard face. Ile dribble you all over with goo and saliva, you beautiful, petulant child. And what lovely little teats you have, like naughty little puppy-dogs, like a 12 year old girls tits, budding like rose buds, ready to be bitten off and eaten.

Im so full of puss, Bernadet. Im drunk and my knob is

going soft. Quick, Bernadet, turne around, stick your arse high in the air and let me lick at it again!

I rub my knob up and down the split. Ah, if we'd of been in the SS together, Bernadet, with your black SS britches round your shinny jack-boots and a little Nazi dagger at your hip. Christ, ile whip your muscular arse for you, you BDM slut! I want to spurt on it, to fuck it and come all over it, to drown you in spunk.

Suddenly the door handle turnes and someone tries to barge in. The bolt slips open. I drop my book and lunge at the door, trying to hide my cock.

"There's someone in here!" i sob, pushing the door shut on his horrible leg. I kick at it and throw the bolt, crouching here breathlessly, holding my cock with my trousers round my ankles, listening. Hes gonna wake up the whole house banging on the door like that. There is a sweet, sickly smell as Al Mersin lites up one of his mint flavoured cigarets.

I listen, fearfully at the door, praying for him to go away.

Is that a little piece of string i spy hanging from your cunt, Bernadet? And you reach between your legs, pull out that swab of bluded cotton and let it drop heavyly to the floor. Oh, so your on, are you, you little SS slut? You little murderess.

I raise the open whisky bottle to my lips and chug it back, the hot liquid is suddenly in my mouth. It surprises me, fighting its way up my nostrels untill i snort like a bull.

Really… Please… That i am so shy… That i blush… that i'm scared of the powerful race of women. But oh, how this one worships me.

I lean over her pale back and kiss her hard mouth. So youve read poetry just like mine and seen drawings just like mine? And now i'm fucking you in your cunt, then in your arse, in your cunt and in your arse and you are crying softly, biting the soft flesh in the crook of your arm.

Yes, soon my book will be printed, Bernadet, it will sit in all the book shops of London, Munich, Berlin and the world. And it will confound all those who dare to speak my name disrespectfully, Bernaddete. No, William Loveday will not be made a mockerey of, and all those who have damned him, been unkind to him and wished him ill and to amount to nothing, all those will have to say sorry and beg for his forgivness, (viz). Mister Bennit and all my teachers who never beliv'd in me; my parents whos eyes have never admired me, thay to will have to apologise. And it will be a spit in the eye to every book shop who has said 'Oh no Sir, our policy is that we can only display books on our shelves which have spines!' Fine, you fork-tongued traitors of art, if you want a spine then you shall have a spine – here is your fucking spine!

And you and all the women of the world will crawl to me upon your bruised and damaged knees, Bernadet, and kiss my blud heavy cock, imploring me to read you my poems, which will fall like stones into your ice-cold harts.

Bernadet, uh-uh-uh-ahhh! And i stagger, my thighs cramping. 'Achtung, ich comer!' and i pull my cock out and feed it spurting into Bernadets upturned mouth. It covers her lips, it drips like glue. So beautiful to see a cock spurting and to no that it is yours and to no that the tongue wants to love your taste and to drink it in torrents.

I fall broken to the floor, kissing away her tears. Dont cry, my sweet Bernadet, my poor little SS princess. And she smiles bravely up at me 'Dont you cry when you come?' she speaks. And i droop my head and kiss her teets, thay have my spunk on them, like icing on 2 little cup cakes. I lick the cherries. Collapsed there on that cold, tiled floor. Alone.

Suddenly there is a fearfull pounding on the door and it sighs on its hinges.

I have to go now, Bernadet. The Devils running after me. Maybe there will be another sweethart like you, Bernadet. Weighting for me, to help me to destroy my desperate hart and loneliness. But of course, she could never really match you, Bernadet, for you aremaculate, you are alive, trembling with life. And you have given me everything so willingly. And besides, women hate me, Bernadet, and give me nothing. Can you belive that? Such a fine person as me, a poet and an artist to boot, so capable of love, if only i was allowed to show it.

"What the hell are you doing in there?!"

Im scared that i mite lose Karima, Bernadet, lose all the women and be left with nothing. Becouse there can never be enough women, Bernadet, to blot out the cold stare of my mothers disapproval. Hurriedly i turn back the pages, trying to clean them with toilet paper.

Bernadet, pull on your black stockings, we have to leave. It is then that i notice her poor brused toe. One of her boyfriends tried to push you under a tram? Aw! Its black and blue.

You should mind who you go with, Bernadet. Look after

yourself, get yourself a nice fellow, an English poet, like me.

There is the smell of mint and Al Mersin really dose try to shoulder the door down like some kind of insain bull.

Oh, if i could just stay and fuck you for always, Bernadet. But no, the SS would be too fine a place for the likes of me. And besides, i am an Englishman, and even tho' i despise my own race, i can not deny my creed of moderation in all things.

Yes, i must go now, leave you and this bathroom, and you too must go back to where ever it is that you come from, Bernadet. I am 1stly a painter, tho' of course i despise all painters. 2ndly, i am a poet, tho' poets stink worse than the worst, most villainous scum.

Actually, to tell the honest truth, Bernadet, i only rite out of boredom and to be adored – that is it! I do everything to be adored. But that dosnt necessarily mean that i worship success, Bernadet. In fact i despise it. You see, if somebody offer'd me success, i would vomit on it befor accepting so much as one stinking crumb off their humiliating plate.

No, rather than be applauded for my genius, i will crawl under the floorboards and become a pea-bug – do you hear me, Bernadet? – I will become so small that nobody will even be able to find me! Thats my ultimate ambition, Bernadet – to become a nothing. To become a zero. Becouse it may seem that i am afraid of you, Bernadete, but ultimatly i am afraid of nothing but my own power and imence intellect.

That amuses you? Then good, becouse it was ment to be funny. Becouse, i am above all else, a commedian and will never be caught out or be surprised by anything,

Bernadet. Becouse the only way to be truly safe is to never give anything away and to remain always closed. But that is also the way of the Devil, Bernadet, and to be a true artist you must open every vain in your body, untangle every last nerve and be surprised by everything, absolutely everything! So that is what i will do. Go ahead and mock me if you wish, Bernadet. I am above all else a contradiction and we artists down the ages are used to ridicule.

Bernadet pulls on her leather mini skirt, sticks her poor foot into her stilettos and hobbles out of the bathroom, me following. I wave my sweethart good bye. Shes a tough one, stood there, all sex, pale broken and lost. A lovely one, one full of gonorrhoea and herpes.

Al Mersin is standing before me, waiteing to fight his way past me. I have to look away out of decency. I push back my hair, hold my nose against his hateful cigaret and walk past with my magazine tucked down my shirt front.

34

A Fathers Leggercy

PREHAPS, becouse i was so mercylessly bullied by my father who diddn't no how to love me – and still i am terrified of him, to the extent that i will nessisarally have to kill him –

is the reason i rite this small history.

My first memorys of my father are his beared and the next is his face sat oppersite me trying to make me eat my dinner, which i couldn't.

"Eat it. All of it!… Not with your mouth open! Breath thru your nose!"

My nose was blocked so i had to chew with my mouth open.

"Eat with your mouth shut!" Which ment that i was being ordered to die.

My big brother joined in, he told me i was disgusting.

35

A Testiment

KARIMA HAS TALKT with the print teqcknitions and it has been agreed that thay will print my book during the skool hollidays. I have left all spelling mistakes, ritten down all lies that i have been forst to ingest and spoken of all bad things i have done and that have been done to me.

I am the namer of names and now no one will ever be able to forgive me.

I am very anxious to see and feel my testerment in my hand. Whereas most books cater for the cultural elite, mine will cater for the downtrodden, de-harted and the scum. I would like my testiment to be seen as a glove in the face of art.

36

Our Heros Returne

In meny ways i have cheated my own hart. One day i will have to pay for all my evilness, even tho' i am as much a child of God as any one else.

Karima, i long for sex between your large, sexuel buttocks, to lose myself tottaly in oblivion. I want to talk with you and shear the blackness of my wretched hart with you. For us to find a way to finnaly arrive here together as humens. I long for you to hold my head in your razzor-sharp claws and kiss me, to absolve me of all my past sins, but you dont want to no the truth and would rather hear lies. So be it, i will tell the most butiful lies the world has ever heared, recounting delvilish sex with unnown whores.

Someday soon i will marry Deep Snow – that is my secreat plan – just to spite you, Karima. To fix you for being so misserly with your cigerets, hart and money. For spilling my secreats to the world and for aborting our baby without even telling me you were pregnant. Yes, i will marry Deep snow, to prove to myself that i am still loveable, swashbuckling and brave. To be a dark mystery, but above all, to excite myself at my own wickedness.

To have sex with a german prostitute then lie naked in the bath looking down into the dirty water at myself and wounder what those sores mite mean. You will sit on the edge of that bath, Karima, soaping me and i will turne and bite at your brests thru your blouse, making the mattireal wet with my dirty, English serliva and you will giggle and look down at that part of me and your eyes grow very serrious.

"Did you sleep with any one?" you will ask.

"There was a girl in Germany who slept with everyone. She had dark blue eyes – midnite blue."

"But you diddn't sleep with her, did you?"

And you will look up at me and i will go to speak but you will stop me. "I dont want to here the truth."

"Yes, i slept with her."

"Your lieing to me, you wouldn't."

"I did."

And i will kneel up in the bath, hold your small chin in my hand and mock your little girls voice and look at your breasts and breath in thru my teeth.

"Who was she?" you will ask, your eyes unable to meet mine.

"Her name was Bernadet."

"I dont want to no her name. How old was she? What did she look like?"

"I dont no… she was 20, 22."

"Was she blond? I bet the slut was blond! What did she wear?"

"She had a broken toe and lookt a bit like like Miss H—."

And you will drop the soap splashing into the water, your chin will start to tremble and i will stand, step out the bath – the water cascading off my body – and lift you from your knees, find your mouth with my tounge and place one of your hands to cup my balls and the other to wank me off. Then i will turne you, lift your skirt and bend you over the tub.

Yes, Karima, no that i am the sort of man that runs down empti streets praying for roasted pigions to just fly into my open gob and the sky to rain golden pennys. Then looking angryly up at the empty gray buildings and tumbling clouds beyoned, i shake my fist in the face of God, turne and dash on like a mungerel dog, truely expecting that on the very next corner there will be a butiful woman lying there, her legs parted, willing me to have sex with her. But even if such a woman really dose exist, Karima, and that, as i round the corner she really is just waiteing with her legs grotesqkly hacked apart – so to speak – then i will still have to grin maniacly, tear my filthy eyes from her body and cast them to the gutter, for i can not abide the touch of strange hands, blud, or degridation of any kind!

To say that i am sceared of what lies between a womans legs is a monsterious lie, but who nos what terrible evils i mite be capable of in the futcher? And isn't it quite possable that the seeds of my own distruction – and that of my potencial victims were sown – all be it unintentionaly – in some inocent act of our sheared past?

I am not afraid of the futcher but it would be true to say that the past is panting down my neck, pushing and urging me into the very teeth of the storm. Yes, the futcher is stood with its arms folded upon its garganchian chest, waiteing for me to make just one false move, so's that it has the perfict excuse to smash me with one of its talon-like claws.

I am, like my father befor me, an alcoholic, you see. Tho' all the students at the Acadamy would laugh to here me say so. In fact thay would ridicule me spitfully and i would have to look away – stareing at the floor – pretending not to be blushing with shame.

Then there is my family, who have all changed their names or moved away from these towns. Thay have detached themselves, or obsolved themselves, and now there is just me and my mother – who werks up at the fish 'n' chip shop – and soon it will even be time for her to move on. My name i have also forgotten. Like all things childish i have given it up and now i am an alltogether different person. I pretend to do nothing. I am an artist you see and a scally-wag. In truth, a waister. Actually, on the dole and people say that i look like a student, which fills me with disgust becose a student is really a nothing appart from new and 1/2-formed. A student has no depth, no experence and therefore no charicter. Yes, i am a student, but i refuse to look young and fashionable for anyone and will instead become a musseum piece.

If i ever was this other person – whos name i have forgotten – i was quiet and obedient. In fact i was bullied and down trodden, but underneith that facarde of being just a sex object for an older man, i was all along contriving to get the upper hand on my betters and trample them underfoot.

Later, as i started to metermorphsise, i cut my hair short and answered my esteamed educaters back, actualy swearing rite in their horrified faces. Naturely, i diddn't swear at those teachers who i lov'd most, for thay were the most male, and therefore the ones that i feared and respected.

When my cosy time at skool finnaly came to an end, i went to werk in Her Majistys Dockyards, where i stayed for several months. Then tyering of the hours and of meanial labour alltogether, i smashed my own hand and quit; much to my mothers bewilded sorrow. After this, it is all history: i went to the Acadamy, was expelled and became arrogant. Thats something that i have always contrived to be: a great and bitter disapointment to my mother; to allways meet her expectations; to always remain backward.

Where as now… Well now i look out into the world with anger, tinged with sentimental self pitty.

37

Concerning Cats

I LIE IN BED smoking cigaretts, i am normaly quite cearfull not to inhale the smoke, the same as i will often tip my whisky away or make myself throw up when drunk. Now i have a head ache and a hot rash of pimples covering my tounge. The cigarett smoke drifts into my gob and agrovates them, prickling like a lot of hot little insects. Everything in the world is made up of sensations but it is impossable to have only good ones. I have also masterbated, which calms my mind temporaraly. Tho' of course, my mind will rage doubly for it later.

If i lift the blankets the smell of my own body raises up to me, which excites me. My mother has all sorts of false belieths about me. About my ignorent background and my impending doom. One of the things that she is most happy to state is that i take after my 'soddin, bleeding father!' Another is that i am 'argumentative by nature' and a 3rd is that i'm 'for the high jump!' How i hate her, yet smile when she talks this way.

Strange as it may seem, i am going to make a painting of the woman i intend to marry and hang it above my bed. Yes, i will marry Deep Snow. It is becouse of her – a woman i have not yet found – that i no i am still cappable of something like love. And to feel that you are still able to love means that you mite still be a little bit human and that not everything is lost. We have not had sex which makes our relationship somehow holy.

Karima has an 18 inch waist. If she breaths in i can just touch my finger tips round the back, then we have sex, then i leave Karima in her deep, dark cave.

"I want to go into college in the mornings and not be able to walk propperly becouse you've fucked me so hard!"

I pretend not to have heared. The Troll has only recently started using swear words and it dosnt suit her. Insead i concentrate on my drawing. I have compleated the painting of my futcher wife and Karima hates it, all tho', stricktly speaking, she dosn't no that i am going to marry Deep Snow, or in fact who she even is. After 4 or 5 minits of her pestering me i purposfully put away my pencils, roll up my drawings and leave.

One of the reasons that wild animals dont just come up to me to feed out of my open hand is becouse thay can smell the anger in me. In their tiny squirel-like minds, thay no that the hand that today offers them a tasty chestnut, mite next day wring their necks in rage and incomprehension.

On my walk thru the park i call all manner of wild birds to fly down off of their perches and settle on me, but to no avail. Thay just chirp their warnings to each other and fly off, prehaps even lifting their tails and dropping something nasty from the branches.

Cats are a different matter and are, on the whole, far more easy to train. But there is small triumph in getting a domestic pussy-cat to walk along a wall and sniff your fingers.

38

Cypriet Sauspans

At 7 o'clock in the morning i wake up from a feverish dream with the bedcloaths stuck to my body. Karima is not in bed and sombody is trying to get into the room.

I listen out into the darkness. The door handle turnes then there is a gentle scratching. Who ever is out there then puts their shoulder to the door and pushes. I sit up and stare feafully. The door sighs but it is bolted from the inside.

I climb from the bed, shivering as the sweat turnes cold on my body. I put on my coat and listen at the door. It is Al Mersin, demanding that i marry his 'princess'.

I explain, thru the closed door, that i am not some rich art student but the son of a theif.

"I dont have money, Al Mersin. I'm on the dole, my father is in prison and my mother werks nites serving in a fish 'n' chip shop."

As i speak i picture my mother up there on the W— Wood estate, her hair sodden with chip fat and the abussive customers demanding their food be vinigered and wrapped in such and such a fashion. All in all, treating my mother like some second rate grecy Lill. And meanwhile my father is relaxing himself in prison, drunk on illicet whisky.

"Your mother is where…?"

"She serves behind the counter in a fish and chip shop." "And you wish to marry my prinsess?"

Al Mersin will be stood on the other side of the door with his ginger mustash, his dark glasses and his hair, greeced back over his small ears. And i think of my sweet Karima, she has those same ears and i am sorry that i bit them and set lite to her butiful hair. I look down at my naked body and nurvously pull my coat closed. Karima will returne soon and we shall have sex.

181

"Ah, your wounderfull English fish and chip! Think of your poor mothers delite when her... belov'd son marrys my precious daughter and brings her these wounderful, Cyrpriet sauspans... as her... dowery and your mother is able to cook your father the finest fish and chip in all the world!"

"I dont want your sauspans, Al Mersin. I dont think you understand, my father is in prison."

"When he returns there will be a banquite!"

"When my father returnes, there will be a punch up!"

"Pardon?"

"I must sleep now, Al Mersin. It is 5 o'clock in the morning."

"Waite, my English friend... Do you think that I, Al Mersin, would dream of selling my futcher... son in law, something he cannot afford? For you, who will marry my butiful Prinsess, i will make a special price. I will personaly loan you the money... so's you can pay me back, just as soon as you please... A little every month, for instance."

"Its cold, i am going to bed now, Al Mersin."

"And dont forget... you not only get these sauspans, but i will still give you the carving knifes as well... Absolutly free!"

"I am tired, Al Mersin. Karima will be here in the morning. I must sleep now. I have to get up at 11 o'clock and sign on."

"Where will you live?... how will you support my butiful princess?"

"I have no where to live, Al Mersin. I have no money for

rent so it naturally follows that i wont be marrying your daughter or be buying any sauspans."

The door handle goes limp and i here Al Mersin sniffling to himself. Then i smell him lite up a mint ciggeret.

"So… you dont want these sauspans?"

"No, Al Mersin, absolutly not."

"Nor this set of… carving knifes?"

"Im tiered. I'm going to bed."

"Okay, i go now… Tell my princess that i am flying to Cypress to buy her a beutifll vinyard by the sea… With olive groves and a black, black horse… so's she can gallop on the beach… Thru the butiful rolling surf!"

"Ile let her no."

"My daughter is very, very… loyal."

There is a silence, then he asks one further question.

"Who is the landlord of this… flat?"

I think for a moment. "Mandleson."

"Mandleson?"

"Yes."

"And what dose this… Mandleson do?"

"He's a chemist… i think he lives in S -."

"Really? This Mandleson, is he a Jew, does he have money?"

"I dont think so, he's German."

"Will he sell me this… building?"

"I have no idear, Al Mersin, you will have to ask him."

"Maybe he would like to buy some… kitchen wear?"

"He does not want sauspans, Al Mersin."

"Oh no? How do you no what he wants… He's a

landlord isn't he? Does he have other... properties? His tenents have to cook... dont thay? And what about his... wife? I have sold just such sauspans as these to the Turkish Prime Minister... for his wife!"

"He rents un-furnished. Now i'm going to sleep!"

There is a deep sigh from behind the door.

"So... i am finished then, kaput!... i am to go home... a broken man. There will be no... vineyards by the... sea."

I listen at the door. He mutters on to himself for a moment, then falls silent. I wait till i here him shuffel away. Quickly i unbolt the door.

"Al Mersin!" i call after him. He has only gone a few paces and is stood there, degectedly at the bottom of the stairs. A soft, dark looking hand on the bannister rail. "Shall i tell Karima you will be coming in the morning?"

"Do not worry yourself about me, my English friend, i will go back to my... homeland. You have no rent! Well i have no fucking rent either!" He speaks bitterly. "But I, Al Mersin, do not ponce off your English... wellfare state in your disgusting English way!"

"But Al Mersin, you are, after all, a distingished sauspan salesman and it is only fair, by rites, that you should pay for your own living expences out of your own pocket and not try to sell me useless Cypriet sauspans that i carn't afford."

"German sauspans!" He corrects, surn, survaying me from behind his black Turkish sun-glasses. He then takes out a large purple, silk handkerchife and blows his nose. I listen to his heavy breathing, then he coughs.

"I dont sell any fucking Cypriet... sauspans!" he spits,

"I sell German sauspans! And anyway, there is no way for an honest man to make a living in this stinking… country of yours!"

39

Lemons

SOMEHOW, it is true to say, that at 7.30 this morning i signed a promissary note to pay Al Mersin 60 English pounds in 6 monthly installmaents of 1o pounds, plus 3 pounds interest on the 1st of every month. And that he, in turne would diliver me a set of German, stainless steel sauspans – and a set of extra sharp chefs knifes – as soon as further stocks arrived from his whare house in the Black Forest.

After signing my name i close and bolt the door. I waite untill Al Mersin has left the building, then put my arm behind Karimas cloaths rail and extract the stollen fruits from their hidding place. I unwrap the bludy looking pomigranit and roll it harmlessly onto Karimas bed. In the early morning lite these fruits seem to take on a new, viggerious energy, thay are not 1/2 as dryed out and usless as i'd first feared. If expertly packed into a box with small wires and a battery of some sort attached, who nos what catoclisim thay mite unleash.

40

Comunication

AFTER WRAPPING the lemons in tissue paper and placing them cearfully in an old shoe box, i sit and rite a warning note in the form of a manifesto, directed towards my family, the Acadamy and Mister Bennit in particular.

WARNING!
EXPLOSIVE DEVISE ENCLOSED.
Do not tamper with. This box contains a
sophisticated warning system.

For the crimes commited against him in his short stay at the acadamy (namely his expullsion and humilation at the hands of 'the buricrats of art'), the ex-student (whos name is signed bellow), calls for the imediate resignation of all of the tutor's therein, (viz). Mister Bennit, etc.

The same ex-student also reminds the said authorities that he never wanted to attend their Acadamy in the first place and was in fact forst to do so at their insistance, being told that he was 'a studdent who showed outstanding artistic potential' (unlike his tutors who only gained their positions thru bribes, nepotisim, base servile flattery and fawning, hypocritical deceit).

The same ex-student (William Loveday), also demands his reinstatement at the Acadamy, the withdrawl of all claims for moneys from the County Council, a full grant and a ritten appology from Mister Bennit, begging the said ex-students most gracious pardon. Once reinstated at the Acadamy, the ex-student (William Loveday, by name), promises to resign on these conditions:

1. That his ex-tutor (Mister Benit), relinqishes his post and retires forthwith and cease from this day in any further 'dallying' in the field of art. (It will be found, upon inspection, that the only reason this drunkard was ever employed in the 1st place, was to pay for morgages on studios and grand homes that he can ill-aford but which his repelent greed compelled him to own. Thus, indebeted up to the neck, he is unable to respond to the needs and requirments of his more talented students (the ex-student, William Loveday being one of these).

2. The ex-student (William Loveday), asks, politly and civerly, that Mister Benit stops pretending to be a praticing artist, or to love art or his students in anyway (which he certenly does not!).

3. The afore mentioned ex-student (William Loveday), also pleads that it is wholy unacceptable that the afore mentioned tutor (Mister Bennit), be

abusive, arrogant or demeaning to the ex-student, (William Loveday) just becouse he is unemployed, his father is in prison and his mother is forst to werk nites serving behind the counter of a fish and chip shop.

The ex-student, (William Loveday) now humberly puts forward some sugestions for the enlitenment and betterence of the staff of the afore mentioned Acadamy, where he was once proud to be call'd a student and to be labled 'unco-oporative', (viz).

1. By their abuse of the power invested in them, the tutors (Mister Benit, Mister T— and Bill H— , respectivly), have shown them selfs to be unworthy of further leadership. Far from softening their harts, power (and the acompanying over-blown wages), has given them the notion that thay have leave to ride rough-shod over the rites of others, (most notably the talented ex-student (William Loveday).

2. Artistic expression has been strangulated at the hands of these Burocrates of art. Their love of the cult of succes has driven them to terroise the ex-student (William Loveday, by name), and drive him into an artstic and pennyless, wilderness. It is in protecting the rites of the ex-student, William Loveday, that he (William Loveday) proposes a 4 point plan for the destruction of the vile creed of success, (viz).

1. The true patheticness of the tutors shabby ego must be exposed and the violence of his success smashed. (Mister Bennit, take note).

2. The ex-student (William Loveday), hereby calls for the imediate and total disbandment of all art skools and the sacking of their repugnant tutors. He (Wiliam Loveday), also calls for the abolition of all professional bodies and organisations and the installation of a purely amateur society, where people are allowed to express themselves, regardless of their ability or so call'd lack of it!

3. The Acadamy will be destroyed.

4. The tutors (Mister Benit, Mister T— and Bill H—, respectively), must be forst to their knees and made to apologise, in public, for their deceitfulness and the error of their ways, to the ex-student William Loveday.

Signed
William Loveday (ex-student).

NB.
The ex-student (William Loveday), is happy not to fit in to the rediclious dictates of what the Accadmy belives constitutes art, culture and finance.

41

A Reacuring Dream

I HAVE ANOTHER reacuring dream. This dream takes place in the futcher:

If, in the futcher, i was to meet a woman who, unlike Karima, diddn't want to destroy me and wanted to instead hold me and talk to me in a genuinely loveing manner, it wouldn't be impossable that she would fall pregnant and give birth to a strange, small living creature. And bringing it into our bedroom with her, we would no doubt look upon it and wonder what to do next.

After 2 or 3 days – realising that it was unable to fend for itself and unnowing of how to love or to feed it – i mite, out of some peverse sence of mercy, take a small peice of metel and knock a small hole in its fragile scull. With the strange looking human form now dead on the floor in front of me – and realising that i will now have to be rid of it befor the authorities find out my crime – i mite then endevour to dismember it. Prehaps jointing one of its tiny legs, and even its disproportionately large head. Wrapping the seperate cutlets in newspaper i mite then surepticiously try to dispose of them in verrious locations about town.

Of course, the tiny corpse of a baby would be relatively easy to hide compared say to the carrcus of a young woman. In all probability this evil – tho' in many ways innocent act of infanticide – would go unnoticed and un-recorded. Soon the act itself would pass from my memory into forgetfulness, untill that is, the day i awake in a cold sweat with the memory vividly playing befor my minds eye, and i then would realise the certainty of my guilt and inevitability of my incarceration.

After all, even the murder of a new born infant is frowned upon by socioty. And no matter how cearful or clandestine one is about dumping the remains in seperate hidy-holes about town, ones movements dont always go totaly unnoticed. Inquisitve old hags, in particular, are allways on the look out for the tiny dismemberd corpses of children and can often be seen picking about in dustbins – and under the comunel stairways of flats – in the hope of finding some 1/2 mummified shin bone or a bag of childrens teeth. On every street corner of every minor town in England, there lives at least one ex-policman who keeps an ever whatchfull eye on the comings and goings of shabberly dressed young men – just to check that thay are not depositing a pair of severed arms in the top of their nabours dustbin.

Yes, there are many ways in which the truth of a murder will eventualy come and find you. Haddn't the women i procreated with arrived from somewhere with the little egg-head? Prehaps even at this very moment a nurse, or maybe a nosey pedeotrician who was present at the birth, is scratching his hooter and woundering to himself about the baby that was born in his surgery one day last August and then the mother and child just up'ed and dissapeared. The fact that the mother never returned with the child for it anoculations may have been enough to alert his suspisions. That it never had whooping cough, measels, mumps or even so much as a common cold, mite just strike the midwife as currious, and that curriosity would then no doubt grow into susspission. Yes, it is a fact that Doctors are nosey by proffesion.

Of course, it is only my fear of capture and incarceration that now keeps me awake at nite. Surely i was inocent? I really beliv'd that i was doing the rite thing, how was i to no that, left to their own devisses – even helpless, egg-headed babies grow up and count as being alive? Not noing what it means to be born or to be alive, i was acting out of total iggnorence.

And so i awake every nite, certen that i am guilty of a crime i have – as far as i am awear – never commited.

42

The Rite Not to Werk

SINCE I AM now all but pennyless i have ritten to the Local Arts Boared for a matirels grant for paints and canvasess. After several weeks, thay have sent me a form asking many inquistive and probing questions. Namely, thay want proof of my 'qualifications' and details of 'collections in which my werk is held'. I have ritten a letter back pointing out that if i had 'qualifications' and my werk was being 'held in collections' then i would hardly be in need of a matirels grant. After this letter there has been silence.

Midmorning i go into town to sign on in the new social security buildings. Previously, i signed on once a week at the Old Drill Hall, with its battered wooden floors, naked lite bulbs and desks from the last centry. But now, thanks to the astrinomical rise in unemployment, thay have been relocated into a larger, vile, 80's style office, with its gray carpet tiles, strip lites and security gaurds dressed in cheap uniforms. The one consolation is that i now only have to sign on once every 2 weeks. Also, the gray old man with specticels – who used to sit behind the counter and ask nothing – has been replased by an old harpy who cross-questions everything you say and does everything in her power to trip you up and set you on the path to utter destitution. She has also tryed to change my signing on time to 1/2-past 9 in the morning, which is rediculious. I read the instructions on the slip of paper she has handed me, then walk back to her desk.

"Excuse me. This can't be rite. I've allways had the mid-morning slot." I hand her the pink form. She reads it and looks at me over her specticels.

"You are ment to be up and about early everyday looking for werk, mister… Loveday. You will sign on at the time specified." And she trys to give me back the pice of pink paper, which i refuse to take from her painted fingernails.

"Surly there's an afternoon slot available?"

"Sign on at the time specified or your claim will be canceled."

"I havn't recived a single check yet. What am i ment to be living on, fresh air?" This was my joke. But instead of laughing she shone her furrios eyes at me.

"Your claim is being prossessed, Mister Loveday. You will hence forth sign on at 9.30 on the date shown below or you will be removed from the registar and will have to make a fresh claim!" And she pushes the pice of paper towards me, and starts ripping threw her card index with her blud red finger nails. I leave the slip of paper on the desk and stand studdying her, she looks up sharply and asks if there was anything else that i reqire.

"Yes, is your name Pam?"

"It's none of your bussness what my name is, now kindly leave. There are other people in the que."

"Your name tag says P. Imogen. I just wondered if the P stood for Pam?"

It was then that she made a phone call and a security gaurd came over to the desk, whispered with Mrs P. Imogin, then stood and asked me to leave the premisses.

The security guard has a hat on. As he leads me away i introduce myself but apparently this man either dosn't have a christian name or has never been taught good manners.

"My first name is William. She has it ritten down on my file so i just wondered what her first name was."

Once he gets me outside he declines to shake hands with me and instead roughly grasps me by the rist and elbow and marches me along the pavement in front of the building. He is no bigger than me and i could easerly overpower him, but i choose not to and instead allow him to carry on abusing me. He pushes me away and tells me to get lost. I tell him that i am very greatfull for his assistance but i would prefer to stand by the door way.

"That part of the pavement belongs to the Social Servisess Department and you would be tresspassing and i would then be forst to make an arrest."

"Are you allowed to arrest me?"

"A citisans arrest!" He says it loudly so that the people standing near can here him comanding me.

"The police stations just over the way, maybe you could call on them for re-enforcments," i offer helpfully.

He squints at me from under his peek hat but is afraid to look in my eyes.

"You just keep off our pavement!" Then brushing his hands he looks up and down the street and strolls back in thru the plate glass doors with the air of a man who has completed a very important task. How is it possable to be friendly in such a world? I waite untill he is gone then put one foot onto the DHSS's pavement.

There is a bearded man stood on the steps selling newspapers. He has a worried expression and smiles at me weakly.

"Fascist barstards!" he croaks, nodding at the building.

I look at him and try to defy him – with my eyes – from speaking with me again.

"We'er from the Socialist Werkers Party," he ventures. "We'er demanding the rite to werk for all unemployed. Do you wan't to sign our pertition?" And he holds out a little clip board with a biro attached by a small piece of string. There is a scar on the mans neck, just bellow his adams apple, and some food trapped in his beared.

"But i dont want the rite to werk," i explain, "i want the rite not to werk."

"Yeah, but 1000's of others dont, do thay?" He says amiably.

"Well, get them to sign it!"

He looks at me sulkerly. "Buy a paper then?"

"I dont want one."

"Well, make a donation."

"To what?"

"The SWP."

"Im sorry but i've got other things on my mind."

I hurry across the street then off up M— Road chuckling to myself all the way. I really had out-foxed him.

It was quite hard battling aganst the wind.

43

Youth in Pub

JUST AS I CROSS at the lites by the bank i catch site of some glossy magazines thru a shop doorway. Now i have to make a dessision. I stand in the street whatching the lorries go past, breathing in their powerfull fumes. I feel my coins in my pocket – woundering if i can really aford to starve myself for the sake of an indecent magazine – when the pub doors open behind me and an old man comes out and stands on the pavement, smoking a little strand of cigarete. The blue smoke rushes away in the wind. Up the street a dog barks and a lady with a pram passes by. The baby starts to cry.

I have just determind to cross the street when i catch a glimps of Kajii thru the pub doorway. He is sat mysteriously alone in the back, drinking a glass of yellowish liquid. I recognise him at once and then the door closes. Yes, it really was him – the very one who stoll the lemon from my grasp. I push open the door and can just make out the top of his head. He is bowed, reading. He has on a pair of my old boots, no socks and even his hair is cut in the manner of the mad.

So, this imposter has been running around behind my back commiting all manner of unspeakable crimes on my behalf – so to speak – untill people belive that it is me who is the villan of the peace, not he. All along, this sharleton has been stealing fruite in my name and i have been compleatly inocent. I nod – so not only dose he dress in my manner but he is lemon theif to-boot!

I slip into the pub behind the old man and let the door swing closed behind me. I walk and stand directly befor my impersonator but he just lifts his beer, takes a small sip and pretends not to notice me.

The Victorian interiour of the pub has recently been

ripped out and then re-done to look 'oldy worldy'. I peer around the dark empity bar and back to my nontchulent friend sat here. Of the stollen lemon there is no trace, but then he is hardly going to march around the streets brandishing a stollen lemon, espersherly when 1/2 the town is out hunting for it.

Only last nite i had given up all hope of ever finding Deep Snow and truly beliv'd that everything was lost. Never would i wreek my terrible revenge on Mister Bennit and the world of art. Never would i find happyness in the arms of my Japanese Princess. But now, on this cold and windy morning, fate herself has thrown my Japanese accomplise rite back into my path.

I keep an eye on him and order a 1/2 pint of black beer at the bar and pull up a chair oppersite my Japanese freind. I lean over the table and look closely at the dark discs of his eyes, but it is impossable to dessern – by his expression alone – the where abouts of the stollen pomigranite. Obviously, on this count, he is keeping his hand close to his chest.

I smile, but he pretends not to recognise me. Really, he seems to be consumed with fever and shortly his illness will kill him. As his eyes drift away i speak his name loudly in his ear and force him to shake hands. I am determind to ingage this rapscallion in conversation and to learn the whereabouts of the missing lemon. Kajii finnaly looks up and nods in recognition.

"The wind is a terrible thing," i remark to him, sipping on my beer. Kajii traces round the wet circle left by his own beer glass but dosn't answewer. His fingers are quite yellow and it is obvious that he smokes a great deal. Then why dose he not smoke now? I offer him a cigarete but he declines.

"I dont no about you my friend, but one thing that will set me to becoming a murderer is the wind." I raise my eyebrows and wrinkle my brow at him but still he says nothing. I look at my white boney hands, which are shaking.

"If you stop to think about it, the mind is quite like the wind. First the thoughts are blown this way and then the next. One moment there is a gental brezze blowing thru the spring flowers, the next moment a rageing hurracan has ripped them all to shreads. I dont no about you but my mind just wont stop thinking these days, even in my sleep it punishes me relentlessly, tormenting me and ridiculing me for my inadiqueses."

I look at him pointedly, becouse i no that he follows and understands everything that i say implisitly, becouse he is like me and i am like him, we are one and the same.

"Dont you have that?" I speak, "a repeating dream that thumps away at you nite after nite, like a nasty little devil? It keeps on nagging you and wont let you have a moments rest, it really is like a tooth ache. All nite long you toss and turne on the edge of sleep, but this devil keeps you awake with all manner of nonsence. Repeating over and over again the same piece of idiotic jibberish about injustice and how you are to go about reeking your revenge on your tormentors. But actually, upon awakening, you realise that the revenge you have plan'd is meaningless but in the midst of this nitemear, some quite harmless inament object suddenly becomes pregnant with possibility. Untill finaly, in your delussion, you belive that touching your nose 3 times befor crossing the road will settle your enimys hash for him once and for all! This madness runs on and on thru the entire nite and you are convinc'd that it is increadably important and must not be forgotten. But by morning the dream has evaporated and no matter how hard you rack your brains it is impossible to remember the very thing that fill'd your entire consiouness and bedeviled you all nite. In the cold lite of day the whole dream retreats into a fog and is – to all intence and puposes – tottaly meaningless and may as well be forgotten. And all the while you have to remind yourself that just becouse you dream that you have murdered some child and buried them in a shallow grave, it dosnt mean that you nessisaraly have or that 'ghost policman' are going to arrest you for it."

At this point i have to actually stand up and follow this theif to another table as he trys to get away from me. He moves rite the way over to the other side of the pub. I pick up my glass and follow him.

"Let us just say, that if somone who has been sexually abused as a child is statistickly more likely to commit sex attacks on children in adult life, then isn't it better to elliminate them at sorce, when thay are still meerly victims and befor thay themselves pupate and emerge as abusers? Is a crime not a crime simply becouse it has not yet become manifest? And these dreams, are thay the nitemears of the past or halousinations of the futcher. These crimes of the futcher will no doubt be commited by the emasculated, but those people will still be people in the ordinary sence of the word, won't thay? To feel justified in killing those previously classed as 'victims of abuse' these 'new murderers' will have to be convinced by God and State that thay are destroying the criminels of the futcher, but won't that in itself be a crime?

"What shape or form will these 'new murderers' take? No doubt thay will be evil and grotesque. Benieth their external apperence of flesh and blud, thay will be 'sex robots' wired by the devil. Oh yes, they will be cunningly dissguised!

"The more we protect our children, the more vunrable to attack thay will become. The emptier the streets the more dangerious the streets – and meanwhile 'kindly uncles' and 'cearing teachers' will have free rain to lay their disgusting hands on the spines of children. Naturally, parents and familys will at all costs deny all abuses being carried out in the cots and kindergardens of Merry England, least they themselves should have to point their finger at their own family and feel 'a little guilty'.

"If such 'sex robots' exist, and by examination, thay must - for somehow, somewhere, thay will have had to come into existance – if only thru the course of our collective anger and denial – then we must accept that thay are allready here and perpertating unspeakableness amongst us and within us.

"As surely as everything must rippen, so too have these destroyers of childhood, creativity and life, been gradually taking shape in our conciousness and are ready to seed – all be it unbenownst to us – and sooner or later our socioty must suffer thru our denial. By this means, many will come to no intemitly these 'sex robots' and feel their hot breath on their childs cheek, and no their wrath.

"Another important consideration is, how does the mechanisim or mind of a vampire werk? This can not be shown untill we have the chance to monitior one in action. But it is clear that all models will have 2 functions in 1. 1stly, that of sucking out the victims sexual essence and 2ndly, dissposing of the empity husk. The final death of the victim is a simple matter of the absence of their core, or humanity.

"It is our fear of life and our love of instertutions and burocracy which have created these 'others', these 'sex robots'. And for this reason their nature and physiology is obviously quite ordinary and uninspiring. If it is mans will to create such monstrositys, can it really be claimed that man has challanged God? Would it not be truer to say that God has challanged man? Or even himself?"

I follow Kajji round the room as he serches for yet another seat. I refuse to belive that he is trying to shake me off and instead reason that maybe he's looking for somewhere a little more private so's that he can hand over the stollen lemon to me in secreat. I look to him encourimagingly but he makes no attempt to give me back what is ritefully mine and instead sighs rather heaverly as i sit down next to him. If i can only take this fellow into my confidences, then he will soften up and tell me his sisters address and maybe even introduce me to her.

"Listen, i will tell you a dream i had. In this dream there

was a girl who had fallen from grace with God and had thereby incured the spite of her wretched landlady. This dream is real – in that i really drempt it. Some time befor, the poor girl had had an illergitamet child and her body – which had previously been young and firm – was now turned into a saggy, white sack. Her flesh really hung off of her torso and gave off a bluish-white glow, like the body of a squid. I lookt at her poor belly and the flesh was just a little skirt hanging over her boney hips."

My Japanese friend doesn't look at me but i can tell that he is listening very intently to my interesting dream.

"She bid me to lay with her on her dirty bed, which i did. No sooner have i layed down than the wretched baby starts to cry in a horrible screech, like a seagull. That baby was so tiny that you could of lain it in the palm of your hand and it's apperence too was also more like that of a squid, or an axilottel, than of a human being. The girl then took her tired breast and fed the little tyke, rite there in front of me. The baby was translucent and i whatched as it fill'd up to the top with milk. Its mother then put it to bed in an ashtray, which stood next to the headboard. The ashetray was one of those chrome afairs on a stand. Of course, for the sake of the babys comfort she had lined it beforhand with some pieces of old rag or cloth. Once the baby was settled she then lay back down beside me and i felt myself growing aroused."

Kajii takes a nurvis sip of his beer and i too refresh myself.

"Look, i dont no why i'm telling you all of this, its perverse. I will stop. Afterall, i've only just met you .and dont even no your name. But when i saw you sitting there and the way you just happened to glance up at me, well, in that exact moment it was as if we recognised each other, dont you agree? I can see that i'm making you feel uncomfortable, but belive me, that is not my intention, it's just that i must talk to someone, and you feel passionately about life and art just like i do, dont you? You mite not no it, but you do. You ask questions of yourself constantly, dont you? You dont have to answeer me becouse i can see its true. You no what it's like to be ignored and abused by dirty crowds of ignorant art lovers, dont you? Whether you no it or not you are a kindred spirit, otherwise how could we be here talking this way, like old friends, when only a few moments ago we hardly new each other? Maybe your sister has spoken of me? I no you, and you no me, you'll see if i'm wrong.

"So anyway, i'm lying in bed with this dibortched young thing and then somehow she drops her squid child onto the floor in the corner. I no that just now she had placed it in its little ashe-tray crib, but somehow she had hold of it again and then dropped it, by accident, in the dust. Did i tell you that when she was breast feeding it, that it got its little sucker latched on her teat and then all around her nipple small glands started to swell up into hiddious bumps and cankers? Anyway, after accedently dropping her little axolotle in the corner she snatched it back up, dusted it off, placed it back in its lined crib and climbed back into bed with me. It was then that i realised that i was 1/2 naked and had an erection.

"You dont mind me being frank with you, do you? I have had sex, many times and i can assure you that this isn't the dream of a frustrated virgin. There was a door just opposite the big iron bed that we lay in, and behind it i could hear the sound of her disapproving landlady banging about in her abomnible kitchen – crashing the lids on sauspans, kicking the bread bin and what not. All the while i was fearful that this horrendous old dragon would barge in and discover me in the arms of this wanton strumpet.

"This girl, who i somehow felt sorry for, then ask'd to see my stiff cock. She jumped up, pulled back the bed cloaths and insisted on stepping on it with her bare feet. Ile admit it, at first i was shy, but seeing that she was only going to be stepping on it against the soft mattres of the bed, i tho't i would give into her demands.

"I no it sounds insain, but this was only a dream, and surely everybody dreams something strange sometimes? So anyway, she stands on it and to tell the truth, it does nothing for me and i begin to lose my erection. Then she stops trying to stand on it, snuggles up to it, licks it and tries to fit it into her vile snatch – which i simply will not allow her to do. You see, i have a fear of that sort of thing, especially with strange unnown women. The girl, of course, is wild at me. She gives me such a tongue lashing. She nos all the dirt on me from day one: the exact type of dispicable cad i am, and exactly who i've wronged, with dates, names and addresses. Shes a real little man hater and all becouse i wont give her a good seeing to. Just then the door crashes open and the old landlady comes stomping in, wanting to no what all the racket is about.

"Still 1/2 naked i slip from the bed and hide under the table. I peek fearfully out at the landladys swollen, bandaged ankles as thay stomp about the room. More and more people flood into the room, adults and children. Whole familys suddenly appear as if from out of the wallpaper. One of the children stairs intently at me, hidden in beneath the shadow of the table cloth. At first it seemes that i am invisable to its penertrating gaze but my face and hands glow in their pale way."

I show my companion my blue-white hands. I turne them befor his eyes, so he can get a good idear of their paleness and elegance.

"Im lying there surrounded by strange legs and the enimy landlady, and terrified that i'm going to be discovered and exposed for my wickedness at every moment. The old landlady comes round the back of the table and i have to tuck my legs in still further in case she sees my boney white feet. Then the child who had been staring unseeingly at me, steps forward and looks directly into my eyes. In my hart i am terrified that this little boy is going to finger me and i curl my fingers into the sleeves of my shirt so that my white hands wont be seen. I try to shrink back even further into the shadows. I lower my face, but he peers even closer untill there is nowhere left for me to hide. And that is when i decide to expose myself and give myself up. My fear falls away and i fly out from under the table and perade befor them in my nakedness. I realise that i can face all of these fears that pursue me and render them harmless.

"Hasn't that ever happened to you? That you are in the clutches of some dreadful nitemare, then, quite suddenly, you become aware that you are dreaming and that you can force the dream into another direction?"

My new found friend puts his fingers to his eyes, rummages with his eye ball then lifts his pint and sips on in a way that shows he dosnt even like beer and is only clinging to this life by a thread.

"You must no what i mean? You've had many dreams yourself, tho' maybe you carn't recall any of them rite now." I really do try to see things from his point of view but Kajji tottaly ignores me.

"2 nites ago i dreamed that i was an archioligist investigating the seen of Custers Last Stand at The Little Big Horn." I check my friends face to see if he nos who Custer is. "I was stood in a low mountinus terain and an Indian guid was by my side. He pointed to the place where we should dig. The site was not, as historians had erroniously beliv'd, the small bluff ahead of us, but the larger bluff behind, on high ground. There, he told me, many braves were burid. In a blink of an eye we were transported to the location. Me and my unnown companion werk'd hard and soon we uncovered a square metal lid on the earth benith which lay the mumyfied remains of an Indian Prinsess. She was tattoed on her upper rite arm with a picture of herself bound for mumification in a sitting position. Naturally, there was an authority figer who was in charge of the dig. We call'd him over to show him our wounderful find. He nodded his aprovel and quickly we uncovered the rest of the Princess. As we cleaned the last of the dust from her moccasons she arose from the grave and call'd in strange voices to her sisters and brethrin who inhabited the spirit world in the hills that surrounded us, and thay in turne ansewed back to her with equally strange calls. She then took me by the hand and led me away, up the hill side and into a wooded arear on the edge of the wilderness. As we entered the trees somone call'd out to us and we lookt back and saw that we were being trailed by a man who thought that it was very wrong for a wight man (myself) and an Indian Princess, to be together. Of course there were boulders and lose scrub all around and as we lookt we could see that the trees were really a little orchard bearing fruits. We waited and let the man trailing catch us up. He told us that we must turne back, that i should go with him and how we would 'not be able to survive in the wilderness'. But all around us were fruiets hanging from the trees. Pairs, to be presise. Not all of these fruits were ripe or large but then my Indian Princess spoke to me telipathicly. She smiled in my mind and said 'This man thinks that we can only live off of the large friuts, but it is the small fruits that my people live off.' Actualy, she let me no that thay were to be mixed, or suplemented, with some other food stuff – bufalo, in all probebility – anyway, my Indian Prinsess then wanted to have a little fun at this mans expence and ask'd him, in his opinion, which were the finest fruits on the trees? And like a fool he walks up to a tree and shows us several large, ripe pairs. Naturally, me and my Indian Princess smile to ourselfs, becouse we no that it isn't the large fruits that we needed to live off, but the small fruits – the man had got it all wrong, just as my Indian Princess had pridicted."

Kajji says nothing. But i can see that i have made quite an impression with my story of the mummified Indian Princess who came alive.

"This was not the first time i have been visited by this woman. In another dream i was a rebal in the Americas at the time of the War of Indipendence. I had been fighting against my own country and the war was all but over. Then a British Man 'o' War sailes into the shore to arest me and take me back to those heathen islands in chains. I was stood on the quee, manicaled by the wrist to a bullish fellow – who lookt for all the world like Jon Bull – stood there as pompus as you like – dressed in a Navel officers uniform. We waite for the ships liter to come alongside to transport us abored, when suddenly this wounderful Indian Princess springs from out of nowhere, takes me by my free hand and dives off the queeside dragging me and my captor after her. She swims down and down, pulling myself and the Captin along behind. He, of course, fights all the way, desperatly tuging on the manical by which he is chained to my wrist, but nothing can compeat with my resquer who swims with the strength of a mermade. In fact, i'm sure that is partly what she is.

"After swiming way down to the bottom of the seabed she strikes out for an underwater caven – which we shortly enter – my Princess swiming strongly, and all the while the Captin still wriggling and cursing me. 'My God', i thought, 'he even talks under water!' I can here his voice shouting thru the bubbles but eventually the Captin can go no further and has to pull his wrist out of the chain or die. He gets free – and shouting that he will be coming back for me – swims back down the subterainean tunnel and returns to the surfiss.

"Meanwhile, me and my Princess swim on till we finally surfiss in the cellar of a large building. There is the sound of merry-making coming from above. It seems that a party is in full swing. My Princess holds my hand and leads me up some stone steps, at the top of which is a trap door, which she opens. She goes thru and i am to follow. It was then that i awoke."

My japanese friend looks to the door and doesn't even smile with me in my triumph.

"Look, you dont just want to sit in a pub like all these others, do you? You could become a painter, and why shouldn't you? You must still have some fire left in your belly? Cos answer me this: how is it that every child dreams and paints quite naturally and automatically, up untill thay are 7 or 8 years old? Then somehow, once their educators get their stinking hooks into them, thay allow themselfs to be tricked out of painting on the grounds that 'thay are not talented enough' and 'it is time for life to get very serrious'. – In short, thay are talkt out of painting and dreaming and by the time thay are 11 years old thay are meer husks. In defence of this stance, their techers and educators declair that this violence is meated against their charges purly for their own benfit; to illustrate their inadiquaces; to show them their missrable futchers; and not let them waist vaulable lerning time with 'imaginings', when they cannot draw and are clearly 'not good enough' to be allowed to even try. And what the hell does 'not good enough' mean? As if being good at something is laudable and being bad at something is somehow inadequate.

"No, you must paint pictures again – and not your silly abstract doodles either – but pictures of the sole. I myself have a serries in mind, you could borrow my idear if you like. The 3 pictures will all depict the stages of a crime – a crime of the futcher! The 1st in the series will show a grassy field, to the left of the picture is an old gnarled oak tree, beneath which lies the slashed and dissembowled figure of a woman. Her belly has been split open and a man in his early to mid-40's is kneeling over her headless torso. In one hand he holds an old, blunt kitchen knife, in the other, her severed head held up by the hair. His flaccid penis hangs from his open flys and there is an intense look in his eyes.

"Imagin, if you yourself had just committed such a crime, wouldn't your eyes certainly be intense at just such a juncture? Or maybe the look in the eyes isn't one of madness, but instead betrays realisation. The head is off the corpse, his penis is flaccid and now the terrible inevitability of his capture and incarceration comes crashing into his mind like a steam train. Is there remorse or pity for the crime he has committed? I think not. At least not yet there isnt. Now only excitement pounds thru his veins. His lips are thin (and also his hair is thinning), his nose is too big for his face and his chin too small. By the way, the picture is not painted in an old fashioned intricate style, yet it is not painted in a modernistic or showy way either. No, it is painted more in the style of that which the murderer himself would employ – in simple colours, with simple lines. Art should not be allowed to muddy the simple brutality of this murder painting. As to his redemtion, maybe this very painting is the 1st step on that path.

"The 2nd picture would show the sex murderer's kitchen. Such a kitchen would be in the basement flat of an old Georgian building – not unlike those that run along the boundary of the castle, down by C— Hill. When people first look at this 2nd painting thay would only notice the sulphur-like glow of the murderers face peering out at you from the gloom of his den. His lamp-like eyes – do thay show fear or amusement? Or are thay somehow innocent? There would be no real definition in his expression or in the rendering of his features. That's the wounderful thing about paint, dont you agree? – it lacks all certainty – it is pure subjectivity – becouse all true creativity is subjective, or else its boring and a waist of time, isn't it?"

I look into the hot, pale face of my new friend and have to stop myself from clasping his Japanese hand in mine and squeezing it till he yelps in agreement. His eyes, in this lite, are not Japanese in the least but rather big and doe-like, the lashes dark and wet. There is something soft and disgustingly palpable about his whole being. He dips his head and assents to my description. I carn't be sure that he really agrees with me or is just avoiding a clash of idears, so i demand that he put his own case forward, his own argument for or against my description of the pale yellow face of the sex murderer, painted peering from out of the depraved depths of his kitchen.

"Is there, or is therc not a partially dismembered torso of a young woman lying butchered on the shelf behind him?" i ask. "And would you say that her head is green with mould and the mouth agape? Dose the torso lie on the shelf to the left or to the rite? And should the ragged neck stump still be seeping blud, or has it long ago dried up? In short, have all the corpses bodily secretions ceased and is it now in an advanced state of decompersitsion, or not?"

My friend nods and i have to point out to him that he carn't just agree with me glibly, as i have expressly put forward 2 very diffrent propositions in regard to the state of the severed head. On the one hand, mumification and on the other, decomperstion.

"My friend," i carry on earnestly, "we are talking about art here. We are not talking about drugs and fashion but about all that matters in this world. Do you realise that culture is the only thing that sets us appart from the chipanseses on the streets? Now, are you interested in this murderers kitchen or not?… You must at least agree that the tiles in the background of the kitchen are certainly obscured by a build up of years of grease and grime. Once, i grant you, thay may well have been a pristine white, but long ago thay became caked with unspeakable filth. The colour purple could be used to convey that. Purple and a putrid green that would shine thru a dull wash of dismal grey and all the while the murderers face would gleam forth like a hellish beacon, becouse art is always about people and communication and not about technique or cleverness, isn't it? And i for one refuse to impress idiots with my skill."

I sit back and fold my arms in defience. The Japanese boy sits there with his eyes closed, no doubt meditating, prehaps trying to counjour up a mental picture of my wounderfull discription. I look at him for quite some time and wounder weather to lean over and touch his elbow.

"Of course you dont have to listen to me. No doubt you beleive me to be some kind of deranged mad man, but what is life for if not for shearing our idears, our dreams and inner most secrets? Look around you, i have not contrived to build myself a nest aganst lifes triels and tribulations, have I?—No! I have desided to align myself with the mad, thru choice. And now you think that you can go around dressing like me, stealing lemons and getting me into all sorts of trouble with the police and the athoritys. Well i can tell you my friend that it has got to stop!" And i slam my fist on the table so hard that i nearly spill his beer.

I turne round and survay the room. The landlady has come to the end of the bar and is looking pensivly at us. A young couple come in holding hands and smiling into each other faces. I turne back to my Japanese friend, who has his fingers to his temples and his eyes shut.

"Look, dont you understand that nobody is happy? Of course thay appear to be happy on the outside but on the inside? On the inside everybodys true inner state is one of supream missary and unhappyness. Becouse no matter what thay think thay own and possess, really thay own and posses nothing! thay can build themselfs the biggest and most fancyfull castle in the entire history of the world, but inside it thay will still be lonely and woundering how to avoid facing death! Only God can save them, and where is he?"

The Japanese boy stands, excuses himself and trys to leave to go to the lavitory. I jump up double quick, there is still the possibility that he will lead me to his sister, Deep Snow, and i am not about to let him go to toilets so that he can escape me thru some hidden back exit.

"You no perfictly well that you stoll that lemon, so stop pretending that you diddn't!" I have to clentch my jaw to stop myself reaching over the table, grabbing him by the leppeles and giving him the shaking of his life.

"No, my friend, God wants you to encounter the vileness of your underbelly, and encounter the vileness of your underbelly you will! – No matter how fast you run!"

His way is blocked by some chairs. He stands there divering for a few seconds befor realising that he will have to come back past me to get out, and i will be standing here ready and waiteing for him. I really am wondering if i dare wrestle him to the ground when suddenly a flabby arm grabs me from behind, its soft bycep filling my mouth, acompanied by a sickly smell of sacrin. The old landlady has me round the throat. She pushes her iron hard tits into my back and i have to stop wriggling or she will choke the life out of me.

"Go on, get out! Go on, run for it!" She yells at the Japanese boy. And he looks to her fearfully befor edging

215

past us and scampering towards the door. I kick out at him as he passes.

"Quick, he's escaping!" I shout, but the old dragon tightens her grip on my adams apple.

"Oh no, you dont!" And i really do start choking. I peer out the corners of my eyes at her, trying to loosen her arm from round my kneck but she's as strong as a horse.

"You aren't leaving yet. You let him alone."

"He stoll my hat and my shoes. He's a lemon theif!"

Only when the door is swinging and the Japanese boy is streets away dose she push me away from her giant tits.

"Now finish your beer and leave!"

I look at her sulkerly "I dont want it, i want my lemon!"

"What lemon?"

I realise that in my haste i have given too much away.

"Its alrite, Its nothing. It was just a joke, we were just joking, thats all."

"Well not in my pub your not. Now clear off, and i dont want to see your face in here again, either!"

She goes back behind the bar and starts wiping it down with large, brutle strokes. She really has got some arms on her alrite, just like a wrestler. She looks up at me again and i try to smile. I dont finish my beer, i just leave it there. Really, i tip it into the ashe tray. It overflows onto the table top and i whatch it dripping down onto the floor. I tread the suds into the carpet, then leave.

Outside the sky is purple black on one side and blinding lite on the other. The wind really has gotten into my brain today. I turne my coller up and peer down towards the P—

shopping centre. I think the Japanese boy took a rite when he left the pub but there is no sign of him now. Then suddenly the pub door flys open behind me and i have to duck as the landlady takes a swipe at me with her dish rag.

"Get out! You horrible, disgusting little pervert!" She is holding my empty glass in her hand and i wounder if she is going to throw it at me, but she dosn't.

"I never, ever want to see your face in here again!" she shouts and i have to scamper off, doddging between the trafic, ashamed of myself and my clever trick.

44

Money Dosn't Grow on Trees

ON THE NITE of my fathers arrest i climbed the stairs to his bedroom and quietly open'd the door. It was drawing towards dusk, there was no lamp on and at first it seemed as if the room was quite empty. I stood in the doorway, an iron poker concealed up my sleeve. There was a faint movement and i saw the black shape of my father move from beside the curtens and become silhouetted against the window.

Since his unexpected arrival i'd aproached him and ask'd several times for the loan of a 5 pound note and each time he denied me. Twise with an inclination of his head and the 3rd with an almost inaudable 'no'. Really, i was again penniless, he was threatening my mother, and i had again decided to kill him. The reason that my father never offers me a helping hand – in any way whatsoever – is becouse he belives that a mans off-spring, like the tadpoles of a frog, must fear, fight and fend for themselves in the pond of life. 'Money dosnt grow on trees!' Is one of his favorite maxims. Which is a stupid thing to say, as i have never once suggested that it does.

In truth, whether or not my father wishes to give me 5 pounds or not, is now of little consequence, for one thing is for certain, i will not be nown as a beggar who has traipsed all the way from C— town to visit his fathers house, drink his mothers tea and leave cold, frozen and empty handed. I am not allowed a grant becouse of my fathers exhorbrant lifestyle and yet my father keeps his earnings soley for himself.

As he crosses the room to his wardrobe and fusses with his Edwardian suits, i step silently into the room and let the poker drop from my sleeve into my hand. One of my fathers many obsessions is to have a knife-edge crease in his trousers. I watch as he holds the trousers in one hand, the hanger in the other then – taking the bottom of the trouser leg between his teeth -feeds the trouser legs threw the hanger, all the while ruffling the legs untill the creases fall perfectly. As i move round behind him a floorboard squeaks under my weight, but my father is intently studying an invisible stain on the cuff of his drape jacket and dose not notice my presence.

I peer into the peroxide curls that fall over his long ears, willing myself to raise my arm and smash his brains in for him. I tighten my grip on the poker and raise it into the air. Just then my father steps sideways, picks his suit jacket from the bed and walks back towards the wardrobe.

If i am not ment to kill him, why does he steadfastly keep his back to me, as if inviting me to cosh his blond head? And how is it that he dosnt feel my terror and turne to face me? Doesn't he hear the blud pounding in my head? Such a terrible thing – that i should be driven to kill my own father? And why has he never held me in his arms or told me that he loves me? Why did he leave and allow that 46 year old man to step on my hart and touch me in that dispicable way when i was just 9 years old? Why wern't you there to protect me, old man, rather than feeling-up strange women in strange bars? And why should i be afraid to strike you now? You were never shy of hurting me as a child, of banging me and my brother's 'bludy heads together', just to vent your frustrations. Then you left home.

And even now, as i stand here ready to kill you, you turne your face sharply away and humiliate me yet again. If God dosnt wish you dead then why dosnt he turne your head and make you speak with me, like any father would his own honest and most loyal son? And why for that matter dosnt he stick your boney old hand into your tight pocket and make you cough up 5 misserly pounds for me when i have nothing to eat and you have an attaché case full of brand new 20 pound notes?

I breath him in, my nose almost brushing the golden

hairs on the back of his neck. I stand back and stare into his parting, rite at the point where i will strike.

No, you dont love me, old man and you dont see me, do you? I am the ghost you have never seen or lov'd, or spoken to, nor uttered a single kind word to. The only reason you are here now is to get your wifey to do your stinking laundry for you, starch your collers and beat her into not devorsing you. Thats rite, isn't it? Your on one of your famous visits to check we'er still pennyless and missrable and for you to bathe and to mow your pathetic lawn.

No, you are not here out of love or even duty. Whereas you wear the finest, newly laundered linen, i wear the second hand cloaths of the dead. Whereas your many dozens of shoes are hand-made and polished to perfection, my single pair of ex-army boots are scuffed and reek of a deadmans feet. Whereas your teeth are brand-new caps, fitted by a private dentist, my tusks are drilled and packed with mercury by an NHS butcher. Where as your nails are meticulously manicured, mine are raw, bitten and torn. Where as your suits – hand tailored by Mister Driver of Newcombs 'Shirt Makers to the King' – hang in the wardrobe in neat procession, my single jacket dosnt even have matching trousers becouse the man who owned it befor me shat himself when he conked-out and died on C—High Street.

Old man, on several occasions, whilst staggering between London brothels, you have been mugged and robbed blind, so it is almost inevitable that one day you will be robbed and murdered by someone, and why shouldn't that someone be me?

Again, i weigh that poker in my fist and it is only Gods intervention that stops me from killing you here and now, for you quit shaking out your suits and go to the chaise longue to fondle the gold coloured locks of your attaché case.

There is no curiosity in me; i already no what lies hidden in there: a cellophane packet containing 3000 pounds in freshly printed bank notes and several hard-core pornography magazines. The reason that i no all this is becouse i have already broken into your case, pocketed 20 pounds and removed the magazine of my choice whilest you were in the bath peroxiding your hair. So this is what it is to be a man: to have a briffe case full of pornography, money, and to fuck as many women as you can and to come and go as you please. Very well, i will become that man.

A single lock of hair curls over your celluloid collar. Above that is my fathers scull, just an 8th of an inch benith his scelp.

Outside the window, silver birches wave to me in the twilite breeze and small birds are still singing. Thay are all whispering for me to kill you, telling me that you have never lov'd me, that you hate me and have never protected me and that you deserve to die. Which i already no. I grip the poker in my hand and raise it. 'It is not murder; you will scarcely get 2 years for manslaughter.' I reach out my hand to touch the hem of my fathers coat. My fingers brush against the expensive cloth.

It is then that my mother calls up to me from down stairs. "Your teas getting cold!" and my father turnes. His eyes find my chest.

"Yes?"

I push the poker back up my sleeve.

"I just came to ask... I havent any money... I was woundering...?"

"What on earth are you twittering about?"

"I need some money."

"Then go out and earn some, like everybody else does. It dosnt grow on trees!"

"I no." There is a silence.

"Your mother is calling you."

"Yes."

"Well, run along then."

I look into his bulging blue eyes. His fingers come up, touch his neatly trimmed beard and i see his small tounge in there. This is the body that seeded me and the 2 eyes that lookt down at me new born. I turne, leave the room and walk down stairs to drink my cold tea.

45

As Bad as His Soddin Father

LATER THAT NITE, my mother calls me at Karimas: my father has been arrested. I have to walk back up to W— in

222

the heavy rain. My mother makes food and we open a bottle of my fathers vintage port, which we steal from his pretend wine cellar under the stairs.

The Troll is quiet and friendly, its only during the meal that she takes the opertunity to humiliate me, gain sympathy for herself and spoil the food that my mother has prepair'd.

The reason the Troll chooses the dinner table for her assault is becouse there is no better stage to exposse me on than here – in front of my own mother! Also, Karima is in need of sympathy becouse i refuse to have sex with her, which she has allready discussed with my mother. Apparently, my mother told her the reason is most likely due to my being a homo sexuel, like my father.

"His father had books with men in." She says, pointedly.

I eye her coldly and carry on eating.

"He's seeing a slut call'd Deep Snow!" Speaks the Troll.

My mother looks at me nurviously.

"I dont want any fighting. Now shut up, the pair of you!"

"Im not seeing anyone," i reply.

"Then why did you rite her name down?"

"Its just a name."

"Who's name?"

"Just a name. Anyway, you told me that you would never look in my note book."

"Well, you shouldn't leave it lieing around then, should you."

I carry on eating.

"Why does he want anybody else when hes got me? What's she got that i have'nt? Why dosnt he live with me and why dosnt he sleep with me?" Karima asks my mother, then pouts, her dark eyes filled with tears.

"Leave him, then. Dont bludy put up with it!"

"I dont live with you, becouse i dont want to!" i state, "becouse your allways on me."

"He hasn't slept with me for 2 whole weeks." The Troll shouts trumphantly, this time actually nodding at my mother.

I throw my knife and fork down.

"Oh yeah, well has it ever ocured to you that its possible that a man mite not want to have you forcing your disgusting old cunt on him every nite!"

At this my mother stands and starts to tiedy away the 1/2 eaten meal.

"His as bad as his sodin father!" she says, clanking the spoons. "He had those books in his breif case. Not the normal ones but ones with men in!"

"What books are thay?" i say mockingly.

"Dont think i dont no about those books. And he had friends who were… Poofy."

"Poofy?"

"Well it wouldn't come as a surprise to me if he was one of them."

"One of what?"

"A homosexual," she whispers softly.

At this Karima smerks at me and tilts her nose in the air.

"So what if he is?" And i laugh out loud so as to shut

them up about 'my father'.

"Well, he smuggled drugs and those… Poofs, use drugs, dont thay? And heven only nos what he has been bringing in and out of Amsterdam on his bissynes trips. He ask'd me weather i thought he should, you no – smuggle dimonds! And when he took me with him that time he gave me a suit case to carry and told me that if any body ask'd to serch my bags, that i was to give them the number of his friend Sven, the Director of the airport. I diddn't put 2 and 2 together at the time but now, well, it seems obvious. And to think, we were starving down here whilest his Lordship was living it up with his mistress, in The Ritz, of all places! And there's a Rolls Royce sitting out there in the garage, and a yachet in the south of France. Now i 'spose his criditors are going to get it all, as well as the house! And ile be out on the street, when i'm the only reason that there's anything still left! Becouse if i haddn't stayed and brought you kid's up he'd of squandered the lot and there'd be nothing!"

"So that makes him a homosexual?" I sneer at my mother.

"Oh, shut up, i'm sick of the bludy lot of you!" And she slames the plates one on top of the other and sits back down.

There is silence and then the sound of heavy rain drops pelting against the window pain, like as if someones chucking gravel. Their 2 female faces look across the table at me thru the candlearbra and the flickering candle lite. I am guity becouse i am my fathers son.

"You married him – not me!" I speak. I see her face made ugly by the shadows.

"And the reason i dont want to sleep with you," i say, pointing my knife at Karima, "is becouse youre allways on me, pawing at me and you dont listen to anything i say. And you dont wan't to talk, you just want sex. One minit your all puffed-up with your silly 'art talk' and the next its more mindless drivel about being a little person living in my pocket! Well i'm not a teddy bear and i dont want to be talkt to in the voice of a fucking glove puppit!"

Karima throws her chair back from the table and runs sobbing from the room. The table shudders and a heavey stream of blud-red wax casscades down from the candlabra, spattering the table cloath. I hear the front door slam… She passes the big front widow then disapears into the nite.

My mother sits silently for a moment, then pours herself a glass and takes a mouth full of my fathers gut-rot.

"She'll be back," she says, "you mark my words – you wont get rid of that one in a hurry! Besides, she'll be soaked to the skin in 5 minits."

We sit and drink. I lite a ciggeret and listen to the pouring rain. And its true, almost at once the Trolls face re-apears in the window and trys to smile at me. I go to the front door, open it but dont let her pass. I stand and laugh at her, her large brests showing thru her wet blowse and her maskara cracking her face. Then she pushes past me and into the front room.

I laugh to hurt you, Karima, becouse i too have been laughed at and ridiculed. Laughed at by the world of art; by my mother, brother and nan; by sluts in the street. Laughed at becouse i am my fathers son; laughed at becouse i still wet the bed when i was 12 years old; laughed at becouse i said that i wished that i was dead, Karima. And thay laughed in my face, not noing that the reason that i still wet the bed – couldn't read or rite and had to sleep with the lite on – was becouse i had been raped by a 46 year old man when I was 9 years old. So, dont tell me about humiliation, you gluttonous bitch! Yes, thay thought it was hellerious and I ran from their laughing faces and smashed my head against the tiled wall in the bathroom. And do you no what, Karima? – thay diddn't run to comfort me, or tell me that thay were sorry, or ask me for forgivness, or ask why i cryed, nor tell me that thay lov'd me. No, thay saw my pain and just laughed all the harder! So forgive me, Karima, if i am less than human but i have been made so.

Later, i set Karima's hair alite.

46

Kissing the Silver Lady

THE HOUSE is silent. My mother, upstairs asleep with her bottle of Guinnes. I had burned my hand quite hidiously with a cigeret. I lift Karimas head from my lap, go to the bathroom and run some cold water into the wound. I look in once more at Karima, curled on the sofa, grab my coat and step out into the nite.

I walk slowly thru the rain to the garage and lift the waighted door. There's no lite in here but as the door comes up my fathers Rolls Royce shows like a huge ghost under its dust sheet. I have to press myself between the car and the wall to get in out of the rain. The car doors are all lock'd, as is the boot.

I serch about in the darkness for a hammer. On the bench by the window i find a torch and on the shelf bellow, a tin of paint stripper. I squeese back passed this car that i have never been allowed to even sit in, and roll up the dust cover, exposeing its vast gray bonnet and silver lady. I put my cheek to its cold sefis and lick it. Then, opening the tin, i empity the paint stripper in thick globbs all over the bonnet of this car, which my father loves beyond me, my brother, my mother and all life.

47

A Blatent Fib

ONE THING that makes me unbearable to myself is my crulety, which seems to ouse up from my very insides and overtake me. It can not be Karima who makes me cruel. It is only her charickter and attitude that have awoken these base instinkts in myself, and caus'd these poisons to hatch out. The first thing is her sickly loyelty. Shortly, i shall prove, once and for all, that she has never truely lov'd me and that her devotion is nothing but a contemptable entrapment, and that her decleration that she will always love me and never love another, is a sick, premeditated lie, only uttered to make me hate myself for loathing her.

Of course, it is wrong to constantly test somones love, purly to see if it will break. But why then dose she tell me that she wants sex only with me? She has, after all had sex with many others befor me and can hardly claim to be a virgin who has been saving herself for me alone. And just repeating something, over and over again – in a sacarine tone – dosn't make it true, or any more belivable. No, i have come to belive that her love should be abused untill it is broken and useless, and it has been proved beyond all reasonable doubt that this person – who swares everlasting love to me and to me alone – is a lier and a fraud.

Actually, it is no wounder that her speech is sickly and tainted with death as she has learned it from her father. I am talking of Al Mersin, who has returned from his 'bissness trip' and has once more taken me into his confidences.

Foolishly, I had allowed myself to be tricked by the Troll into staying the nite for sex. In the morning, Al Mersin lets himself into the flat and accosts me in the kitchen.

"My Karima is sweet… so sweet," he says thickly. His tounge moistening his lips. "She is my… Princess. She is… Loyel. Very, very, loyel. Make sure that you make her… happy." And he wrinkls his forhead at me.

Next, the door opens and the Troll comes in.

"Ahhh, My princess."

"What are you doing here! I've told you you have to bludy knock!"

Al Mersin takes not one bit of notice of his 'princesses' rudness.

"Today, i almost died." Al Mersin pauses for effect and looks sulkerly at Karima. "A head-on collission . . . in my car, princess. It was the other drivers fault... not myself. This is the way thay drive nower day, isn't it... young man?" And he looks to me for agreement. Both Al Mersin and i no, that what he is telling is a compleat and utter lie, but Karima just smiles and nods and seems to be in full agrement with Al Mersins blatent fib telling. The truth is, Al Mersin has failed to buy Karima a vinyard in Corsica of any discription what so ever and has almost caused an horriffic car accedent by being impatient and pushy, which is his nature.

"Look, i've bawt you a present." He says, rumeging thru his trouser pockets. He pulls out a fat wad and peels off a 5er. Imedeiatly the Troll starts cooing. She clasps the 5 pound note in her hot hands, so happy and greatfull. Basicly, thay're like a pair of love birds.

"Ahhh, My princess." And he takes her small head in his hands and kisses it. She pulls away.

"You do have to knock when you come round. You do no that, don't you? Now you can say good bye. You can go over to the castle and look round. You can come back in an houre, if you like."

Al Mersin nods, smiles his big face and looks at me meaningfully. I watch his back as he hobbes off up the basement steps. We here the door go.

"You tell him not to talk to me anymore. I dont want him round here!"

"Why?"

"I dont want him speaking to me."

"Why?"

"Becouse i don't need to here him telling me how loyel and sweet you are."

"But he loves me."

I go out into the hallway to look for my cloaths, and leave.

48

Thinking of Murder

IF I AM BAD it is becouse i would like to be nown for my specialness but have grown into a rogue. If a man carn't be King he will be a murderer and if he was truly brave then the killings would start dispite himself.

I have a list of all those i wish dead, my father and brother shearing the place of honour, rite at the top. Next is Micheal Crowsfeet who bullied me at skool. Norman, my abuser, would also need to die in an accident. Back then, in the olden days, i prayed to God to kill them, but now it will be me who cuts their throats and leaves them grinning with 2 mouths.

When i was a child and first saw child sized graves i was fill'd with horror. The fact that children die seems against God. The M— Murderes kill'd children spersifickly, and Miss H—, it can be prosumed, helped tape their mouths befor the sexual asults and death. By and large, sex crimes – as commited aganist myself – are rarly done by stranges but by 'uncles' and 'friends of the family'. Norman did once try to intice me to drive with him to the woods after skool, and if i had of gotten into that car that afternoon and gone with him, then he would nodoubt have murdered me in some kind of sexual frenzy and left my childs corps to be found next morning – 1/2 naked and scratched by brambles – in a small clearing in the woods. (As it was he had to make do with feeling me up under my mothers neglectfull gaze). After refusing to drive with him, i ran home into my mothers kitchen, where she lookt at me, her face crumbling, and told me that Nanna Lewis was dead. Norman then walk'd in 10 minits later, look't gravely at me and started consoling my crying mother. And even tho' i knew the truth of him i still kept 'our little secret' – as he instructed me – for over 10 years. Rite up untill, in fact, i was ripe to murder.

The reason socioty looks down upon sex murderers is becouse it is afraid of its own dark hart. And rather than kissing and embracing these 'lost sheep', socioty would rather deniy them forginess and thus increase evil. The

232

truth is many would like the power to commit state murder and there by help nurture even more darkness in those already thrown to the margins. This is becouse our socioty is run amoke with deniers and hippocrites who call for the peace of Jesus but also love murder.

When i kill my father – rather than seeing it as a son killing he who gave me life – i would see my job as killing the man who murdered my hart. Next, i would kill anybody who thinks themselfs superiour to me. But all this is just empty talk. Above all else, i am broken. This is why God sent the Troll to me: so's that she could fit her broken self into me and then together we could prehaps make up some sort of 1/2 human monster together, which i shall not allow. First of all she must accept every evil i have to offer and then mabe i will forgive her for lying when she says that she loves me.

I have surgested to the Troll that she befriends a skool girl and that we become child murderers together. To be a child murderer, afterall, must be as far from God as one can possably get. Also, i have told her that she can become a prostitute and that i will 'run' her. If she was indeed to become a prostitute and eat the seed of other men, then it would prove beyond all doubt that she loves me, tho' i would still hate her for it.

My father will have to die, then Karima. Once dead, Karima will never be able to leave me, all tho' there will still be the problem of her rotting corps which i would not be able to tollerate either. And if i become the murderer of children, will God still love me? And will Jesus be able to forgive me? Afterall, the whole point of Jesuse is that nobody is beyond redemption, so, in a way, there is nothing that cannot be forgiven.

When i was aged 10, every nite i had a reacuring vision, (viz). Whenever i shut my eyes i saw a disembodied womans pelvis, 1/2 rotted to soap, floating befor me, glowing faintly in the darkness, and where the cunt should be there was nothing, just a great void in which hung a great drip of snot.

My fathers death will be thought of as just a random mugging. Karima, i will throttle, wrap in bin liners and store in the coal hole that sits outside her basement windows. From there i will stuff the corps in a trunk, drag it down the hill, under the cover of darkness, and toss it off the side of R— bridge into the black river bellow. Of course i wouldn't have the stomach to cut up her body, so i would have to keep it whole, which would mean that i could still have sex with her corps.

All this is meer speculation, but one thing is for sure: Karimas ghost will be very chatty by nature and will probberbly drive all the other dissemboded spirits at the bottom of that river to distraction with her inane whitterings. It will also be quite likly that she will still somehow manage to smoke 40 ciggerets a day and refuse to offer the Devil even so much as a drag on a dog end.

At nite time she mite well come crawling, trapsing blud and seaweed along the esplanade, all the way up the hill, in thru the door and back to her cave, where she will lie her disgusting, rotting head on my pillow and ask me to hold her in my strong arms and tell her that i love her. Her lips will be cold and blue, her hair reeking of black river mud and she will put her icy fingers on my cock and demand that i kiss her, which is simply something too intermet to do with somebody i already no and have conqoured.

49

Meeting Karima

THE DESIRE to stamp on peoples heels, kick pigions and spitfully kill insects is once more upon me. But even in my rage my naturel good manners force me to run and hold open doors for compleat strangers. Despite willing myself to be rude, i am unable to let the door go in their ungreatful faces. In short – the poetry of life, instead of calming me, makes me want to vomit. I walk the town day and nite, scowling.

If, on one of my nocternal walks, i should here voices and laughter drifting out of some upstairs room, i stand bellow in the shadows, bearly able to contain myself from pickin up a rock and hurling it thru their infernal windows. If a woman passess me on the street, i stair after her trying to guess weather or not she has seemen in her anus, just by her walk. Then, chomping down on my thick, steak-like tounge, i turne on my heel and march away from the trashy noise of her heals to the other end of town.

So Karima taunts me as a homo-sexual? – Just becouise i like to take a moment to myself, a chance not to fuck like a dog on the street. Actually, sex repulses me. Yes, rather than filling me with liteness and joy, the Trolls love fills me with the utter futility of life. Where once i lov'd buti and harmony, i now seek pain and rejection. I have entered a season of hell.

What has become of the girl who i once beliv'd could save me with her love and admeration? That nite we met i fell down upon my knees befor her. 'You saved my life tonite,' i said. 'The nite would of kill'd me, or i would of kill'd myself. I carnt bear to live any longer in this world of aloneness.' And it was true – but for meeting Karima, for her adoring eyes passing over my body and my paintings, i would not be here now.

'I no you, your the artist. I've seen your werk,' she spoke, 'I love your pictures. You use such… thick paint.' And each word was like the caress of a gentle hand, for at last i'd met somone who could trully see me and my specialness. I held her in my arms and lay with her on my bed. But i diddn't love her. If i said earler that i did, then i am a lier. And if i claim later that i love her, then i am a lier and you must tear out these pages, and i will tear out my togue at the root! Of course i diddn't love her, i only lov'd her admeration of me.

'I love you,' i said and lookt down into her smiling

pug-face and already i was planing how to change her, how to re-mold her and make her new. To cut off her nilon black hair - specifickly – which she wore in a great tangle on top of her head. A snip here and a snip there, and i would make this girl into who and what i needed her to be.

The Troll sighed and her arms entwined round my waist and her head pressed into my shoulder. Her hair is in my face. It is dyed a dissgusting shade of matt black and has been purmed to oblivion. Greatfully i breath a lungfull of its cheep perfume. I gag but still i hold her tightly to my body.

This dress you wear Karima, i no i will change. You are a lowly fashion student and belive in that world, this also will be stopped. After all, i am a real artist and a hater of students, having once been a mock student myself. Also, i despise the life of all agree'ers, of the sain, of their teachers and the educated. Yes, i will make you into the imeage of what i desire, or i will smash you, you little Troll.

Of course, i am being romantic, becouse only a romantic sets his girlfriends hair on fire then maimes himself horribly with cigeret ends and hides from the girl he loves. Tho', some nites, i cannot resist the temptation of her body, for i am addicted.

So, i contemplate crimes that will mark a mans sole forever. Crimes that only somone who feels that we are not truly alive could commit.

50

An Impertenent Letter

MY MIND RACES on and never lets me rest, becouse i have been cut too deeply to be able to repair myself. Becouse my mother never smiled at me, but instead lookt sternly down at me as i stoll her milk. Becouse my father bullied me and never admired me. Becouse i was left un ceared for and was abused by the hand, tounge and cock of a 46 year old man. God bless him.

1stly, Karimas aderation will have to stop. Her copying of my werk will have to stop and her fawning to Mister Bennit will have to stop. Why i taught her to give me what i desire i do not no, for now i have snaired myself and i have a vission of her tiny, Turkish waist and muscular buttocks, lifting to take me again and again and i cannot stop.

Actualy, i have been implicating Karima in my plans. When choosing a murder weapon it is as well to get an axe with a rubber handle, as blud is greecy stuff and it can be quite hard to maintain a good firm grip thru out a frencied attack. An old fashioned wooden handle is useless. You carn't aford to slip.

I have ritten a letter to Miss H—, at the local prison, here's how it goes, (viz).

> *Dear Miss H—,*
>
> *I am very much interested in your carrier as a child murderer – or mass murderer – and i was hoping that i mite be able to come and visit you one Sunday afternoon and have a little chat over tea and scones.*
>
> *Yours Sincerly*
>
> *William Loveday*

I have ritten Miss H-'s name and the words 'personal', very clearly on the envelope. This is to make sure that the letter go's strait to Miss H—, and dosen't get caught up in some buricratic system, whos sole purpose is to make life a tangled web and make more money for its self.

Of course my letter is outragious, but it is also true to say that i have a genuine interest. My mother is of the oppinion that it is the type of prose that is bound to generate hostility.

51

A Very Pritty Lady

I MET KARIMA in the park next to the Acadamy. She has

befriended a young Indian girl call'd Netka. Netka is eleven years old and thinks that the Troll is a very pritty lady indeed. Netka even runs up to Karima after classes then skips beside her as Karima walks down the hill.

Karima introduses me to Netka and i try to say hello to her, but i am sceared of her, as i am sceared of all children.

I then try to shake her small hand but Netka withdrew it and lookt at me very coldly from her black eyes and hated me on account of my deformaty befor God.

As we walk'd on Netka lookt up at Karima with glowing admeration and told her again that she was 'a very pritty lady.' There were a few things that i could of told Netka about how butiful Karima is, but for the moment i desided to keep my thoughts to myself.

For one, Karima has stollen a cat which belonged to a young child.

52

Karima Wants Me to be a Cripple

I AM DRUNK and pretend to of passed out. I let her unbutton my cock, take it out and wank it, but then she stops herself and puts it away again. I lie with my thighs parted, watching from benith my eye lashes, all the while i pretend to be unconcious.

To be unconcious and not responsible. To get drunk, pass out and be molested. To be a corps that is fucked by the living. To pretend to be dead and feel the same pitch of fear and excitment that i experenced the day i was drawn into the dark world of adult sex by the hand of Norman. His hairy brown fist on my childs body, and my mother sleeping unawears in the next room.

This one time that i truly want the Troll to molest me and i carnt induce her. I see her shadow leave the room. Later, i pick myself from the sofa, walk along the dark corridoor and enter her Trolls cave and sleep. In my dream i am fucking with a stranger. I chase this naked girl-child across a broken and destroyed landscape, my excitement is at a fever pitch, and finnaly i catch her. I am strong and manly in my dream and she sercomes to my every command. I am about to squirt, when my conciousness returnes and i relise it is not a pubecent girl lying benith me but the Troll. It seems she has mearly trimmed the hairs on her cunt. With this realisation i instantly lose all desire. Freeing myself from her clamping legs, i roll off and sleep.

I wake in the morning 1/2 lite with the Troll's damp body clinging to me, its nostrels snoring in my ear. I lift its arms from round my neck. Ah, Karima, has your mustash grown in the nite? I count the tiny hairs that grow there on your twisted little lip. There is no gap, your lip joins strait onto your nose, your nostrels like 2 torpido tubes.

You little submarine! I stick my fingers in there to shut her up, but she just snorts, pushes my fingers away and rubs her face with the backs of her paws like a rabbit, and then her arms lock back around my kneck. You little Troll! All in all, with her little mustashe and side-burns, its a charming effect. I cearfully climb out from her death grip but she crys out and starts fumbling for my cock. I skip from the bed and start to dress.

"Where are you going?" She asks fearfully.

"Home. Have you seen my vest?"

She reaches under the covers, pulls out my dirty under shirt, lifts it to her nose and smells it contentedly.

"Give it here."

"No!" she lifts her arms and puts it on.

"Why are you wearing my vest?"

She looks at me and smiles in a teasing child-like way. Which makes me want to smile and play but i refuse to allow myself. I have to get out of this room.

"I need my vest!"

"You come and get it."

"Look, i'm cold and i dont even have any socks to wear. And i'm ill, so please, stop tormenting me, take off my vest and give it to me." I lunge at her and pull it off over her head.

She sits there on the bed pouting, lifts her little pug – really as if she is a small ermin – and sniffs the air. I should point out at this point that she is in fact blind. She peers round the room to find out who it is that is disturbing her.

"But i want you to stay. We can have brakfast."

I grab up my jacket.

"What's the time?" She says in a very small voice.

"It is 1/2 past."

"Just stay a little bit longer, please!"

Then she stands from the bed and shows herself to me. It is true that i once punched her, but not as hard and as oftern as i have let her punch me.

No wounder that i am unreckognisable, that all of my finner qualaties have been ruinned. I have been forsed into fighting for my very existance, to punch kick or be swamped in goo. For she would prefer me to be a cripple, to feed me baby food, bathe my stumps for me and then fuck me.

53

I Have Become My Father

MY MOTHER isn't really in a position to talk about relashonships. Since my fathers arest i have been trying to force her into devorcing him. I have told her that she will be left with nothing but the pittence she makes serving fish and chips to the unemployed – of which i am one – on the council estate. If she continues to refuse to do as i tell her, my fathers creditors will take everything.

"But i couldn't devorse him, not now, could I? I

couldn't. Its wrong to kick a man when he is down, isn't it? Even if for 16 years he has lied and desived me, time and time again? It is allways possable that he is about to 'turne over a new leaf', isn't it? You dont think he could change, do you? None of this would even be here if it wasn't for me, would it? Shall I devorse him?"

"Yes."

She walks over to the mirror and examines herself. Her voice is very quiet and she has to play with the lose skin about her neck. I have had a terrible dream where i tryed to have sex with her in the bathroom, but it wasn't possable to pennitrate her as there just wasn't any substance to her form. It really was as if i was trying to fuck a ghost made only from skin.

Yes, in many ways my mother has become invisable. Tho' she is probebly the angryist person i no, her anger is held like a great stick above her own head and she whispers in fear of it, but harshly, almost louder than ordianry talking.

Ever since i was a child i have had to make sure that she is alrite and to keep my own sufferings hidden, otherwise she will take them over and worry herself till it is me who has to comfort her again. Also, my mother will not talk about anything that she dosn't want to talk about and will walk out of the room if anything is said that displeases her. This is how she gives her anger away: as presents.

"I carn't devorse him, can I? Not when his down on his luck, what would people think?"

I lead Karima out of the kitchen and upstairs to have

sex. Say what you like but there's something magical about the way that girls arse sticks out. I hold her head by her platte and ride her like a small pony, little twists and tugs, and her neck drawn back. She likes to whatch, over her shoulder, with her penciled-in eyes, to see it going in, just the head. Her arse grows taught, she pulls at the cheeks.

After, i sit benith my fathers chanderleer and pour myself a glass from his Nepoleonic decanter. In many ways i have become my father in his absence. Trying to be him, trying to make him live. This is another way Karima has beaten me.

54

A Lump of Jellyfied Fat

WITH THE 3 POUNDS that i own i go to a pub and drink 3 pints of vile guiness, 4 glasses of foul whiskey, a hiddious rum and then force myself to smoke 10 ciggerets. Afterwards, i stair into the full ashetray in front of me, then it is time to leave and i go and visit the Troll.

Outside, i go into an ally and piss against the wall. There are 2 policemen coming down the other side of the road and i have to speed up to finish, a trail of piss snaking across the pavement. As thay come closer i can see that thay are not real policemen at all but what thay call 'Specials'. I button up and step back out onto the street, lower my neck into my coller and steer towards them. What would happen i wounder, if i were to bump them 'accidently' into the gutter with my shoulder? I quicken my pace and cross the street. I have my hands in my pockets and my shoulders hunched. The 2 Specials stop gassing to each other and look at me questioningly and i am forced to abandon my experiment. I mutter good evening to them under my breath then hurry off towards the bridge, taking the long way round to the Trolls cave.

As soon as i enter the building i can smell food. I bang on the door and the Troll lets me in. Downstairs i sit to the table and wait for her to serve the poor little bar-lamb. She brings in the roasting dish to show me.

So, Karima, you want to play mummy's and daddys? So i get to carve the meat. 1st i lift it from the tin and onto the plate, then i have to re-sharpen my big knife. Karima smiles at me.

Truthfully, there is no meat on the joint, it is just a lump of jellyfied fat. I throw down the knife.

"I carn't be eating this!"

"Why, whats rong with it?" And her small chin trembles, her little pug crumbling in front of my hard eyes.

"Its just a piece of fucking fat!"

"No, its good." She whines, "It cost me £1.50 thats the best piece thay had!"

"But look at it. Its fucking inedible!" And i stick my finger into the glue "Its just baked fucking lard!" And i lift

246

it up and slap the whole carcuss down onto the carpet in front of her. I take a piece from my mouth and wave it under her nose and it feels wounderfull to see her trembling, terrified face, just like real mummys and daddy's. I sling the meat down and turne on my heel, my brain screaming in pain. I must leave this fucking dungeon, the land of dripping, ghastly sheep! I stagger up the stairways, vomiting of that vile fat, that the one i love should try to treat me so – should try and choke me. And then shes upon me, clinging round my thighs. I shrug her off as she flayels at my legs, begging me, clawing at my trouser leg as i try and wade past her and up the stairs. I heave on the banistairs, draging her up on her tits behind me. Yes, she is the one i love alrite, shes the one i must destroy and crush. Clawing at my ankles, i kick at her with my free foot. For a second i wounder weather to stamp on her face, i lift my boot but really, i carn't.

"Get off of me. For fuck's sake, i just want to go home!"

"No you musn't! You musn't leave me, you must come back and eat. Sit down again. Please! I've made a lovely tea, please sit down! Come back, you carn't leave me. Please, please! Ile cook you something else, something different, something you like! We'll go for a drink, we can have some wisky. Do you want a wisky? I 've got money, just a little bit, that i've saved."

So shes got money has she? – the cunning cow! But i pull away and push on up the stairs anyway. You see, i have to have her beg me, and she a woman and me a man, but not just any man, a man despised by her evil race – the tribe

247

of artists and women!

Yes, on your knees you bitches, all of you! Come and beg and crawl in my wake, and maybe, just maybe, i will condescend to turne and spray you with my precious sperm. So please cry Karima, prove your pathetic love for me, clawing at my strange pretruding ankle bones.

Is it really possable that a man can have such thin ankles and wrists? And have the wrong type of hair alltogether? I really do push my foot aganst her face. She scrunthes up her nose into such a funny fizog that i have to concentrate not to laugh and there by ruin the whole situation.

By rites, i should have the sort of hair that curles up slitely in front and then waves back over my tiny ears, which aren't tiny at all. Or if not that, then hair that at least stands up on end, of its own acord, like my elder brothers, or that is somehow naturely unruley, becouse that is how i am and – as everybody nos – a man should have the hair, eyes, ears and nose that suit and express his innermost charickter.

I may laugh at Karimas abonimble face but really it is myself i see as ugly, and secretly long to be sombody else, which is stupid. If i was a woman i'd want to wank a cock that was a foot long!

I shake her off my foot at the top of the stairs, get the door open and bundle out into the darkened passage. I get to the front door, which is open onto the street. I hear her wimpering in the shadows, stumbling after me. She screams and lunges, i side step her and dash out into the nite, her following 1/2 naked, her nitie billowing out behind her like a ghost. It makes me want to bite her tits.

I cross the road in front of the Cathedrel and slow down a little, so's that she can catch me up. I waite till shes about 20 paces behind, then run on again. I play tag with her, cutting thru the avenues of trees across The V—'s. In all probability there is a man hanging by the neck in those bushes, his legs kicking out into the nite. I run on, holding my arms out in front of me, protecting my face from his visious boots.

55

The Gods

WHEN I GET to my gaff i dont go in but instead cut down the side ally onto the street bellow and listen out for Karimas footfalls. After a short while i hear her banging on the front door. There's a pause befor she comes down the ally and goes in the side gate. I stay hidden in the bushes. I hear her harsh voice shouting and then the ping of little stones being thrown up at my bedroom window. I put my hand in my trousers and feel my cock. I wounder weather to double back and lie in waite for her at her place: to be sat there in the armchiar, rolling a ciggarette, having a cup of tea with a fist of rum in it, my cock already out, waiteing for her returne.

I pick myself from the bush and hurry off down hill. I hear her calling but run on, my hands stuffed in my thin pockets. At the bottom of the hill i'm caught in sombodys headlites. I see the drivers face grimicing thru his dirty windscreen. He 'bibs' at me but he's too slow to get me and i jump out the road, leaping up the concreat steps out of his reach. I turne and look down at him passing. I am not afraid of cars. After all, he isn't a policeman and dosn't own the street. I take the steps 5 at a time. You see, my feet have to be above the hight of the roof of any passing cars, i dont no why, it is important, that is all.

I climb up onto the field, shivering with cold. The river laid out below me, the old chalk pits, the docks, the wounderfull crains and the stinking towns. All the street lites shining out and glinting, piss yellow. Every sailor and every whore who ever liv'd is down there. The whole town is winking at each other indecently, trying to make a pound.

If i was somehow magickly catipulted from this hillside into those ici deapths, i would certanly drown and be trapped there up to my neck in black river mud, kissing the flesh tenderals that waft from the fish-net stockings of drowned whores.

I walk past the Acadamy and then pick my way down onto the High Street. There's this old MT boat there – behind A—House – that used to be home to all the dancing girls from the C— Empire, back befor it was bulldozed. The whole boat is in gray, mornfull darkness. A small piece of yellow net curten hangs limply from out of a broken port hole. I climb over the railing and reach out to touch it. I hang from the railings with one hand and sway out over the inky water clutching at empty air but it stays a whole yard out of reach. I look to see if there's a gang-plank but it's fallen into the mud. There's some old bits of timber sticking up out of the water bellow. I pretend that i am going to jump, cling onto the side of the deck with my finger tips and pull myself on board but the fear of death stops me. I climb back over the railings and pull on the mooring roaps. I inspect the knots, which are really huge and impossable to undo by hand. I kick at them. If i had a knife i would cut clean thru them without a hint of remorse. The girls are dead and gone now, their home is too, lying here rotting. Soon there'll be nothing left but shopping complexis.

Further down the High Street i pull up in front of the old Theater R—, which is also completely derilickt. Maybe i can force some old tramp into letting me in under the pretext that i have come to restor the building. Round the side there's a door slitely wedged open, which i manage to jam my head and shoulders thru. Inside you can see the stars clean thru the roof and the flutterings of nite pigions… 3 tears of balconies like a wedding cake, luminous white, incrusted with 30 years of pigion shit.

A torch shines out feebly thru the gloom, and wakes me, then a little fellow comes up and asks me if i would like a tour of the theatre.

"I'm the old door man, thay never retired me. I used to werk over M— way. Of course, that was in 1947. Becouse i liv'd over here, I'd pick up the tickets, take them back home and sell them for all the maternay and evening shows. Bigger than all the London theatres this was."

I look at him, stood there in his glasses, a little ticket machine slung over his shoulder and a peeked cap on.

"72 i am. 72. Have i shown you my photos?"

"No," i answer vaguly. "I was looking for somewhere to sleep, how do you get out of here?"

"I'le show you, this is the way to the cellars. Thay had the big stoves down here, big enough to supply hot water for the whole theatre! That was the back stage over there, with dressing rooms for over a hundred performers! Thay had to strengthen the stage with steel girders when thay brought on the elephants. Biggest stage in the United Kingdom it was. Now look here," and he takes out his wallet and shines his torch.

"This picture here was taken when i was just 3 years old. That's me and that's my mother and in the background, that's the Benbon Brothers Arcade. And this one's me and my father, he was in the Marines. Thay were taken just over the road, 'What's on at the theatre mum, what's on?' He tugs at an imaginary sleeve and looks up to where his mothers face would be. Judging by the photos she was a hatchet faced old dragon with a nose like a mans. "Thay were taken just over the road, outside the Bernard Brothers Palace of Variaties. That burned down in 1936… No, 4! 1934. Thats me, holding my mothers hand."

Why on earth this old crock thinks i give 2 hoots about the date of the Bernard Brothers Palace of Doom burning down, i carn't imagine.

"I suppose youre the sort of man who hangs around bus stops trying to anoy people?" i ask him.

"Youre in an awful rush aren't you?" He answers. "Thats the trouble with your type these days, you've got no time."

"Well, thats the type of person i am." I afirm, flatly.

"Well, you should try and change. Not that its my business to tell you how to behave, its just when you get to my age…"

I nod, understandingly and look around at the desolation. "You need to get this place done up a bit, its leeking and drafty."

He looks at me.

"Well thats what we'er doing, isn't it! But i tell you, we'er not restoring The Gods. I'm a grandfather you no, 72, i've got 2 grandchildren. I'm the nite watchman. No, really i'm restoring the place… the 'Monday man'… Sweeping up the mess… All those rotting balconeys will have to be repaired… Then rebuild the stage. Then there's the roof. But i'le not be putting The Gods back in – the place is too big already, with this amount of seating, its not necessary, is it?"

I look up to the furthist point of darkness, a patch of lite and then the sky, where the pigions come and go.

"I like The Gods," i tell him, "there my favorite bit."

56

An Appology

FORGIVE ME, if you can, Karima, that i threw your nutrissious and wounderfully tasty roast lamb onto the floor. I appreciate that you bawt it for me with the last of your grant check and that you cookt it for me with love and afection. And even if it was a little on the fatty side that was no reason for me to pick it up out of its watery gravy and throw it, viberating onto the carpet.

Proberbly, you will never want to cook for me again (which would be quite understandable), and now i have ritten these aufull lies. I am a cripple, Karima, and deserve nothing better than to be starved into submission. I hand you the loaded revolver. In truth, i am not even worthy of the crumbs that fall from your table, let alone your tasty lamb. Maybe i shouldve said nothing and have meerly made you more angry with my apology.

But dont think that just becouse i have appologised that i have made some kind of admission of guilt. I will not force myself to live with you, or play mummys and daddiys with you becouse in my home daddys threw the dinner on the floor and slapped mummys stuppid face for her. No! I refuse to eat such foul and dissgusting fat as that which you served me. And unfortunatly this is how i honestly, truely feel.

57

Police Seek Alibis

I HAVE STOLLEN a newspaper bill from outside the local newsagents. Checking that nobody's looking, i un-do the wire mesh, fold the bill away inside my jacket, turne and walk away, compleatly unditected.

The bill is in regard to a young choire girl who was murdered up on the G— L—'s last Sunday whilest on her way to sing in the Cathedral chior. But she never got there becouse someone was lying in waite for her up on the hill.

After the attack the girl managed to crawl a 1/4 of a mile down the footpath to the police station, but befor she could get inside she bled to death on the pavement. There was a trail of gore that had to be covered with sawdust. I have bought a copy of all of the newspapers regarding this crime and studed them most thurerly.

Is it nessisaraly a crime that i love all women? I dont think so. What it feels like to be a theif and a lier is something we have all experenced, but quite what it feels like to stick a cold knife into sombodys soft under-belly, i dont no. I imagin it would be important to view the victim as nothing more than just meat and offal and also belive that your own life was very unimportant. Acording to the newspaper report, the choir girls hands were terribly cut where she tryed to grasp at the slashing blade.

As i walk along i have to keep clentching and unclentching my fingers, forceing myself to imagin that i am a the choire girl and it is me who is being murdered and am helplessly grasping at the blade of my attacker, but just making his blade all the more slippery with my black, insolent blud.

58

To Here My Name in Their Exciting Mouths

I WOUNDER if it is possible to find out who i truly am and the reason for me being alive. In everything i contrive to no myself but also i long to become a great mystery, which really, i already am.

When i was a child my dearist wish was to silently

dissapear and keep my enimys guessing. Espersherly my parents and teachers. And then, when i had finnaly dwindled from their memorys and was only a vague flicker at the back of their minds – to the point of almost not existing – i would suddenly emmerge like a firery phenix. To be thought dead and then be alive – for people to grieve and sorrow for me, to apologise to my corps for all the wrongs thay have done me – then open my eyes and be upheld, worshiped and adored. To come from nothing, grow into nothing, then suddenly turne into a topic of conversation. Then, just as people are at their most currious, to mysteriously dissapear again. To die and to see ones own funneral. To make everybody sad. To become some sort of a legend, then fade into the grave. To be forggotten, then to come to life again with a vengence. To be dead but be able to read of my own youthfull exploits. To be dead and for Mister Benit, and all the women, to wish that thay had been farer and kinder to me. For them to wish that thay had kissed me and lov'd me instead of scorning me. To hate themselves for their callousness. To be a ghost, step onto a train and overhear beautiful, unnown women talking of me. To hear my name in their exciting mouths. To feel it roll against their girlish tounges and be bitten by their hard white teeth. To almost live in their mouths, yet all the time i am standing rite next to them, pretending to be reading my newspaper, chuckling to myself becouse thay really do not have any idear just what sort of a monster thay are actually sitting next to. Then, befor thay get off at the next stop, to suddenly reveil myself to them and thay drop to their knees

257

and take me into their cool, wounderfull mouths.

I walk along just in this manner. Remembering my youth; my skool days; the murder on the lines and the wolf-like faces of the women at the Acadamy: No one will ever no my true identity, and the joke is just too pressious for me and i have to fall to the ground and lie there laughing out loud, pounding the earth with my fists, crying amongst the fallen leafs. Some passing skoolgirls look over their shoulders at me in fear. And really, i am laughing at them, for their ignorence and pathetic buiti, for if i just said one word then thay would all become instantly mine. I am a mystery, but people should not laugh at me.

59

Heads

MISTER BENNET was in the Acadamy refectory wearing his loud tweed jacket, a red tie and boldly telling the serving lady which dish he wanted. I, by contrast, was shyly looking at the food on display in the glass cabbernets. I hear my name spoken and turne. Mister Bennit is moving towards me, his mouth opening and shutting and his eyes bulging. He is talking at me and i stand with my back against the skool notice boared.

"I have lookt at your birth chart, Loveday, and i can see from your alighnments that you are an egotist!"

I am ashamed to amit that i mearly nodded as i diddn't then no what an egotist was. Mister Bennit was then served his mash and gravy. As he turned and walk'd away, i noticed that the skin of his head had the apperence of having been soaked in vinagar. Really, his whole head was 1/2 hanging off on account of the red necktie garotting his neck. Why does he speak to me in such a manner? Surly i, a meer student, can not be deamed a threat to such a man?

By comparison, Karimas head is tiny, almost fist-sized, with an astonished rodent-like expression. If you put the 2 together thay would make a fine pair of ghost heads, and would also show the evolution of man from rodent to ape.

When i was 5 years old, i was playing over the road at Anthony B—'s house. Me, Anthony and his sister were leaping across the gap between the ancieant, iron bedsteads in their bedroom. Below, in the hard lenolium floor, liv'd a sea full of man eating crocodiles. Anthony was chassing me as we bounced from one bed to the other, squeeling with fear, my hart high in my chest, my whole being singing with excitment. Then, my small foot caught in the ida-down and i pitched forward, hitting the floor with my head. I was badly concussed and Anthony B—'s mother had to take me home still crying. She held my hand as we crossed the road and carry'd me to the front door. My mother thanked her, closed the door behind her and lookt coldly at me.

"Stop that God-awfull noise!" She ordered.

I was dizzy and still spinning.

"Do you want me to have to call an ambulence?!" She shouted as a threat.

I lookt at her and screamed all the louder. What i needed was for her to hold me, to comfort me, but my mother diddn't cradel me in her arms and tell me everything would be alrite. Instead she walk'd over to the telephone and lifted the resiver.

"Do you want me to call an ambulence? Becouse if thats what you want, i can, and then thay will come and take you away! Becouse if you dont stop your bludy screaming, thats where you are going!" She waves the resiver at me and i suck on my snot... Stars filling my vission... my head pounding. I was really very unsteady on my pins... 5 years old.

My mothers neck has moles on it and the skin is soft to the touch. It will be necessary to shut my eyes and imagine that i am peeling a potatoe rather than sawing thru her soft neck. Her expression is slitely dissdainful, slitely sad and horribly worried. She has a pudding basin haircut and drooping earlobes.

My fathers head (which intrestingly shears the same birthday as Karimas), is bewiskered, baggy-eyed and drunk. Its neck too, should prove to be simple to slice thru and snap off. My brothers head, (and really i do have a big brother) is large and bulldoggish, with bad breath. Its neck is slitely on the robust side. 2 large hacks with a meat cleaver just bellow his arrogant mouth should be enough to remove it. And then there is the Japanese boys head: the lemon theif. The Japanese are well aquainted with be-heading, almost turneing it into an art form in itself, which means that stealth will be of the upmost importance. His face is sallow and the expression is of someone who is already for the bone yard.

Finally, there is the ridiculous, Cypriet head of Al Mersin. His great grinning mug should look pretty amusing, sitting there on the dresser looking ghoulishly out the window, its mouth 1/2-open, its silly orange mustashe drooping slitely and a thick wedge of toiletpaper stuffed into its neck stump to soak up his insolent, Otterman blud. It will be a matter to see if it has a taste for insest.

'Ah, Al Mersin, and how would you like to kiss your 'Prinsess' Troll's purple lips? Sure, shes your daughter, but after all you carn't make babies by just kissing, can you?' And i lift Karimas shrunken skull from the floor by the bed and shake it at her fathers face. I make her lick his neck stump and her nose gets all messed up with his thick, Turkish sauce.

At first Al Mersin appears very bashfull. As i pick him up he closes his mouth tight shut. I have to pull at his chin but he keeps his jaws locked together and stairs at me with a look of intence hatred in his eyes. I take a soft clot of blud from Karimas neck stump, force apart his peeling lips with my thumb and forefinger and smeer it onto his disgusting old gums, but still he refuses to open his mouth and copperate. In the end, i have to take a screw driver and jemmy his teeth apart. There is a loud crunching sound and one of his teeth falls to the floor and rattles under the bed.

'Naughty Al Mersin! Please, for the sake of decentcy, keep your teeth in!' i reach my fingers into his dark mouth and fish out his black, slug-like tongue, and then make him lick Karimas dead eyes with it. I smear his kisses all over her small forehead. Once he gets warmed up he really does start to enjoy himself. You can tell on account that he wriggles his ears with glee and grunts like a naughty, Otterman pig. Then suddenly, without warning, Al Mersin's head is smashed across the room by the jealous head of Mister Bennet. Al Mersin's head hits the wall and falls to the ground, face up, looking confusedly at the revoling cealing. In my left hand i have Mister Bennit grasped by the hair and again use my full force to smash it into the skull of Al Mersin. The ferocity of the attack is so intense that Mister Bennits cheek bone is quite badly brused and starts to give way, his left eye dribbling down his cheek thru the slit of his eye socket.

'Al Mersin, you really are a number! I have told you, you are not to abuse the other heads or you will be made to go back up on top of the wardrobe untill you think you are ready to mix with polite socioty once more, do you understand me?!' Mister Bennet, whose hair is falling out in great tufts, then tries to mount Karimas head and have sex with it, which again, is illegal. Mister Bennet sneeks up on her from behind, pushing his fat jowls into the back of Karimas skull. He raises himself and pounds up and down on her like a tortoise untill i have to lift him from her blud sodden hair and punch his face in for him. Unfortunatly, his nose breaks and collapses into his face. I really have to beat his head into an unrecognisable pulp, but still he looks smugly and trumphantly up at me, so then i stamp his head into the litter-bin.

I clean my shoe with a sheet of newspaper and undress. I stand there breathing heaverly threw clentched teeth. It is i who will have sex with Karimas severed head, no one else! I hold her face to my crutch and try to put my cock between her wonky teeth without her biting it. I thrust my hips and a sob of blud drips from her neck and splashes my foot. I feel eyes watching me and look up. My mother peers down at me from a'top the wardrob and gives me one of her worrid looks and i hide myself in shame. The floor is littered with tuffts of old hair and dark smeers of blud. Actually, my mothers eyes are closed, but i can still feel her pupils burning thru her eyelids, accusing me of being a naughty boy. Cearefully, i place Karimas head on the floor, stand on the chair and turne my mothers head to face the wall. My fathers head is asleep beside her, snoring on its side. Some green ooze has escaped from his overly large, bulging eyes. I wonder, if i wake him up will he tell me that he loves me? I lift his head and stair into his face. I sqweeze it quite tightly in my fists then toss it down onto the bed where it bounces 3 times but still it dosnt wake up. Instead, it just lays there, face down in the ider-down, still snoring, its rubbery nose bent slitely to one side.

It is Godless to think of murder and plan murder but i do so becouse i want to feel alive, not caught in a soft dream. I want to meet the edge of God.

60

Sex Ghosts

ANY SEX CRIMES of the futcher will no doubt be commited by people and not by ghosts. This is becouse there are no ghosts. Belief in ghosts is a backward idear, a superstion and a sign of cowadise that went out of fashion years ago. This is a matter of common sence amongst modern people.

Of course, in the olden days people took an entirely different view. Back then, loads of people beliv'd in ghosts and were afraid of them. There is nothing strange in this. This was befor man was able to comprehend natural and social phenomena in the lite of sience, so he inevitabley had all sorts of superstitions. All the more becouse of the ruling classes delite in fooling and fritening the populus with ghosts, so as to strengthen their rule. So, let it be understood, once and for all – any sex crimes of the futcher will not be commited by ghosts, but by 'ordinary people'.

Tho' these 'ordinary people' will resemble ghosts by nature, thay will still, in fact, be mortal beings. What i am saying is this, (viz). These 'sex ghosts' will not be demons hidding in cellers and up dark allyways but will meerly be 'uncles' and 'friends of the family' who, from the 'goodness of their harts', offer lost children their help and guidence, and all becouse these childrens fathers – and theirby their harts – have been voided.

So, just becouse these 'uncles' resemble ghosts, it dosn't nessiserally mean that their bodys are not of flesh and blud. Thay are part of us but opperate on a level so low and debased, that we only see a glimps of their shadows. And the authoritys, at all costs, deny their very existance. But make no mistake, these 'sex robots' do exist and have already taken form within our midsts and it is only a matter of time befor we all reep the conciquences of denying their terrifying capability. Yes, sooner or later, even the worst deniers amongst us will suffer their displeasure and come to no intemitly their exact mechanism.

The more efficent these 'sex ghosts' are, the less able we are of assertaining their true existance. If, for example, the remains of their victims are walled up, or prehaps rendered down into slurry, it becomes impossible for us to ever definatly trace their path. And, as more and more children are 'iniciated' and made 'ghosts', it becomes harder to no who amongst us is the dead and who the living. So, it remains hidden and few detect these dark deeds as the werk of ghosts. (On refection, it is highly proberble that we will never become fully conscious of these 'sex robots' existence or whereabouts and will allways suffer in denial of our 'sexual uncles').

How the mind of a 'sex ghost' werks can not be nown till we monitior one in action. But it is clear that thay have 2 specific functions: 1stly, sucking the victims sexual essence from them. 2ndly, spitting out the husk. 3rdly, the emotional death of the victim, which is a simple matter of absence of self, or God.

It is we who have created these 'others', these 'sex ghosts' and it is up to us to recognise the enimy is ourselfs. This is also the reason why their nature and physiology is quite ordinary and uninspiring. The rule is: everyone keeps their filthy trap shut about it becouse nobody wants to admit to them selfs that we've been 'diddling' with our own children and denying it for generations. If it is man who has created such a monstrosity can it be claimed that man has challanged God? Would it not be truer to say that God has challanged himself?

61

Karima Goes To Holland

FOR 7'RAL DAYS now the Troll has been absent from her cave. Her room is in darkness and her stollen cat runs away whenever i aproach it, or try to feed it. I have left it out some food which apears to have been eaten. Some days the cat is sat there on the back of the setee, rising it's heckles at me but on my next visit i can find it nowhere within the building. It seems that this devil cat has its own secreat means of entry and exit. Also it has taken to shitting and pissing on the carpets and the whole flat is alive with hopping, bitting fleas.

About a week after her mysterious dissaperence a post card appears at my mothers house. It is from Karima. Apparently she has gone on a trip with the Acadamy to Holland, under the direction of Mister Bennit. My mother pours tea in my cup and sets a packet of digestive biscits down in front of me. I am upset that Karima should leave me; that this girl who proffessess undying love for me, and apparently can not spend a single nite without me; who loves me and only me, can now set off with the Acadamy to Holland, without even informing me – or asking my permission – beforhand.

So, you think that you can act independently of me now, do you Troll? That you can make these pleges of love and desseperation then breake them at will? I blow on my tea and sip at it. On the front of the card is a picture of some blond haired girl, wearing platts and clogs, stood in front of a tulip field and in the distance a windmill. I turne the card over in my hand and try to read the back. I stair into the scrawl. The gist of it is this: Karima calls me 'Mister' and says that she is living on a barge in Amsterdam. I toss the card to one side, tear the wrapper off the digestive biscits and dunk them – 2 at a time – into my tea and hungerly feeding them into my mouth, using the palm of my other hand to gaurd against them flopping into my lap. I really eat them as if i am a starving dog, which i am. I dont quit till there is just a pile of crumbs on the table in front of me, which i then scrape into my palm and stuff into my open gob as well. I then sit back, wipe my hands on my trousers and congratulate myself on having eaten a whole packet of biscits.

So, Karima, i will now take what is most precious to you and break it. I push the chair back. Now it is time to leave. My mother follows me out into the hallway. Just as i get to the door i turne and ask for money (which is the real reason for my visit). She looks at me with her hurt, worried eyes. She is smaller than me and can no longer threaten to take my trousers down and spank me in public. Instead she abuses me by telling Karima that i am a homosexual, like my 'soddin father', which amuses me.

I walk from my mothers house into town. I have no money for the bus so stick out my thumb as i walk. There's a bitter wind blowing and its clear that i am not warmly dressed. (According to my mother the wind was once again blowing in from Siberia), but still no one stops to pick me up.

I get all the way to the top of W— W—'s Hill and not a single bus has past me – which shows how useless it is to stand and wait for such things. I stand with my eyes closed and count up to 60 slowly, but still no bus apears. As i walk on, a red coloured car pulls out from the W— Estate and speeds towards me. As it comes along side, the car slows and the passanger winds down the window as if to speak to me. It is a youth sat there with glowing spots. He really opens his mouth as if to ask something, then gleefully spits at me. I jump back but the juce goes up my leg. The car then speeds off. I try to wipe the gob from my trouser leg aganist some leaves on a bush but is thick and yellow and adheres to me in great strings. In the end i have to scrape it off with an old lolly stick i find in lying in the gutter. I imagin being able to leap to the otherside of the hill, grab the car off the road and hurl it down into the vally bellow, broken and burning.

I meander on, studdying the broken tarmac path where a small tuft of grass, at the moment, is winning the war. I have no money and am apparently the type of person who deserves to be spat on from passing cars. When i get to the bottom – by the old water werks – i again stop and check up the hill behind me. If a bus was to come now then surly the driver would take pitty on me and let me ride for free. Afterall, the bus has to go to C– anyway with 42 seats all empty, and if i were to board it here, it will hardly make any difference to the amount of deesil it has to burn, will it?

But no matter how hard i pray for a lift i dont get one. There is no bus and i turne and drag my feet up that impossable slope, each step feeling like my feet have been nailed into the pavement. Suddenly, there is the grinding of gears. I terne and whatch a big green bus start labouring up the hill behind me. Joyfully i stick out my hand and wave, looking directly at the face of the driver – it is important to establish eye contact; to shame the person into recognising you as a fellow human being; so that he can see that you too are alive and have feelings, so that he may at least take pitty. But the driver studiously avoids my gaze and drives past. I run along side, waving at him, but still he keeps stairing directly ahead, a trick he must have learned in his previous life as a hangman. I stand and watch untill the bus dissapears over the brow of the hill and is gone, stick my hands in my pockets and trudge on.

Suddenly, at my feet in the dust is a dead bird. Its yellow feathers are all ruffled and caked with grime, also its small feet are drawn up tight like tiny fists. I look round for something to pick it up with but there is nothing. In the end i have to use my bare hands. Its eyes are closed, the lids gray and bulging slightly and there's a little line of blud at its beak. I lift the yellow coloured bird carfully across the pavement and chuck it gently into the bushes. This is the type of fellow i am: a lover of small animals and insects.

62

Burning Love Letters

WHEN I FINNALY get to the Trolls cave i at first enter the building and bang on her door. She is'nt there. So it is true, she has left for Holland. Not to live – as she grandly claims in her postcard – but on a babyish skool trip with the Acadamy. I walk back out thru the entrance way, skip over the railings and lower myself down in front of her basment windows. I lift the sash and peer into the darkend room, which now reeks of cats piss. Even tho' its not tottaly dark down here i am still sceared by the dismal atmasphear. The black coal cellers gape in the wall behind me like devils mouths and i make myself think of spyders and hands that will cling to my anckels and drag me into their black depths. I jump in, slam the window shut behind me, cross the room and click the lite on.

By the bed is a magazine rack in which Karima keeps the only 3 love letters that i have ever sent her. I have not broken in here just to amuse my self but in order to retrive my ritefull property. All 3 letters were sent in the 1st weeks of our relationship and are there for highly rare and the Trolls most prized posessions. Never again will i rite to her or tell her my innermost feelings. The letters are still in their brown envelopes. It is my spit that sealed them and stuck on these stamps. This one is from Germany and this one has my mothers address. I take them over to the lite. Yes, it is my hand writing and this is a German stamp. I read them one at a time then fold them away in my pocket.

One thing that can be honestly said in my letters favor is their abrutness. The script is large and there is bearly more than 5 words to the line. No, there are no sacrin lines here. No novel length discriptions of the blindingly obvious. No seeping, disgusting sentiments spoken in the langwige of imberceals.

At the back of the rack i also find her diary hidden inside a magazine. I fish it out and sniff at the damp pages. This is where she attempts to emulate my writing. I leaf thru untill i find a story apprently involving me. If it is ment to be great litrichar it has failed missrably. My charicter has the name of Kurt. Her story goes like this, (viz).

Kurt comes in from the bath. Karima, (the heroin) wants to speak to him and tell him that their relationship is all over and to stop having sex with him. But Kurt ignores her and just lifts her tits out of her dress and starts sucking on them. Then Kurt makes her suck his fat cock befor bending her over the arm of the setee and fucking her in the 'backside'.

I snigger inwardly to myself at her absured use of the word 'backside'. I lie back on the bed reading her idiotic diary then have to take my cock out and masterbate. At the last minit i sit up and squirt it over the dusty floor. Then i hate her.

So, Karima has deserted me in favour of the Acadamy? She has left me here with her flea-ridden, stollen cat, when she clearly said that she wanted sex with nobody but me. So now she is in Amsterdam with my enimys, enjoying herself, no doubt drinking with young Dutchmen and possably laughing in their arms and pretending to live on a barge.

I wipe myself on her bed sheets, take my love letters from my pocket and burn them in the grate.

There is something sorrowful about love letters and my mood is affected all day.

63

Spining Wheel

FINNALY, THE DOLE OFFICE have decided to pay me my dole money. It is not quite all that i was expecting, becouse there is allways some hidden cost that thay steal back from you, but in the big picture this is of little conciquens as, including all of my back pay, i now have the grand sum of 96 pounds 27 pence in hard cash, which will go a long ways to paying for the printing of my wounderfull testiment.

I have to que at the post office to cash the check and then it is refused on acount that i dont have any identification. I look at the cashier with hatred but still i have to trudge all the way back to my rooms and serch out my birth certificate. So it is 7'ral houres later that i dash outside the post office, sit on the bench and count my money very cearfully, 6 times over. It is definetly 96 pounds, or there abouts. I also have another 5 pounds which i lifted from my mothers purse when i 'visited' her last week.

There is an old newspaper on the bench, which i have been using to warm my arse against the cold. The front page says that a 21 stone lady, who werk'd as the radio opperator for a local taxi firm, has thrown herself from R – bridge and that 2 policemen 'Specials' – who were trying to save her – were all but dragged in with her when she jumped. Her body has not been recovered and she is presumed drowned.

Money means nothing when your dead and i get a strong impulse to give my money away to the first needy person i see on the street.

On reflection, i have decided to keep my money. Of course, i have many nobel intensions in my hart but really i should pay my rent, which is allready 2 months over due, but that would be just plain stupidity, becouse if i pay my rent i will have virtualy no money left at all. No, i will pay my rent all in good time, maybe with my next dole check. For the moment i am in need of some 'new' second-hand shoes, as my hobnail boots are cutting my feet to ribbons and skid all over the shop when i am trying to dash along. Also a packet of filterless cigarrets would be lovely -the harsh kind that hurt your lungs.

The great thing about my room is that it is barren, apart from my paintings which hang indecently from the walls. At the Accadmy i refused to paint, but here it just courses thru my body. To be free of women and sex is wounderfull. To not wake to there noises. It is all very well to paint but without the Troll to spend the nite with, it is depressing. And this room lacks the female touch. 1stly, there is nowhere for a nude woman to sit and show herself to me, and all tho' i am happy to be alone, allready i can feel myself being cornered into oblivion. It is hardly my fault if i was born under a strange and enigmatic star.

Sometimes i sit on my bed and look to the empty corner and say out loud to myself: "Now a nice antueque chaselonge would fit in very nicely under that window." Other times i fancy that i should live in a large tudor mansion house with as many naked women as you like. When i was a child i would sit on my mothers dressing-table as she polished it. Actualy, i was allowed up onto it with the duster and she'd pour on the cream polish and i'd rub it in. Somehow, in my simple, child's mind, i grew to love the smell of furnitue polish.

None of this is sillyness, smells are what draw us back to our mothers and our gentleness. What a man needs, in my condition, is to go on long, lonley walks thru the empity streets of nite, stepping thru the darkness like a ghost. I get my coat and enter out onto the street.

Apart from a couple of drunks sat on the benches outside the post office, the streets are all but empity, the shops being in compleat darkness. I pick my way along the Banks, occasionally stopping to peer into their dank, dusty interious.

On the second to last Bank, just after the tattoists, there's a shop which still has a lite burning, (it is past midnite). The name Wally Hangman is ritten above the door. The sign says that thay specialise in 'House clearenses, Quick sales, Furnishings and Antiques'. Then i realise why my legs have unconcouslly walk'd me here this nite. I scrunch the bank notes in my pocket and stair in thru the window, my eyes serching fearfully. Thank God, the 'spining wheel', come 'lamp stand', is still here, but as to the

Neon Bible, it is gone. So that roge of an ex-miller, or what ever he fanced himself to be, has returned and snatched it away.

I peer into the back of the shop, checking to see if thay havent by chance got another neon bible tucked away in there, or that the old one hasn't been moved into the back. The interior of that shop is like one long cave full of the worst junk imaginable, but there is definatly no sign of a Neon Bible – it is gone.

From what i can make out in the gloom, one whole side of the shop seems to be dedicated exclusively to the storrige of second-hand mattrisses, that pile upwards towards the cealling, each with a more elaberate and disgusting stain on it than the last. The other side contains a load more junk that Mister Hangman has presumidly perloined from the dead. And this is the man who had the nurve to bang on his window and shoo me, William Loveday, away!

I turne to go, then the antique 'spinning wheel' come 'lamp stand' catches my eye once again. How i could of ritten off such a masterpiece befor, i dont no. It is surly made of the finest oak. A magnificent example that should be the central disply piece of a high quality Museum, not rotting away in this dump. I place my fingertips to the glass and eat it with my eyes. Putting my shoulder to the door, i am surprized to find it open. Theres a tiny point of fire up at the back of the shop and sat hunched over it is the same blown-up old man who threw me out. Mister Hangman looks up when he hears the door, stands and comes rubbing his emaciated hands towards me.

"All rite, cocker?"He shows me his set of yellow, crumbling teeth.

I smile down at him and then look back to the spinning wheel. His pale eyes follow mine

"Ahh, thats a lovely piece youve spotted there, cock. I can see that your a man of decernment."

I nod, slowly. "All those holes in the wood look fussy to me."

"No, thats all in line with the current fashion. Thats what everybody wants these days – real woodworm, not fake! thay prove its true antiqity." He raises his eyebrows at me mysteriously. His actual eyes are such a pale hue of gray that their colour almost blends in with the rest of his skin.

I look away. "Still, its not really my thing."

"Its antique Flemish, very rare." To prove his point, Mister Hangman takes his cap from his head and wrings it out in front of me and stands there noding his head. "I wish i owned such an item myself."

"But its for sale in your shop?" I reason.

"True, that's as mite be, cock. But things arnt all ways what thay seems, are thay? Its for sale rite enough, i grant you, but ive only got it on consignment. Selling it for a Gentleman up town." He looks at me suspiciously, to see if im swallowing this fairy story. I nod at him sarsasticly.

"No, truely, cocker, honestly, id weep for joy if i owned such a thing but that just isn't the case. Tho' it would be wounderful to do so." He adds ruefully.

"Well, i find the whole thing too… French!" And i turne as if to leave, but really i am playing a great and cunning game with this weasel of a shop owner. I see it like this, (viz). One day i will have to buy a house. And a house needs furnishings. I could do far worse than bying this antique, which is sure to increase in value. Yes, i must begin buying furniture and i see no reason why this spinning wheel shouldnt be the first peice in my collection. Then, if i save wisly from my dole money, i can plan – week by week – on bying a dressing-table, a shase-longe and finnaly, some dinning chairs. All tho', stricktly speaking, i have no where to store such furniture, to my mind it makes perfict sence to snap up a bargan whilest it is still alvailabe. Afterall, if a person owns one piece of furniture then the rest is sure to follow. Everybody understands the flock instinct? Well as it is with birds, so it is with furniture.

My shoulder has bearly turned when i hear Mister Hangman give out a little gasp of fear.

"I can give you a very good price on it, cock. That is, if your seriously interested?"

I let him arrest me but instead of looking at the mesmerising 'spining wheel', come 'standered-lamp', i start absently studdying a pile of filthy suit-cases, picking my way thru them and examining the handles for any faults or signs of undue wear.

"No, no, really i was looking for something quite different. Something a little more… African." I turne on him, "have you any Congonese atache cases?"

"What?"

"Have you any Congonese atache cases?"

"No," he says doubtfully, "we aint got nothing like that.

You carnt get quality stuff like you used to. If you carnt see none, then we'er all sold out."

"What about a monky- scull pipe?"

"Pipes? Yes, we've got a pipe. Now where did i see it?"

It is obvious from his reaction that he is trying to hide something from me. There is also something strange about the way that he said 'we'. Suddenly, i am wildly currious to no if his twin brother is hiding somwhere out the back.

"Maybe your brother nos, your twin, maybe you should go fetch him, bring him out here and ask him. In fact there is nothing i would rather see than the pair of you stood shoulder to shoulder." But Mister Hangman ignors my requst entirely and instead fidgets nurvisly with his pale eyes.

"Pipes... Pipes..." he muses, "we used to have some, but not lately."

"You dont seem to understand, im not looking for just any old pipe, what i am after is something quite spasific: a monky-scull pipe. Prehaps your bother can help us, if you'd just go and fetch him."

"I aint got no brother, cock. You said you was looking for a pipe, made out of a monkys head?"

"Yes," i continue, "one with a hollowed out monkys scull, the scull sits in the palm of the monkys paw and you puff at it thru a hole in its forarm."

"His forearm?"

"Its been especially hollowed out."

"No, no, i dont think that we've ever come across one of them."

"But surly you must have? There not that uncommon.

Thay have several in the East G— museum. You must have seen them?"

At last there is a look of confusion on his face.

"Not for sale tho'? thayer just in display cases, rite? We've not seen one, not on the open market, anyways."

"Well, Mister... Hangman – thats your name, isnt it? – that is a disapointment." I try to look pieacingly into his eyes but i carnt on acount that i am lyin and have made the whole wretched story up from beging to end. "Look, what if i give you my address and if you come across one at auction, you could contact me? You no how it is; you dont see one in years and then suddenly a whole shipment comes to lite and you carnt move for simian cranium tobacious."

"I can keep an eye out for you, cocker, but i dont think ile find anything, its all in the museums."

"I assure you that i am prepair'd to pay the highist prices, mister Hangman – if you can just lay your hands on one for me – even double! My father has money."

Mister Hangman disslodges an old bent nail from the floorboards with his boot, picks it up and flings it rattleing into the coal scuttle by the fire place.

"My father was a bissniss man... and all tho' we arnt on speaking terms, im sure that he will loan me whatever sum is nessisarry, upon his realse from gaol." Mister Hangman remains silent. I look at him to see if i should continue. "Sometimes the sculls come with a little cranium lid on top, with a hinge – to stop hot ashes flying out in the wind. The eye sockets are sealed over and inlayed with precious stones, prehaps a pair of rubys or emaralds... Now, how much was it that you wanted for the Flemish spinning wheel?"

"15 nicker to you, cock. Call it a 10'ner – cash!"

I look at him stood there, his tounge playing over his cracked lips.

"Its the only one like it youll ever see. Thats home made, that is. You carnt get the wheels, not like you used to, and if you do find one, thay cost the earth!"

"Why?" i ask scornfully.

"The conversion, cock. thay 'aint gonna be cheep, are thay? Theres fitting the lamp, the lampshade, then wiring it all up – putting a plug on it – it all costs money! Sombody came in earlier and askd if i could keep it for them till the weekend," he looks at me crafterly, "thay put a deposit on it, but to you, for cash, ile let it go."

"I only have a certen amount that i can spair." I say, still carresing the notes in my pocket.

It is true that i have no intention of buying this butchered spinning-wheel for such an exstorshonet sum. No, my money is to pay for the printing of my book. I turn my back, take my cash out and count it cearfully from one hand to the other. If i do indeed buy this Flemish monstroserty i will not be able to breath a word of it to anyone. I will simply pretend that it was given to me or say that i found it in a skip on the way home and i have no idear of its true value, but 10 pounds is out of the question.

"You understand that if you do happen to come across a monky-scull pipe that the paw-stem must still have all of its orginal fur on it, i dont want a bald one! And be sure to check that its little human-like hand still has all its little claws, and also the lid, that too must have its little tuft of hair standing up on top, other wise its of no interest to me." I bang my fist on the pile of old suit-cases for emphersis and Mister Hangman nods hastily in agreement. "becouse i warn you, Mister Hangman – or whatever it is you call yourself – i will not be sold some ramshacle, 1/2-broken, false pipe that carnt be smoked by the devil or his wife!"

I start towards the door, to say goodbye and never returne to this vile, vipers nest ever again. There is no point in it. For people like me – an artist and thinker – an antique spinning wheel converted into a lamp-stand is a rediclious affectaiton.

I stryd puposfuly out thru the door and march back over the banks towards S— Hill.

At the bottom of S— Hill, i stop to rest under a bus shelter. The real question is, is wether such a piece of furniture is an essential purchace or not. But also, i dont feel like just going home with my 90 pounds still intact. It would be terrible not to have spent any of it, and the spinning wheel is definatly an old one. Why, i could probebly sell it tommorow for double the money at the flea market.

I step out from the shelter and look back up the empty High Street. From here i can just see Mister Hangmans shop front, his sign swinging there dismally in the nite. Drizzel has started to fall and a prostitute walks grimicingly towards me. Suddenly, i jump up and set off, snaping my fingers and cursing myself for nearly letting such an obvious bargan slip from my grasp. And all the while i am stareing at Mister Hangmans shimmering sign and berating myself as i walk along:

"What does it matter in the end? One peice of furniture is very much the same as another, isnt it? The way you go on about it youed think that this was the last 'spinning wheel', come 'lamp-stand' on earth. But surly it is best to show caution?"

By the time i get to the shop front, i am having serrious doubts about purchasing the spinning-wheel, and dither about getting thoughly damp in the drizzel. All the while the spining wheel is stood there in the shop window – tempting me – in all its glory.

It is true to say that this is a butiful wheel. Each of the delicate spokes – only 2 or 3 of which are missing – have obviously been hand turned. There is a little seat made from an old peice of plank, thru which 4 rickitty legs have been spliced. The lamp, all tho' not expertly grafted onto the frame, still has a certen charm, there being a large rip in its shade. All in all the contraption has the apperence of 2 unreckonsilable obects being nailed togther, regardless of the unsuitability of the match. But somehow, it is still aluring.

It really is rather mysterious how i could fall in love with such an object, when there are 1000's of other staple requirements in my life which are far more pressing, like the rent for instance.

I gaze at the contraption thru 1/2 closed eyes. The lampshade is a good one too. It would be lovely to sit bellow it on dark winters evenings, open a favorite book and be bathed in its gentle, harmonious glow. My book! – i must pay for the printing of my book! How could i even considor waisting my dole check on such a pile of Flemish junk?

"Go on, walk away, you theif," i harang myself, "theres nothing here for the likes of you! Go home to your little room, masterbate and fritter away your dole money on rent and cigarets. Take indecent photographs of yourself! Pretend that one day you will be great, that one day you will paint a 1000 pictures, but dont you dear pretend that you are worthy of such a magnificent piece of furniture as this!"

Without hesitation i march in thru the shop door.

"About this Flemish spinning-jenny of yours, or whatever it is you call it – ile take it!"

"The 'spinning-wheel', come 'standerd-lamp'? Antique French. 15 pounds that is. Like i said – a real bargain. The only one like it youll ever see. A one off."

I feel my hart sink. "Just now you told me it was 10 pounds."

"That was then."

"I can only aford 10."

"Hmm. Allrite, if you say so. A man of my word! To you, 10 pounds."

"Really, i was after a pipe. I want to buy the monky-scull pipe!"

"I've told you cock, we ain't got one. Try the antique shops along the High Street, maybe thay can help you."

"I want that one!" i shout, pointing indignantly, "i want to buy that monky-scull pipe." I point at an empty display cabbinet which contains nothing but a rustey set

284

of keys and a tray of assorted specticels.

Mister Hangman looks helplessly at the empity cabbinet. "You mean the keys? You want the keys?" He dips his hand in and sturs his fingers thru the rust. At the same time he lifts out the tray of specticuls and offers them to me.

"Honestly, cocker, we aint got no monky-brain pipes."

"All rite. Ile take your wretched spinning wheel! Heres your 10 pounds"

"Its not for sale!"

"You just told me 10 pounds."

"I've changed my mind."

"You carnt do that."

"Its reserved, for a gentleman. I forgot. I've got a sowing machine you can have."

"I dont want a sowing machine, i want that wheel."

"It is a very nice example. A Singer, almost brand new."

I snort and glance around. "This is a junk-shop, isnt it?"

"Quick sales and antiques," corrects Mister Hangman, nervously.

"Call it what you like, but i want that wheel, understand? We had an agreement. I will give you money for it, thats what your here for isnt it – to sell things? So sell it to me! Or dont sell it to me, i dont mind, there are plenty of other shops who'll be happy to take my money!"

All the while i am getting more and more werk'd up. I am aware of being a swine, that i am treating this confused and anxious old man atrociously. But i carnt stop myself, i am in a rage against the world and everyone in it. It is this old mans misfortune that he is the only one available on whom i can vent my speen.

"One moment please," stammers the old man, "Ile just have to make a phone call."

He vanishes. I stare after him and worry weather he is going to call the police and have me arrested. I am just on the point of slipping away when Mister Hangman comes back from behind the screen.

"You can have the spinning wheel, cocker," he says briefly, "but the price will be 25 pounds."

"25 pounds?!"

"Its not expensive at all. A 1st-class spinning wheel like that costs over 20 pounds on its own, and then ther's the conversion."

I count thru my money again. Mister Hangman studdys the notes in my hand.

"25 pounds cash, cock. Take it or leave it!"

I look desperately at the wounderfull spinning wheel. I carnt go back now, i simply will not leave the shop with out it.

"Look, earlyer on i told you about the monky-scull pipes. I was lieing. Theres no such thing, not even in the East G— museum. Ive got 12 pounds here, cash. Ile give you that now, for the wheel."

"I carnt cock, id be robbing myself." but he looks hungryly at the money in my hand.

'Its not too late, i don't have to buy this rubish, i can still back out,' i think to myself.

"Just a moment, please," says Mister Hangman and vanishes behind the painted screen again.

The best that could happen is that he refusses to sell this

useless spinning wheel to me. I must be ready to leave the shop quickly. I position myself by the door. Then Mister Hangman comes back.

"I'm a fool to myself but times is hard. You can have it for 15."

"Well…" i say hesitatingly.

"If you hang onto it, in a few years your'll be able to double your money."

I hand over the bills and whatch my money disapearing out of my hands and into his knitted, theaving mitts. He counts it out, licking at his browned finger-tips, then rolls it away into his back pocket.

Outside, i look at the useless lamp. Karima will be back from Amsterdam tomorow, my books will have been printed and the tecknitions will be wanting their money. And i no that i must now smash this 'atrocity against good taste' against the wall and leave its pices lying here in the street.

64

Some Famous Ice Skateing

IN THE MORNING, the street is covered in snow and the outside tiolet is frozen over. I walk to my mothers and meet Karima there. All thru dinner she tells my mother of her wounderfull life in Holland and my mother listens and nods politely, whilest i listen darkly.

"I went skateing on the ice on the cannals. It was just outside my front door."

"That must have been nice."

"It was butiful."

"Did you meet any nice people?"

"I met lots of interesting people. Artists and street performers."

I look at her angerly. "You carnt skate!"

"Yes i can, Frank taught me."

"Frank who?"

"A man i met there. There was a group of artists. It was his friends barge that i liv'd on."

"You diddnt live on a barge," i correct her, "you stayed on a boat whilest you were on holliday."

"I did live on a barge and every morning i had to lite the stove and then go to the bakers to buy 'krentebrood'."

I look at her small mouth talking.

"Krentebrood," she repeats, "its Dutch for current bread. I learned lots of Dutch words. Thats what we all ate for brakfast when we we'er in Amsterdam, living on the barge."

"Listen to me," i say slowly, holding her with my angryist eyes, "you have never ever liv'd on a barge in Amesterdam and no matter what pathetic fairy tail you tell to people, it will never ever be true, you will always be a lier."

"Yes i have," she retorts, "I liv'd there with Frank and he

taught me how to ice skate."

After dinner Karima goes to sleep on the sofa and i go upstairs to paint. In the middle of the nite i come down and make her march home. I force her to wake up, put on her shoes then push her out into the ice cold nite.

"I want to sleep here. Why carnt we sleep here? Im too tired to walk, it'll take for ever."

"It is only 3 miles into town, we'll be in by 2."

"Can i stay with you?"

"No."

"Why not?"

"I want to go to sleep on my own, in my own bed."

All the way she limps along in the snow wimpering. I have to forse her to walk. At the top of W— W—'s Hill i have to stand in the ice for 10 whole minits waiting for her to catch up. She is just a dark speck moving inperseptably thru the snow at the bottom of the hill. It is biting cold and still she wants to drag this out till the bitter end. I have to go all the way back down to the bottom of the hill and drag her by the arms up the icy slope. We get 1/2 ways to the top where i can listen to her no more and push her into a snow drift.

"Come on then, lets see some of your famouse ice skating!" I pull her up onto her knees and drag her across the ice and tarmack. I swing her round in a wide arc and let her go. She starts out laughing, nurvis like, in her throat, but then she has to cry. I leave her sitting on her arse in the road and stryed off into the nite. Soon she will come scampering after me.

65

The Roughs

I WALK DOWN to the cave in the morning. My books have arrived in 2 large cardboad boxes. I carry them down from the entrance hall and rip the lids off, close my eyes, dip in and feel the covers with my fingertips. I lift the books to my nose, sniff at them, then open my eyes – ah, such a wounderful, fresh book. To breathe it, flicking thru the magical pages, writen by me -William Loveday, pheonix of the firery ashes, who has returned from the foul death delt him by the Acadamy to rise once again and destroy them.

It is time to sit back and read the lines, to admire the shapes of all the little letters – perfect. One word follows directly after the other. Then another and another. You turne the page and it carrys on rite the way thru to the end of the book. Sentences and paragraphs pile up, just like real. And all the time my attack on the hypocrites of art is blistering, harsh and relentless. Socking blows to the left and the rite and finally an upper cut, rite on the jaw! I look to my book mesmerized as Karima makes tea, and i pore in a big glug of rum.

Sometimes, i wonder where i would go if Karima was in fact to be murdered. And the answer is of course America, but what would i do in such a place and who would i no? I would, no doubt, be wretched, penniless, and as alone there as i would be here. And even if i was to meet some young, muscular German girl, wouldnt it always be the case that as we were making love i would chance to look down into her blue eyes and flushed cheeks and see the horrible rotting head of Karima the Turk grinning up at me? If i am not really alive (and in many ways i am not) then it must follow that neither are my fellow human beings, which means that its small beer to kill them, for how can the dead die? To be a true artist i must become a forever moving target and shun all lifes gifts and trinkets, but why must i also become a murderer? Isn't to become one of the mad enough? Isn't God satisfied that he has already made me a leper?

As i skim on thru the pages i suddenly become awear of an ocassional mistake in the text. Then another and another. I turn back to the front and start reading again. My whole book is full of errors, nothing is as i wrote it. This damnable book has cossed me every penny i own and on every page there is a glaring error! I read quickly on thru the pages in rising panic – staring from the open book to Karimas gormless, self-satisfied expression.

"Its full of mistakes," i scream at her, "you've wasted all of my time and money that i havent got! These aren't my pages – these are the roughs – what about my corrections? – I gave you my corrections for them to put in, but thay've

291

printed the roughs!"

She shrugs at me and looks away at her stollen cat.

I swear at her horribly, throw the box to the ground and rush out of the cave. I run thru the snow not even pretending to let her chase me or catch me up.

66

2 Specials

I WALK DOWN the High Street, across R— Bridge and stair down into the swirlling current that passes bellow. It seems vastly unfair that becouse of my fearlessness and love of buti, that i, William Loveday, should be singled out for humiliation.

I pace back and forth, peering between the iron girders, positioning myself in the exact same spot where i imagine that the lady from the taxi office must have stood the nite she climbed up onto the balarstrade, then gulping the nite air, lifted her skirt and plunged into the inky waters bellow. I knock the snow off the rail and whatch it drop away to be drunk by the sliding water. I lean rite over and peer into the darkness benith the arch of the bridge. There are corpses down there, the skin of their legs shreading thru their nilon stockings, waving in the current like the tendrals of strange sea erchins.

A voice inside me tells me to throw myself in after her and frolic with her corps. I scare myself with discriptions of the inside of her mouth, the extent of decay she will have undergone, and how i will have to kiss her breasts and cunt after they have been scuffed and gouged by drift wood. The reason her body hasnt yet come up is on account of the trecherious under-currents and the fact she hasnt yet fill'd with gas.

Since reading of the fat ladys suiside, i have often been drawn to vistiting the bridge after the pub chucks out. Instead of walking thru the back ally to Karimas Trolls cave, i come down here to stand on the esplanade in the towering nite and listen to the sounds of the river bellow.

The street lites of the oppersit bank lite up the whole westen sky with a hiddious orange glow and its as if the whole, detestable city is being clensed by fire. Not that i necessarily wish this to be the case, as there is an awful lot to be said for the small minds and petty prejudices of our dull and obedient towns folk. Besides, it is easy to forget that all people have the same needs, feelings and desires as myself and that i am not the only sole who contemplates suiside, murder and death, which of course i no to be true, but somehow refuse to accept.

If i had something large and weighty to hand, or even a small rock, i would toss it off the bridge so's that i could hear it splash in the water, then imagine it sinking down into the black mud below. Twise already this week i have leaned over the edge and tryed to will myself to jump.

I here voices coming: the 2 Special Constables – whos beat this is – stroll past. No doubt on the look out for further potencial suisides. I pretend to be taking the eveing air and nonchenatly smoking a cigereat. As thay pass, i strain to listen. If thay have any undesclosed information pertaining to the missing fat lady, then they are keeping schtum. Thay are apparently talking about some cat that stoll a pice of the Sargents cheese.

Once the Specials are out of site, i again crain my head over the side. It really is quite cold standing here in the snow. On one side of the bridge there is a green lite, and on the other a red lite, other than that it is impossable to discern anything. Then i here a small cry coming up from the black water. I listen out in between a lull in the trafic and there it goes again – most definatly this time – a cry for help. Coming up from under the great arch. I peer into that inky darkness. For a moment i imagine that i can see the gloomy outline of a small cutter dragging in the current, or prehaps, the outstratched arm of a corps braking surfiss. But when i wipe the tears from my eyes with the backs of my hands and next look, there is nothing, only silence.

67

The Nite befor William Loveday Throws a Large Trunk from the Balastrades of R— Bridge.

THIS MORNING at 10 o'clock, i stood benith the snow covered trees in the park, whatching the students arriving at the Acadamy for their morning lessons. When the last students had finnaly trickled in, i did a small circit of the field then pulled up, once again, in the shadow of the Accadmy. Down below, large crains pushed up into the sky and a tug-boat came past in miniture.

Last nite, i dreamt that the flesh had been stripped from my ankles and that i walk'd on the feet of a skellinton. In my dream, i realised that quite soon i would be unable to walk at all and would have to make my way about the world in a wheel chair. How had such an injustice been done to me? I staired at the white chalky bones that protuded from my flapping trouser bottoms. There was absolutly no flesh left below my calfs and instead of tendons, thin steel wires linked my foot-bones to those of my toes. This hopless emtyness was all that remained of the once wounderfuly musseled calfs and feet of William Loveday.

In just such a way my ritefull place at the Acadamy has been taken from me. I alone have been singled out like a bad stone and cast aside as defective. Somone else now sits where i once sat, eats my food and spends my money. It is thay, not me, who stand nonchenotly, talking with their mouths full and walking from room to room, confidently looking down at their well fleshed feet. Others laugh and joke and are reassured in their assperations by the tutors who, rather than admit that it is in fact thay who have failed me, concider me, William Loveday, to be the failer. So, i am left to stand here and walk alone on the feet of a skellington.

My mind has been full of many strange thoughts these last days, most of them relating to feelings and actions that are not permissable. On several occassions i have dremt that i am chasing a girl-child thru the nite in order to have sex with her. At first, i was stood in front of a butchers shop window, stairing in at the red meat that was hacked and piled high to the cealing. Above my head there was a terrible cat-o-walling. I lookt up and instead of dead rabits hanging on the hooks there were live cats. i turned to my unnown companion stood beside me: a dark haired girl of about eleven pouting at me in a most sultry fashion. It was then that i realised that i was dreaming and could do whatever i wished to her. She too seemed to come to this same realisation for she suddenly headed off up the street. I at once gave chase. Paradoxicly, it was this realisation – that i was in fact dreaming – that forst me to wake up and robbed me of the power of possessing her in my dream. And then came the nite that i dreamt that i caught this girl-child and was having wounderfull sex with her, only to awaken and discover that it was Karimas body clinging benith me and not that of some unnown virgin. I imediatly rolled off and detemined, once and for all, to banish this woman from my life and sleep alone.

Why do i dream that i walk with a skellingtons feet? Some people will no doubt say that my dream reflects my inner mental state and that i have in fact removed myself from the comforts, friendship and the warm glow that comes from sitting at the feet of our glorious tutors. Thay will no doubt add that i have robbed myself of a carrier in the arts, and that for my foolishness, arogence and obstenancy, i not only deserve to be ostrisized, but thoughly smashed and made to walk on bare bones.

It is true that i have taken the path of the mad over the path of the sain, but i have been given no choice in the matter, it has been forst upon me by my concionse. I have acted thru deep instinkt. The instink that an animal has to rip out the throat of a sheepherd rather than cringe in an iron cage, or gnor off its own leg to escape from a hunters trap. This may sound dramatic but that does not make it a joke or untrue.

Yes, I have chosen madness over sainty, becouse in my chest still beats a hart that loves trees and freedom and hates buildings and burocracy. A hart that simply loves and refuses to scrape befor success. It is not nessisary to remind me that a cearing man dose not set fire to his girlfriends hair, then maim himself and fall to the floor sobbing on the nite that his alcholic father is locked up in prison, but if you just tried walking in my skin for one day then maybe you would find that my self control is impecable.

I stair up at the Acadamy buildings, no one opens a window, hails me with a joviel hello, or bids me to enter and participate. I look also to the gray steps, but the doors dont fling open, nor a tutor walk out across the snow covered grass, looking first to his left and then to his rite, his hands in his trouser pockets, then coming up to me shame faced, ask my forgiveness. No, no one notices me. There are no familier faces, and any that i do no are hidden in prayer, bowed down in their acurssed studios.

I am about to leave this place when i see a young Indian girl playing alone on the swings at the other end of the park. It is Netka, the girl Karima befriended.

Karima wants us to have children together but how could i ever have children? Me, who is not good enough or holy enough and has only the feet of a skellington. And what if i was to have children, what terrible curse handed down by my family would hunt me down and destroy me? Wouldnt i have to leave them and hate them, as my father has left and hated me? And besides, how could i have children with a woman whos hair i have set alite and who despises me? What type of life is it for a child in a world filed with Mister Bennits as the custodieans of art? How can anyone think of life and enjoyment when all around us death is screaming from the bushes?

No, isnt it better instead to become friends with death and help death, rather than to bring new life into this world? I look down at my skellingtons feet, that i have hidden in my old hob-nailed boots. Only the white bones of my ankels show where my trouser leg is too short. The Indian girl plays with a small stick she has found. Voices of other children drift over towards me, shouting and throwing snowballs, she alone is silent. Who no's if my unatural desires are true or just romantic notions brought on by the humiliation i have suffered at the hands of my abuser?

I walk aimlessly towards her, telling myself that i am not really heading in her direction at all, it just so happens that she sits between me and my destination. I pass quite close, then circle back some 2 hundred yards to sit on the benches overlooking the ici river. Without Karima here to intoxicate her, this little girl will not speak with me. She fears me and even if Karima was here she would snub a man with no flesh on his feet.

It is then that i notice that i am not alone on the field. There is another, an older man, whatching Netka in the playground. I diddnt notice him at first on acount that his drab cloaths blended into the trees and shrubbery in the background. But when he passes in front of the red swings i can see – even from this great distance – that he has blackened and dirty finger nails. He turnes his scull-like face towards me, but it is too far away to see his small eyes. Only his hat is visable, then he self conciously hides his hands in his raincoat pockets. I whatch this disgusting pervert stoop to the ground, pick a stick from the snow and hold it out to the Indian girl. He must call to her – tho' i here nothing – for she looks up and scampers to him. The man then takes her small brown hand in his and leads her away from the swings towards the bramble bushes behind the derelict church. I stand, whatching them in numb fear, already thay are dissappearing into the mass of undergroath. I start to run, but no matter how furriously i kick my feet out in front of me i seem to be getting nowhere in the thick snow. Twise i fall and have to pick myself up. I feel the heels of my shoes thudding into my buttocks as i struggle, as if in a dream, to get to the swings. I must overtake this abductore, grasp him by the lapels and kill him befor this 'kindly uncle' breaths his foul breath into her pure, childs body. I arrive at the swings breathless. There is no sign of them. A small blond haired boy comes out from the derilict graveyard and i ask if he has seen a little Indian girl. I speak in gasps.

"She was playing… On her own… By the swings… She left with a man… Just now! You must have seen her?… You passed them, a little Indian girl in a pink coat… Where did thay go?… In what direction?" The boy looks at me curriously, then slowly backs away. I take a step towards him but he turnes and runs off.

"Im trying to help her!" I shout after him. The other children, playing snowballs, are also too fritened and refuse to speak to me: their savyoir.

I rush into the bramble bushess, trying to find the path thru. I serch up and down a row of impenitrable hedges, but

300

there is no footpath. I have to raise my arms in front of me, to protect my face, and wade thru. My whole body is attack't, one bramble bush cutting my face quite badly.

On the other side of the hedge is the derelect church, sat amongst the trees. It is a very silent and mysterious place, rotting like an old tooth in the snow. I pick my way down a path which runs up by the side of the building. There is a smashed up tomb there with a piece of iron railing sticking out of it. I peer down into the darkness below. The snow has fallen in there. I pull the iron railing and brandish it like a spear. It is ici cold in my grasp and my teeth chatter with fear. I jab at the air, testing its metal. Suddenly, i hear myself shouting. "You touch her and ile fucking kill you!" I scream. All tho' i shout as loud as i can, my voice sounds muted in that snow covered place. I dash on. Behind another broken tomb i find an old matrice which somone has recently lain on. Just at its head is a childs red shoe. I serch in the surrounding bushes but there is no broken body been flung there. 7'ral times i stumble and fall, every second expecting to happen across his male body, heaving on top of the little Indian girl. I will leap upon his back, pile his brains in for him and kill the robbed child that lives within him and which forst him to commit this sin against life.

"Ile get you, you old pervert!" I scream, but my voice comes back to me, quitely from the snow covered stones and earth. "If you so much as touch one hair on her head, ile kill you!" And i bring the iron bar smashing down onto the top of a grave stone, with such violence that it leaps from my fingers. I jump back in pain and stand there, holding my poor, injured hand. There is a noise behind me and suddenly all the deamons of hell are upon me.

"Im sorry, God. I never wanted to fuck your children! Please God, i am disgusting! To be born a man, to have mans filthy desires! To have been corrupted at the hands of perverts! To have the thumb print of a 46 year old man on my childs spine. To have been changed from a child into a hunter of death!"

My whole body shakes in fear of actually finding her small corps laying befor me, her head twisted unaturally to one side, her once dark lips, pale and blue, her cheek smeared with spittle. But i find no one. In truth, thay are proberbly within the church, or he is violating her rite now below ground in one of the hidden morsoleiums. I push open the great doors of the church and stand there in the entrance way, stareing into the impossable darkness, the stench of stale piss choking me. He has spirited her away to his vile, warlocks nest, but i am too feared to enter.

I turne back down the side of the building, forse myself between the burnt out wreck of a car and the wall of the church and run out on to N— Road. There is a huge stream of traffic passing there, i dash strait across, almost being hit by a car, and then decend onto the High Street.

I find a call box, lift the reciver and dial 999. I tell the police everything… Of my obsevations… Of the strange disaperence of the little Indian girl, Netka… Of the matrice and the shoe.

"He is with her now, as we speak. You must go to the church, now! You must protect her." All the while they just

302

keep asking me my name.

"Gus." I tell them

"Your sirname, sir?"

"There is no time for this, there is a child being raped, you must save her!"

"Yes, the quicker that you tell us your name, sir, the quicker that we will be able to respond to your call. Now your full name, please?"

"Claudious, Gus Claudious. You must hurry."

"And your address?"

"I dont have an address, just send somone to the chuch yard and save her tiny sole!" and i replace the resiver.

I come out of the phone box and sit down on the benches there. It is rong to touch children.

68

Deep Snow

ALL DAY i move from one set of benches to the next. Sometimes, heading up to R— to look off the edge of the bridge. Shortly befor dusk a freezing fog rolls in off the river and i see a Japanese girl entering the second hand bookshop on the High Street. Quickly, i run to catch up, cross the street and stand, stareing in at the window. She moves thru the shop, comes back into view, reaches up and takes a large, oversized art book into her lap and sits on the step to read it. Yes, it is her. She turnes the pages and seems to examin the pictures with her small, butiful fingers. She rites something down in a brown note book. That note book is what gives her away, it is the same as Kajii's — she is the sister of the lemon theif!

My instinkt is to rush into the bookshop and arrest her on the spot, but instead i force myself to waite out hear in the ici fog where i can ambush her in the darkening streets.

As i studdy her she shudders slitely. Is it possable that she feels my eyes piercing her body? Her face is flushed, not that i can actrually see her face but her ears have the apperence of blushing.

After over 1/2 an houre, Deep Snow replaces the book she has been carressing and disapears from view. As the shop door opens i shrink back, then — when i am sure it is truly her — boldly step from the shadows. It is quite amusing to see the expression on her face when she realises that it is me, William Loveday, who holds the door open for her. I smile at her, her small fingers are again disserpearing up the sleeve of her kimono.

"Hello," i speak.

"Hello."

"I am Kajji's friend."

"Yes."

"Do you rember me?"

Deep snow looks to the ground and answers 'yes' again, in a small voice.

"Is it really you, Deep Snow?"

Deep snow looks up but says nothing, her fingers absently pulling her kimono closed round her body.

"Ive been looking for you. I mean since we last met. I wanted to see you." I step closer to her, trying to smell her hair.

"I was buying a book, for my brother."

"For your brother?"

"Yes."

"Did you buy it?"

"No, i copied some of it down for him."

"Copying down what some idiot has copied down from some other idiot?… You realise that everyone is just copyng somebody else and that there isnt an original thought in the whole of Christenden? Not that orginality counts for anthing, mind. What counts is not novelty but to be authentic!"

"Yes."

Deep Snow has agreed with me. Quickly, I rush on with my marvilous thoery. "After all, the old masters copied those who went befor them to learn and take forwad the cause of art. Thay wernt woried about petty fashion or impressing the mindless, were thay?"

I realise that i am frightening her and remind her who i am, (viz). A student, late of the Acadamy, and a good freind of her brother Kajii's. But it is not nessisary, as she recognises me already, and i am rite, her name is Deep Snow. Maybe it is becouse of her smallness that i do not feel shy. Whatever, for some reason – that i can not explain – it seems that she is already mine, that she has been promised to me, even that she has been promised to me prehaps in a dream. I take her by the arm and lead her a little way along the street, thru the slush.

"How is Kajji, your brother?"

"He is ill. It is this weather. Our mother wishes him to come home."

"To Japan?"

"Yes, that would be best for him. But first he must finish his studdys."

"Studdying isnt important." I tell her forcfully, "doing things is what counts. You are a riter? Or have ritten a book?"

"No."

"I just thought... Well every college student, tutor, dustman and nobody is writing some sort of novel these days, arnt they?" I draw her close to me and gulp at the air that surrounds her and has prehaps just come from her mouth. Like her silent brother, Deep Snow also declines to answer my questions. I look sideways at her face and want to bite at it.

"We can go for a drink. Then i can tell you my story. Of course i am not really a riter, not like these other charlatens. Too many books have been riten with too much cleverness by too many people. Im not one of those. My story actualy happened, rite here in our home town – to me!"

I lead her into the side door of the G— V—'s Public House, find a seat in the back bar then leave Deep Snow and order 2 small dark beers (which is all i can aford). I wait paicently for the publican to pour our wretched drinks, which he does in slow motion. I am afraid that when i returne Deep Snow will be gone. She will certanly have ample time to slip out thru the side door, nip up the ally and merge with the crowds on the street. All the while the publican nods to himself and i look into the gleaming dome of his head as he prays at the pump. Finnaly, he shuffles over in his carpet slippers and places the 2 misserly little drinks on the wet bar. I give him the money and then have to waite another age as he trys to remember the prices and add them on the till. In exasperation i ask him to please hurry up. At this, he turnes and holds me with a very stern gaze.

"You can leave if you want to. Heres your money back!"

And he goes to tip the beers down the sink. I have to grasp his rists and appologise emphatickly. To tell him that i am sorry, im in a rush, on account of my friend who is waiteing in the back bar. I stammer to a finish, to put my point across.

"Well, they will just have to waite, wont they!"

He stands there stareing at my mouth, his head lowered and his yellow, false teeth showing, then he turnes on his heel, rings up the bill and slams my wet change down on the bar. I scoop up the coppers then carry the beer thru to the back bar.

Deep Snow is sat there waiteing for me, her hands on her lap, just her fingers showing. I put our beers down and tell her my poem.

"I've call'd it 'The Whore Under the Cherry Blossoms in Spring Time'." I look to see her reaction but there is none. "I have another title if you dont like that one. How

307

about 'The Sufferings of a Young Man in Puberty?' Or 'Man Crying on his Back in the Snow'?" Again, she just looks at me from the deep-black discs of her eyes and i feel myself beeing drawn into her sole. It is apparent that we have sheared many life times together, that we have been lovers many times over, over 1000's of years. Looking down at my own large vainy hands i returne to my poem.

"My story ends with a boy, a youth, much like me, or let us say your brother, lying on his back in the snow on a hillside at midnite, overlooking a twisted iron gray river in the begining of march. Bellow, lineing the N— Road, the cherry blossoms are exploading in full bloom. It is one of those feendish 'false springs'. We had just such a one Easter Sunday 1974: The morning broke as a butiful sun-fill'd day, the birds were building their little nests – hidden away from the prying eyes of man – children were already out playing on the new grass – the boys in shorts and the girls in their summer dresses – and just like in my story, the cherry blossoms were in full bloom, thick wads of pink blossoms dripping from their bowed heads. In short – spring was upon us! But by 2 'o clock that same day it was blowing a full scale blizzard. I was only 14 but got quite drunk at the T— R— Public House at U— and had to go and lie in the snow and throw up. So, you see that there is a lot of falsity in nature as well as in man. This 'false spring' i mentioned, had the effect that all the blossoms were knocked to the ground, carpeting the snow like blud."

Deep Snow does not so much as take a sip from her drink. I lift my glass but she only stairs down at her fingertips, which poke coyly from her cuffs. She arranges them in her butiful lap, which i want to curl upon and rest my head.

"Like i say, our hero lies there on his back, the spining snow flakes crashing down out of the blackness of the nite into his open eyes, the tears cursing down his pale cheeks. He lies sobing, crying out to God to either raise him up or come down out of his stinking heaven and smash him; to have the guts to show his cowadly face or just kill him outrite. He is 21 years old to the day and forces himself not to blink on punishment of death.

"'Where is your Jesus, you scoundrel!' He shouts, 'Show me your wounds! Let me kiss them with my tounge and place my hand into his open side. Not till then will i belive, not till then. Otherwise… oh, just throw me to the dogs, you old torturer!"

"He writhes there in the snow, the icy wind penitrating his paper thin shirt, kissing his neck and slipping down his trousers. In short – finding his most sensitive and delicate parts.

"He crys out once again, ernistly beseaching God to show him forgivness, or to let him die of cold."

I fold my arms and look pointedly at my Japanese sweethart.

"Thats how the story ends," i tell her. She nods. There is silence.

"Do you want to no how it begins?"

"Yes." She says very quietly.

"Well, it all starts when he – our hero – is still only a nieve boy, say 16 years of age and just out of skool. His only

309

dream, since he was a small child, was to become an artist in the wounderful tradition of Vincent van Gogh, and like his hero Vincent, he beliv'd in an artstic community, a brother-hood and sister-hood of like minded artists who would paint to enrich their soles and show to the world their vission of pain and buti."

At this point i reach over and take one of Deep Snows small hands in mine. "The Japanes love van Gogh, becouse he understands colour and saw with Japanese eyes!" i tell her. And a flicker of a smile shows in the corners of her mouth.

"Anyway, this nieve boy – who we last saw laid there prostrate in the snow – painted pictures all of his childhood, holding onto his one dream and hope – to somehow become part of the human race. That, or join the ranks of the mad. His life, incedently, had already been one long string of adversity. He had been bullied, mentally and sexualy, in a manner that would shock the devil. As a child he could not read, he could not rite, he could not do mathmatics. He was bullied by his father, his brother and his teachers. The one thing he could do was draw and it is drawing that he instinctively feels will save him. Why? Becouse creativity rules above all other things. And drawing is the hight of all creativity, becouse it is the making of marks in the manner of God! But when this poor, 'raw youth' is old enough to finnaly quit skool, his application to the local art college is turned down becouse of the arogence and the falsity of its tutors. Thay sit in their ivory towers of office and refuse to even look at his werk, becouse he is what our socity describes as 'backwards' and no one feels the least sympathy for our hero, becouse he is not rifind in a way that amuses the librals and isnt quite prepaired to worship at the alter of success as the consevatives demand. Also, he lacks qualifications. As if exam results make an artist!" i spit. "And as for the comunists, well were dose that leave God?"

"His father – a self made man, tyranical dandy and unmitigated shit of quite devistating preportions – left home when our hero was but 6 years old and has never once spoken a friendly word of encouragment to his son since. As our hero grew into a young man the father still catgoricaly refussed to speak to his son or help him in any way what-so-ever! (It should be made clear at this point that this so call'd father of his is nothing but a sensualist, a drunked, a buggerist and a womaniser!)"

"So this is the metal of the father, but what of his mother, surely, his own mother will look out for him, you say? Well, she is a short dark haired woman, who in her youth used to do all sorts of wild things, like ride bycycles and run for busses, but now she has grown powerless becouse she is… Powerless. This ever-suffering woman has neglected to divorce her womanising husband out of fear, cowardness, lack of self worth and a missguided sence of loylty. When her boys were still meer children this lack of 'action', on her part, caused her body to contract terbuculoses."

At the word terbecculosses, Deep Snows eyes flash.

"I no your brother, Kajii, also has this desease, so you can imagine the suffering of these little ones. Whilest their mother is laid up in the hospital, their father is away, involved in all sorts of unspeakable dissapations and thay are left to fend for them selfs. This man, this father; her husband, this alcolic or 'spinless shit!' - as one of his misstresses once described him – tho' absent and living forty miles away in London, still rules the family with an iron fist. How did he manage this? Not thru love, thats for certain, but thru absolute fear. His wife and children are terrified of him. And tho' our young hero dosnt belive in God (the children resived no spiritual guidance at home or skool), he still gets down on his knees every nite and prays for his father to die or be kill'd in one of his drunken car crashes and to never returne again! When the father does actually bother coming home, it is only to keep his quaking, un-fathered, un-lov'd children on their toes. To terrorise his quaking wife and go 'ghosting' about the house, smashing up their property and telling them that thay are all going to go to hell!"

"This isnt all that our 'raw youth' has to suffer. He also, as i think i have already mentioned, has an elder brother, who takes delite in merclylessly bulling him from day one of his childhood. Unlike our hero, this elder brother is an incredible achiver who can read, rite, has all manner of qualifiucations tucked under his belt, and is destined for greatness. In short – he has a brain the size of a dustbin!"

I take my hand from Deep Snows lap and stroke her black hair, which feels stiff and unaturel. "This big brother is now -even as we speak – something of a star at one of the more prostigious art skools in London." A purple shadow

312

flickers across her face. Could it be that Deep Snow no's my brother? This is impossable. I look again at her face but there is no trace of the expression that a moment ago seemed so real.

"Anyway, unable to gain entry into the local art college (thay refused to even so much as look at his drawings and paintings), our hero, this 'raw youth', or 'nieave youth,' if you must call him that, is sent to the dockyard to chip stone for a living, and thats supposed to be the end of him. But it isnt, becouse once there, he doesnt chip stone at all but instead sits in the tea-hut and draws for all his worth. Every houre of every day he takes up his pencils and models himself on his hero: Vincent van Gogh. Thats how he forces his way into the Acadamy – not by fawning to art skool tutors or creeping after exam results but by drawing pictures!"

I say these last words to Deep Snow with pointedness and bitterness. But no matter how hatefull i feel towards the world, towards the Acadamy and towards her own sick brother, Kajji, Deep Snow still looks at me without expression. Or possabley there is some kind of an expression, maybe tenderness plays around the corner of her lips. But i do not cellerbrate, becouse this so call'd smile of hers mite just as easerly be a mocking smile.

"This nieve boy, or 'imbersilic child', as his detractors dub him, really dose belive that if he can just escape the confines of the dockyard and somehow claw his way into the world of art, then he will at last be united with his brothers and sisters in destiny.

"But that is not what lies in store for our intrepid hero. When, on that first dysmel day he climbs the gray steps of the Acadamy, there is no great meeting of harts and minds. Instead of brotherly and sisterly love, of recognition and warm claps on the back, he encounters turned shoulders and averted eyes. In the dockyard he was held in suspission for his aloofness and love of art. In the Acadamy he is ostrisized for his commonness and idiotic love of figrative painting over fashionable abstraction. He has, if you like, walk'd from the world of dulluards into a vipers nest of snobery and deceipt. Far from beliving in the power of life thru painting, these pretenders want to become 'career artists' of the lowist kind. Thay do not give creedence to the brave life of Vincent van Gogh. (It was van Goghs biography incedently, that our heros mother had read to him when he was still an illiterate skool boy, it was that book that set him on his path thru life, seeking art and justice.)"

At this point the Japanese girl coughs violently. She clears her throat, sips the smallist amount of beer possable from her glass then addresses me.

"What do you mean by justice?"

"I dont no. Maybe i dont mean justice, maybe i mean integrity."

"What do you mean by integrity?"

I look at her. "I mean that a tutor should do his best for a student, not try to destroy him." Deep Snow looks down at her hands and i carry on.

"There are 3 threads to my poem and thay weave togther like this: His father, a vulga, self made bissness man,

314

we've already met, his most famous saying being: 'It is the presentation that counts!' Next, his cowardly tutors, who sacrafice him for the sake of their morgages, and lastly his girlfriend who, when we are first introduced to her, is a lowly fashion student who takes our heros beliths in art and sells it in the market place like so much meat. Her sayings are 'I only have 15 cigarets left. Thats 1 for now, 12 for this evening, 1 for bed time and 1 for in the morning, so i carnt offer you one becouse i dont really have any left.' And, 'I want sex and i only want it with you!' and 'I want to be a tiny person , so's i can live in your pocket.' And… well, thay are all either about herself or money… Anyway, this girlfriend and this 'raw youths' father, shear the same birthday and both of them are obsses'd with status, and both of them – in their own little way – are responsible for our hero lien there on his back in the snow, his shirt-front smeered with blud, crying to God. But thats getting ahead of ourselfs. Befor we talk about that, we have to mention that as a young man, our hero was visiting his mother on his birthday – trying to scrape together a few pennys – when something came to pass that is another turneing point in our sarga. (At this time our hero was still studdying at the Acadamy, tho', becouse of his fathers elivated position the council refussed to pay him a subsistance grant and his father, in turne, also refussed to support him finansherly). It was whilest sitting, drinking his birthaday tea with his mother that his father rang from his 'mistresess' flat in London (a room that his father rented at the R—'s hotel). Our hero ansewed the phone, but it appears that his father was so drunk that he could bearly talk. The gist of it was this: his 'misstress' (a term his mother allways used for her husbends girlfreinds), had beaten him to a bludy pulp, thrown all of his hand-talored Edwardian suits out of the window, then locked them both inside her flat and swallowed the key.

"It may seem increadible, but this man who behaved like a tyrent to his own family was but a whipped puppy in the presence of this 'misstress' of his. (It should be noted that on one occassion, whilest stuck in trafic at P— Circuss, this same woman got out from behind the drivers wheel of the car, ripped the wing mirror clean off with her bare hands, then belted him round the head with it, leaving a 3 inch gash above his left eye). The said car was apparently a 'love gift' from our heros father to this gentle and cearing, proffessional call-girl.

"So, our 'raw youth' is stood there on the other end of the phone, listening to his drunken father take a thurrer beating from this 'misstress' (who is, in fact a pettite Indian). Within seconds his father is punched to the ground, the resiver ripped from his grasp and this 'misstress' comes on the line to wish our hero a happy birthday. 1stly, she enqires of our heros build and looks, befor inviting him to dinner with her at the R—'s Hotel. 'I have no money,' stammers our raw youth, 'my father has money, but he dosn't give me any, not a penny.' (Incedently, as you can tell, all tho' our hero is ashamed of this fact of poverty and neglect, he is still somhow proud that he gains no personal benifit from his fathers vulga and ostentashious wealth).

'Dont you worry about money,' says his fathers whore, 'ive got plenty of that!'

"Next up our hero is at the R——'s Hotel being fed on revolting cavvia and primed for dissapation by this Indian harlot. This is how it happens: The moment she gets him into her rooms, our hero crawls into the quilted bed and fains sleep. She undresses him, gets in behind him and he smells her heavy, vulger perfume. In the early houres of the morning he is awakened by her dark fingers fondling him from behind, pulling his cock back between his legs and indecently wanking it. He is excited becouse, as an abused youth, he has been trained in nocternal assults on his body. His mind tells him that it is wrong and evil, but this is exactly what the devil in him craves. But all of these 'sweet feelings' are shattered when she suddenly flings down his penis and leaps upon him, slaming her rock hard groin into his. I told you that she was a proffessional call girl? A woman of the nite who lov'd no man, only the money and power that she could extract from them? Naturally, she ceared nothing for the hart of this meer skool boy, who she has toyed with and corrupted out of a mixture of boredom, curiosity and hatred of his father.

"And where was his father, the brave father whos monica was 'spinless little shit'? – Drunk in some other house of debauchery, whilest his youngest son was raped in his own hotel suit!

Did i mention that his father had meanwhile promised his whore the very house our heros mother still liv'd in? It was the last possetion that he haddnt drunk and pissed away. But try as he mite he could not perswade his little wifey to leave, or manage to disslodge her in any way. No matter how uncomfortable he made it for her to stay. He had the electrisity cut off! The teliphone cut off! He refused to pay the heating bills! But even without heating, food or money, still his obedieant little wifey stayed put. Meanwhile, the Indian whore grew ever more virrerlent, demanding that the 'spinless little shit' devorse his wifey imediatly and instate her as queen of the manor. 'But sweetness of my life, if i devorse my wife then she will get everything – the whole house will be given to her – every bit of colateral that i possess is tied up in that property!'

"So, tho' the 'spinless shit' made lavish prommises, he could not deliver a brass farthing! This is the reason that his whore plotted the 'spineless little shits' downfall. This is how that part goes:

"Her plan was to become a drug smuggler. Our heros father, was to put up the cash and she would fly to Afganistan, buy the cannabis and bring it back into England through diplomatic channels. 'The spinless shit' would then sell it for a vast proffit on the black market. This way thay were to make their fortune and be able to buy a 'love nest' in the country and meanwhile keep up their lavish life style in town.

"How would she be able to bring the drugs undictected into the country? Well, one of the whores other cleints was the Afhanistani Ambasidor. A word in his shell-like and she could bring in whatever she fanced in 'diplomatic bags'. Once our heros father heard this gratifying news, he imediatly went to the bank and drew out 60,000 pounds in hard cash. Being a true nieave – and a sensulist t' boot – the father handed the loot over to his belov'd and the whore set off, leaving that old digenerate to lick his lips in antisipation. (Do you think that that line is too grafic? Of course he had a beard as well, but i dont mention it here).

"Everything went according to plan up untill 'the mistress' arrived back in England and was passing thru customs. Instead of having her packages in 'diplomatic bags', as plan'd, she instead carried them in a plain cardbored box. She then walk'd up to the customs officer and said: 'Excuse me, sir, but i dont think i ought to have this!' She then furnished him with the drugs, the fathers name and address and his list of contacks on the black market. Within the houre the pair of them were banged behind bars. The Drug Squad then prosseded to empity the fathers office of all his files and the contents of his desk was put into black bin-liners and removed. At first his fathers collegues and partners stood gawping in disbelith, then began smiling and rubbing their hands together. Thay had been waiteing for just such an oppertunity to be rid of the 'old sot' and couldnt belive their luck. (He, as a founding partner, had been stripping the company of its assets and drinking himself into obivion for over 10 years). The company also undertook sensitive goverment werk and it was plainly impossible, in their possition, to keep the employ of a common criminal, much less a convicted drug trafficer! All in all his former friends and colleges stuck the knife in and managed to buy him out at a pittence, and meenwhile vastly increase there own percentages in the prossess. It would be easyist to say that everybody, espeshery his youngest son, were celibrating.

"Of course, such a man goes to prison, but not in the same way as a poor man goes to prison. Immediately the father employed a Queens Council, who, as was the father, was a fully paid up member of the oldist Massonic Lodge in England. So he stands befor the judge, (who is also a freemason) and you can almost here love-birds singing. Naturally 'the spinless shits' prison sentence is short and polite, but he is still ruined finacially. With prospect of his release almost round the corner, our 'raw youth' forces his mother to devorse 'the spinless shit,' befor his creditors desend on the family home like a flock of ganits.

"What else was our hero to do? What would you do in such a situation, if not fight? I diddnt tell you, that befor all this came to pass, our 'raw youth' was exppelled from the Acadamy for blassformy; for writting evil texts; for dearing to be a brave artist; for not having 2 brass happnys to rub together.

"And what of the girlfriend of our corrupted 'raw youth'? Dont worry, i havent forgoten her – dont worry yourself on that score. She is now attached to our hero like a limpit and he can not – or will not – escape her.

"How did our 'raw youth' become corrupt? Why, by being born and looking for the guiding hand of his father and there being none! So, hating his father he set out to become his father. Fishing for sex and death, thats how. But is it really nessissary to explain every noble detail?

Whatever, he finds so much missery in love, that he grows to detest love. And his girl friend? Well, she is only in love with the idear of being in love and is also a born victim, so she is made for him. She sees his paintings – as an artist freshly expelled from the Acadamy (and i remind you here that she is a meer fashion student) – and she wants to become an artist herself, so she devours him. Is that all together too impossable? Lets pretend that she is Turkish, has a wasp-like waist and wants sex with him non stop, and follows him round like a puppy dog begging him to abuse her. She is bored with the world of fashion and wants to enter the Acadamy and to become him, yet denies his serch for truth. And becouse her loyelty is split, he wants to kill her. She is, you see, one of those not so uncommon beings who, in delusion, belive thay love what thay are in effect, intent on destroying. There is a duelisim in such peoples minds that means that they can never truely see God and the Devil in unity but only as 2 oppossing wills which must constantly do battle with each other. In short – her left hand calls for art but her rite hand bays for money, prestige and addoration. One has to win over the other and that is that! It is her all consuming hunger for acceptence which proberbly drew our 'raw youth' to murder.

"Naturally, you can say that all of our heros plans are just idle, adolecent imaginings, and prehaps this is how they will remain, if it wasnt for the iminent release from prision of his father and the hurrican that will be unleashed in our heros angished hart and mind. Do not forget that he has no money and his studdies have been curtailed becouse of what the authorties describe as 'his attude of tottal rejection'. In effect – for replying to the abuses he has suffered from day one. And now the integrity of his art is being whored by this girlfriend of his, at the very Acadamy that set out to destroy him.

"His parents devorse is finnaly going thru when the father is released from prison. At first avoiding the show-down, the father jets off to the South of France with his 'mistress', to burn the 20,000 pounds he resived when his partners bawt him out of his company. Once this small sum has been fritted away on alcahole, hotels and genneral high living, he returnes home to fight tooth and nail for his propperty, his wife and to utterly vanquish the son who turned against him.

"But this raw youth – who cuts into his own face with razors and burns himself with ciggaret ends just to see if he is actually alive and still capable of bleeding – is ready to kill. He has been pushed from day 1 to this point of insainty. (It can not be over-stated that this father of his is a depraved sensualist and manic depressive who, when puffed up and inflated with the sliteist notion of his own success, is impossably arogent and unaproachable). Only when he is tottaly smashed and defeted is he cappable of any sentiment. Only then will he reproach himself and blubber about what generious acts he will commit in the futcher, if he can just make more gold. But once that gold is in his grasp, he returnes to his priviouse nature and belives that he is rich becouse he is supreamly smart and deserves to be so, whilest others are poor becouse thay are supreamly stupid and deserve nothing! Befor this cyclone unleashes, the father weeps to our hero: "I only want to get ahead, to earn a little money so's that i can help you." The offer of this loathsome buffon, touches our heros hart and our 'nieve youth', who has hated his father all of his life, wishes only to belive him and help him back to happynes."

I look deeply into Deep Snows eyes.

"Maybe you fancy that i too am insain? But look at me, i am calm and collected, quietly telling you this harmless tail, this poem, which is purly of my imagination and can do no halm to anyone. Tho', of course, the imagination is the most deadly and real thing of all!"

I smile smugly, pleased that i should say such a splended and unrehursed thing. I look around the bar to see if anyone else has noticed me but it is empty.

"Yes," i continue, "our 'raw and naked youth' has been primed for patricide from his first view of the world from the high-chair; from the first abrasive, un-loving words of his father, ordering him to eat with his mouth closed and to breath thru his nose (Of course, his nose was blocked and he could not for the life of him breathe thru it). In effect, his father was ordering him to die.

"But all that is over now. All that is in the past. His father is dead now, take it from me. When the father returns from his latest deborchery he attacks his wife and thats the end of him: Our 'raw youth' kills him on his mothers orders. Cracks open his head and strangles the life out of him. He sooths his fathers kicking body and drags it to rest behind the setee.

"Next, he visits his un-noing girlfriend. Or, prehaps she visits him. Maybe the fathers body is in the very same room, leeking into the carpet, just out of site. Our hero trys to speak with his girlfriend, to make genuine hart-felt contact, but of course she dosnt want 'contact' she wants only sex. So he takes a single match, strikes it and plunges it into the vile nest of hair that sits on top of her grining head. Then, seeing what he has done, he maims himself quite horrobly by slowly burning a hole into the back of his hand with a lited ciggeret end.

"His girlfriend whatches him melitioulsy, without uttering a single word of protest. 'Look what youve done to me!' He shouts, then he falls to the floor draging her down with him.

"He lies there scearsly brething, pushing his tear-stained face into her black, plastic smelling hair. He has to stop himself from squeezing her in his arms untill she too is dead.

"In truth, he wanted to hold her close to him; to kiss her and wisper that he lov'd her and would never hurt her or leave her untill the end of time. Then he feels the softness of her ear lobe between his artists lips. Gently, he sucks it into his mouth, then bites down on it. Instead of whispering sorry and begging for her forgivness, he somehow finds himself hurting her yet again.

"Does that make sense to you? Isn't that just how spite is within ourselfs? Becouse someone wishes to worship us, but not our true selfs, but somone thay mistakenly belive us to be. Well, no honest man can possably tollerate that. Also,

324

quite apart from this, things that he has said to her in confidence, have been distorted and changed into something else, something quite different from his orginal meaning. In fact, she has changed his honest and brave words into the exact oppersite – into some kind of admital of weakness. 'Listen!' he shouts at her, then once more plunges the burning cigaret into the open wound on the back of his hand, 'all art is steeped in falsity! But i forgive you.' She stairs at him in tottal non comprehension, which just makes him hate her all the more. 'You and your fat art skool tutors and their pathetic band of admirers can all go to hell!' He spits. 'But i want sex and i only want it with you!' she whinnys. His fear is that she will leave him, and she mussnt leave him so he must kill her. He sits and stairs at her hairy chin. Her face now is really quite comical to him. Once he tryed so hard to love her (and he really is cappable of quite exteraundanary self sacrifise), but he now nos that she must die. So, he takes her into his arms and throttels her – What do you think of that?"

I tilt my chin defiantly, hoping to hide my fear by brevardo, the fear that my story will not impress her and make her love me but will instead disgust her and make her dispise me. That my admition, far from drawing her into my circle of power, will instead send her scampering to inform the police of my madness.

"I think it is a buetiful tale," i carry on. "Romantic and tragic with a true poet as its hero." I look at Deep Snow again and the corners of her mouth begin to smile at me.

I will make you love me, Deep Snow, then you will

learn to despise me, as all women despise me. If my terrible story does not drive you off, Deep Snow, then you deserve to suffer.

"The reason that he has to kill her is to make room for some gentleness and humility in his tortured sole. To save himself from her bogus, fake love. Her love which is in fact nearer to death than love. Her love which is like triccle and only designed to torture a man and drown him like a wasp in a jar.

"You see, his evilness and so call'd unpleasent nature has only become manefest becouse of her. Our hero looks at her in utter contempt, lieing there on the carpet befor him with her knees drawn up under her large breasts and her wounderful arse stuck up in the air. Now her corps is entising him to have anal sex with her, which he will refuse to do!"

I have said the term 'anal sex' to Deep Snow. I now lie down on the bench and place my head in her lap, which she allows me to do, even absently tassling my hair. It is important that Deep Snow nos the depths of my evil nature and accepts me on all levels. She strokes my forhead as i continue on with my story.

"Leving her for dead our 'naked youth' escapes the room and runs blindly thru the nite. Who nos, maybe he dashes along N— Road. Whatever, hes sobbing and gasping, stareing down in disbelith at his blud-sticky hands."

Suddenly, i sit up.

"Of course, there is no blud there, but still he feels it. It is impossable to describe apart from to say 'her blud is upon him.' Then, looking up, he sees a butiful prostitute stood there in the snow, benith the cherry bloosoms. The snow at her feet is carpeted in pink. Again he sees blud. She is a Japanese, with the skin drawn tight into the corners of her butiful eyes, giving her an intence, quisical and sexual expression. Of course, he falls in love with her at once and steps forward into the lite of the street lamp, and she nods to him. Unbeliving, he steps closser still, but then she scears him with her smile, or should i say with the forgivness of her smile, and crying out in angish, he turnes and runs, slipping and sliding in the ice and snow. He dosnt no where he is running, only that he must escape himself. He sees the darkened buildings of the Acadamy on the hillside above him and that is where he runs to.

"Once on top of the hill, he throws himself down and bites at the snow, forcing handfulls into his burning eyes. Then he rolls onto his back and stairs up into the black impossableness of the nite, the spining snow flakes crashing down into his wide open eyes. Lieing there, he prays, forcing himself not to blink on punishment of death, the tears cursing down his thin, pale cheeks.

"So we are back at the beging of our tail. It is his birthday, to the houre, to the very second. He is born there, a murderer, lieing in the snow. He howls like a new born infant, sobbing and crying out to God to come down out of his stinking heaven and smash him! To show his cowadly face and prove wether or not he really, truely exists, or just stop the world there and then – to give the whole show over to Satan. 'Where is your stinking Jesus, you scoundrel?!' he shouts, 'Show me my saviour now! Show me his wounds! Let me kiss them with my tounge and tast the blud! Let me stick my fingers into his open side and feel his bowls! Not till then will i belive, not till then you charleten!'"

Just then a man trys to enter the bar. He has a large suitcase jamed in the narrow doorway. It is obvious that he is drunk. He notices us, mutters an excuse and reverses back out, the door closing behind him. Deep Snow looks back at my mouth.

"Any way, that is my story... Only... Maybe later, he returnes to despose of the body. Then it is really finished."

At these last words i suddenly start to cry. I sit up and hold my face in my hands. Deep Snow trys to comfort me but i shrug her off.

"Im sorry. Now i must go." I stand and she looks up at me with the worried face of my mother. Suddenly a strange anger rises within me and i pick up Deep Snows drink and fling it in her face. I turne to leave, to run from the intollarable sadness of her butiful eyes but she catches at my sleeve. In truth, i let her stop me. I look down at the cheep, black beer dripping from her face and chin. Then she reaches up, links her arms around my kneck, pulls me down and kisses me deeply. I pull away.

"Look, all i am really trying to say is that hell really exists. Not in a novel, or the bible, or the vileness of everyday life but as an actuel 100 pecent real place. If you carnt belive in God, fine, but youd better belive in the devil or your finished! You see, without hell we have a licence to do anything. Without hell, nothing matters. Where as with hell as our reconing, waiteing there for us, we have to wake up and understand that eveything we say and do matters more than we can ever possably no or imagin and we carnt just carry on bying shopping and new cars into all eternity!"

68

The Lemon is Returned

THERE IS ONLY the tinyist number of black hairs on her cunt, and thay are all gathered at the top, like a little hat. Her cunt smells strongly of sex. On every stroke the innerlips are pulled out to an alarming degree, clining tightly to my cock. I look down at myself in wounder, pleased that i am once more a man and that God has desided to like me again. Also, i pray that he will not destroy me for being a cheat and a lier.

All thru sex, Deep Snow keeps her head tilted to one side and stairs at the wall, which is rite next to her face. For somone whos body smells so strongly of sex it apperes that she hates sex. Her body is strange lien there, her breasts, which had seemed so hard and prominent, now slightly depressed against her ribs and pointing to either side. I pull her up from the bed to face me. On the floor is a bottle of very powerfull, neat spirit – perpotedly brewed by her alcholic grandmother – which i lift to my mouth and then offer her a swig. Deep Snow looks down at my cock inside her and back up to my eyes and again i see a terryfying depth in the discs of her eyes and i no that we have lived many lives together in the past.

"Have you come to save me from the Ottoman Empire?"

"I will do anything for you."

And i feel dirty and ashamed, for somehow i have lied and hurt Karima.

Later, when i am leaving, she runs to Kajii's room and i stand waighting in the hallway. There is an old push bike there from the 1930's. Then Deep Snow comes back with something hidden in the sleeve of her Komono. She places a cool, waxy object into my palm and folds my fingers around it and holds it there – not allowing me to look down and see it – then kisses me goodnite and i walk out into the nite.

I dont open my hand untill she has closed the door and i have turned the corner. There i stop by the wall and look to my palm. It lies there, giving off a faint glow. It is the lemon that Kajii had stollen from me. I recognise it imediatly, its colour is so brite that it throbs in the dim lite of the darkened doorway. Actualy, it is now dried out and useless and i am about to toss it in to the bushes but then change my mind, slip it into my pocket and head off towards the river.

70

The Otterman Empire

THE TROLLS FLAT is in darkness. I peer down into the gloom of her basement windows, scale the railings, lower myself down and climb in thru the widow. There, in the darkness, i can here her snoring.

I undress in silence and slip in under the covers. Karima reaches out for me in her sleep, her arms and leggs entwine about me, then sniffing me, lifts her face.

"Where have you been?"

"Out."

She nuzzuls my shoulder. "Whats that smell?"

"What smell?"

And then suddenly shes awake. I dont see the punch coming, then i bow my head as thay rain down on me in quick succsession, hitting me about the head and neck, her rings cutting me quite badly – a 1/4 of a pound of Turkish gold.

"You fuckin barstard, you stink! Who have you been with?"

And then she punches again. "At least you could have the desentsy to wash befor you come to bed with me!"

She realy belts me one in the ear, and all the time, on the inside, i am saying 'thank you, now i am pure, pureer than you can ever be.'

When she finnaly stops hitting me and is sitting at the end of the bed with a zombie-like expression, i tell her that i have slept with Deep Snow, and then Karima attacks me again.

"You carnt lie to me, youve been with that Japanese slut!"

"Im not lieing to you, ive just told you."

It is all perfictly true, Deep Snow, the sister of the lemon theif is my lover.

"At least you could wash befor coming home to me. You stink of her!"

"Do i?" i sniff at my fingers and then the Troll goes for me again, punching me about the face. Soon, so help me God, i will lose my patentce and land her one rite back!

Instead, i let her beat me up. Really, what i want to prove to this woman – who by some whicked twist of fate has come to rule my life – is that i am fundermentaly un-loveable, rotten to the chore and that she should not love me at all, but rather hate me and leave me. Yes, i am determind to teach her a lesson that she will not forget in a hurry; to spite my mother for having the ordacity of giving birth to me; to spite Karima for making me harm her; to teach the pair of them a good lesson; to smash them for having the temerity to pretend to love me!

In the morning i examin my cuts in the bathroom mirror. Some of them are quite deep from her rings. Yes, i really have been clensed by fire. Next, i make the Troll pay for her insolence by having her bend over the trunk, pull apart her cheeks and display her cunt and arse to me. I observe them. then slowly un-loop my belt and whip her. Next, we make love.

71

The Last of the Acadamy

THIS EVENING i mounted the steps of the Acadamy for the last and final time. Just outside the porters lodge i hesitate, listening out for old Merics transistor radio. He shouts after me as i dash past his cubby hole but i am too quick for him. Besides, i walk in a manner that will disgiuse my inwood apperence, to compleatly out-fox him.

The whole building is deserted. I wonder the depressing and empity corridoors. Almost everyone has cleared off home for the winter, to their small houses, family farms and grand estates. It is only me who has no where to go and no family to returne to. Me, who was once hailed as a genius and marked for great things. Me, who is pennyless and whos dishonarable father never left him a farthing or gave me a helping hand in any way. Me, who has turned from the possibility of great things, to setting girls hair alite and threatening myself with death.

The lift is broken and i have to make my way to the fine art department by way of the stairs. I skip up them – 9 flites. Under my arm i carry an old blue train drivers hold-all.

There is still some lite coming into the studios from the great north facing windows. I stand and look out over the nite time river, the little lites twinkling bellow. There are people who live behind those lites and thay are alive and have familys: mothers and fathers, brothers and sisters, and thay will all, at one time or another, be touched by death. The dockyard is over there, which is also where i dont belong. All in all, there is a sadness that covers this town, the villages beyond, and the entire world. I can safly say that my depression is back in full force.

I have to smash open a door, then lay my broken hold-all on the shelf in the drawing cupboard, rite next to Mister Bennits office. I dont no what force has bought me back here to this very cupboard where Mister Benit stood on gaurd on my first day of college. Back when i was a mock student at this Acadamy. On that occassion i tentitivly askd Mister Bennit if i could use some of the skools acrilic colours.

"And why would you want to do with acrilic paints, William?" He askd me, throwing a mocking glance to those standing near.

"To try them out, sir. To see what theyer like. Ive never used acrilic paints befor." And i smile at him to show that i am not thretening him in any way, and Mister Benit smiled in turn, looking at the others faces for several moments, and i knew that i had pleased him with my inteligent request. Then, with his horrible gray eyes he looks directly at me and speaks.

"I dont think you understand propperly do you, William? One has to earn the rite to use the skools acrilics."

"Pardon, sir?"

"I said 'one has to prove ones worth befor one is allowed to paint with the skools acrilics!'"

I have allways hated the phoney use of first names. Mister Benit anounceated the word 'William' and 'acrilic' in a most effected manner, his thick tounge lolloing about in the cavity behind his old teeth. Then, again smiling, he folded his fat, stupid lips and puffed out his chest, entirely blocking the cupbored doorway. I stood there helpless. Shortly, he gave those very acrilic paints to a girl with large breasts, for no other reason than he admired her clevage.

So, it is to this very same shelf that i am drawn. Those same paints that were once out of bounds to me – and transfixed me from afar with their forbiden, magical contents – now lie here for the taking. I lift a tube of ultramarine, unscrew the lid, squirt the contents into my palm and sniff at it. I do the same with a tube of scarlet-lake, then look at the colours lein there side by side befor angrly smeering them on my chest. In the past such vivid colours would have excited and fasinated me, but now -thanks to the Acadamy and their love of bogus of art – i feel nothing.

I rake a whole armfull of oil paints into my holdall and am about to start filling my pockets when i find the lemon that Deep Snow had given me. I go to toss it to one side when a thought strikes me: Its yellownes fills the whole cupboard with a strange and singular lite. What if i was to put this lemon on top of these insendary colours? I make a pile of the remaining tubes of paint then cearfully place the lemon on top. I look at it balencing there. Then there is the sound of footsteps. Old Merick is hobbling about out there on his wooden leg, looking for me. Quickly, i snatch up the lemon and hide it back inside my jacket and stand dead still.

The store cupoboard door opens and a torch is shone in at me. Old Merick calls to me to come out. I step from the shadows, my hart beating wildly. I look to see if i can run past him but he holds out his walking stick at me. I try to climb up onto the shelf, but it is useless, i have to give myself up.

Old Merick leads me out and takes me to the libery. He tells me to stand by the book case and not move. Then, un-locking the office door, calls the police. This is were i finnaly plant my bomb, when he isnt looking. I take the lemon from my jacket pocket and place it on the shelf behind a book about Kurt Schwitters. Then i make my escape.

I simply walk back out the libery, down the stairs and let myself out onto the street.

I laugh out loud to myself: it really is as if i have become the hero of a novel of the past. A brigand and an anarchist. How devilish – to leave an unexploded lemon in the hart of the Acadamy and no that within 10 short minits nothing will be left of that oppressive building but a heap of old sawdust. Certanly, the police will be on my trail by now.

I walk down under the iron railway bridge and towards Karimas Trolls cave. I mingle with the fog that comes up off the M— river. The fog, that is like an animal and will allways protect me.

72

A Gift

THIS IS THE TRUE REASON i set your hair alite, Karima. When we were walking together on that first evening of our love, you told me of your boyfriend and how you had left him. But i could tell by the tremoure in you voice that it wasnt true and that it was in fact he who had left you. And you were so like a little girl in that nite, as you told me your lie, that i diddnt hate you for lieing to me, Karima. No, it made me love you all the more. And i wanted to hold you, to make it all all rite for you. For you to trust me and for us to shear our weaknessess and there by become one.

So, then i told you my story, Karima, but i diddn't lie, i told you the truth. The story of how, tho' my girlfriend had actually left me, i lied and told everybody that it was a mutual dission taken by both of us to part. I told you that i had lied becouse i was ashamed that it was me who had been passed over and i diddnt want people to see that i was not a man at all, and had no strength to hold and keep a real girlfriend.

This was my gift to you, Karima, so that you too could shear the truth of your sorrow with me and that we could 'grow' together. But then i heard how you had been telling people how i had broken down in front of you and made a confession to you. Tho' in your story there was no mention of what had promted my gift. No mention of your lie and weekness, only your joy at being able to expose me. You threw my wounderfull gift back in my face, Karima, and that is why i set your hair a lite, and that is why i drag this God-heavy trunk out of your basement thru the snow and onwards towards the bridge and the river.

73

R— Bridge

AT THE BOTTOM of the hill i stop to rest. The street is in silence and fog envelops me. From here i carnt even see the bridge. The easyist option now would be to drag the trunk quickly over the road and just dump it over the side of the esplanade. Running backwards i skim the trunk over the ice, bump it up the curb and leave it there behind the bushes. I take a look over the edge. Bellow is just mud, the tide is out. I will have to get the trunk rite up onto the bridge without being spotted. I listen out for trafic. A truck laying salt passes, going in the oppersite direction. I waite untill there is no sound. Then listening to my hart, i again run backwards with short, fast steps, pulling the tunk thru the slush and round the corner onto the bridge. I go in under the ornate entrance and again i rest. Several cars pass and i step well back into the shadows. When the coast is clear again i scurry off pulling the trunk rite up to the center arch of the bridge, the wooden bindings of the trunk splintering on the gritted pathway. I have to get my knees and then my shoulder under it, but finnaly, i manage to haul it up onto the balastrade and hold it there, teettering. I check the clasps are shut and that the length of roap is bound sucurelly. I tug on it and the trunk falls back towards me so's that i have to catch it against my cheast and heave it up again. I hold it there, peering over the edge, into the darkness bellow.

I am sorry sweet Karima, i never ment you any harm. I have to do this becouse you broke my dream, Karima. I sheared my secret with you, not so's that you could trample it under foot like a dirty, discarded rag, but so's that we could be joined in truth and freindship. I exposed my hart to you so's that you too could find the bravery to expose your hart to me. But you dissrespected me and this is the terrible result. Yes, Karima, us 2, barly grown – still children in fact, just a pair of buggerd kids, staggering on in our own fashion – brocken, lost and alone. But i diddnt want to be alone any more, Karima. And when i told you of that fowleness that was done to me by the hand of that 46 year old man, that wasnt so's you could mock me, and make me feel small again and not even a man. The reason i told you my story, Karima, was so's that your little girl could be brave enough to tell her story and we could hold each other in love and in our pain. Yes, this is all your doing, Karima, not mine. I would have lov'd you forever, till the end of time.

I let go the trunk. For several seconds it balences there on its own, rite on the edge. There is a sound from the end of the bridge. I turne, 2 figures are stood benieth the entrance in the fog. Thay shout out, their voices sounding hollow and empty in the nite. I can see the siloets of their policemans hats. Then thay start to walk towards me, befor breaking into a run. The 2 'Specials' come hoofing along the gang way. As thay come nearer i can see the badges on their helmets glinting in the street lites and the seg's in their boots sparking.

One of them is shining his torch. His companion shouts at me to stop what i am doing and to hold my hands up, which i obedeantly do. Thay blow on a little whistle, which sounds mounfully in the fog. I waite for my 2 freinds to arrive beside me, then gently nudge the corner of the trunk with my elbow and it tips into the darkness.

The first 'Special' grabs at the trunk as the other pulls my arm up behind my back and forces me against the balastrade. Meanwhile his mate grappels with the roap but it is slipping from his fingers, then drops away. Still with his silver whistle in his mouth he shines his torch over the side at the trunk as it revolves — caught in its beam — befor crashing into the black water. The whole thing explodes as it hits the serfis, the impact ripping the lid clean off.

I gave it just one harmless little shove and it really was as if my life was one short dream. I watched amazed as the trunk fell away from me. I really wasnt sure if i would push it over the edge at all, but then of course i did, for if i am not brave and fearless, then who else will be?

With my arm still trapped up behind my back, i stair as the trunk disintegrats like old cardboard, the rocks dropping away and sinking into the depths. The 'Specials' lean rite over, currious as kittens. 40 feet bellow, on the dark water, my wounderful books float momenterally on the little wavelets, caught in the beams of the policemans torch. These are my poems, Karima, that one-by-one slip benith the dark surfis, and with them, like seaweed, your black hair and then your face, your bluded nostrels, then you too are gone.

Afterword

It is almost 12 years and 6 months since the events i have related took place in our home town. Of course i am now a completely different indervidual to the youth who set out on those adventures decreeing to 'alighn himself with the mad'. No, that life is dead and over with.

However, even back then i defiantly deny that i was ever truly insain. Afterall, even angels are sometimes driven from heaven by events quite beyond their control and even if from the outside their actions apear to be the hight of madness, maybe if we had to climb into their skins and walk about a bit for a day or two we would see things quite differently. On this point id like to say that during the course of my poem i may have allowed myself to make some dissrespectfull and even scornfull remarks about certen inderviduals whos moral standing and character is high above my own. In my defence i can only say that when i made those remarks, in my imagination i became exactly the individual i had been back then in the moment i was describing; and now as i finish this testiment i feel that if i have re-educated myself, it is precisely threw the prossess of riting down my recollections exactly as they came to me. Of course, i no longer agree with many of the things i have ritten, spersifickly, with the wording and corse tone of many of the passages. Netherthless, i refuse to change a single word or delet anything. I did not kill you Karima, i love you and in the long run i have hurt no one. Becouse despite what you may belive the world is full of love and forgiveness, even for a man who set your disgusting old hair alite.

BORN IN 1959 in Chatham, Kent. Billy Childish left Secondary education at 16 an undiagnosed dyslexic. Refused an interview at the local art school he entered the Naval Dockyard at Chatham as an apprentice stonemason. During the following six months (the artist's only prolonged period of employment) he produced some six hundred drawings in 'the tea huts of hell'. On the basis of this work he was accepted into St Martin's School of Art to study painting. However, his acceptance was short-lived and before completing the course he was expelled for writing what was termed "The worst type of toilet wall humour". Childish then spent some 12 years painting on the dole, developing his own highly personal writing style and producing his art independently.

Sex Crimes of the Futcher is Billy Chidish's third novel.